A Multitude of Sins

The image of Doll formed, unbidden, in his mind. It was as if the sight of her, blatantly astride the car, had chased away the memories of every other vanilla-spiced, sweet-faced woman whose flavour he'd ever enjoyed. His balls tensed and hardened at the memory and his buttocks convulsed rhythmically as he stroked himself. That strange, sweet mixture of hardness and softness she possessed drove him crazy. He wanted at once to lift her tenderly in his arms and to be crushed by her – to feel muscle and metal squeezing the breath out of his body. That afternoon he had had the sensation of cracking open some strange fruit from a distant island – the hard, spiky exterior opening up to yield moist flesh with a flavour that he'd never tasted before.

A Multitude of Sins
Kit Mason

BLACK LACE

Black Lace books contain sexual fantasies.
In real life, always practise safe sex.

This edition published in 2002 by
Black Lace
Thames Wharf Studios
Rainville Road
London W6 9HA

Design by Smith & Gilmour, London
Printed and bound by Mackays of Chatham PLC

ISBN 0 352 33737 0

Contents

Beautiful Creature

If Johnny had been able to read, the sign would have told him:

> Big Tide, Arizona. Pop. 405
> If you pass through you'll regret it
> If you stay here you won't want to come back

He squinted as he tried to make sense of the words. The desert sun tightened around the road like razor wire, the straight highway forming points in the distance in either direction. He could make out individual letters – two S's lay next to each other like mating snakes. But the weird welcome remained impenetrable to Johnny. He knew the name of the place from before – Big Tide. Although there wasn't a drop of water in sight, the name sort of made sense. The town looked like it had been washed up by a wave, leaving a mismatched jumble of buildings in its wake. But he didn't remember the sign from last time. Maybe they put it up after he left.

He parked up the car – leaving it to steam in the heat, sun bouncing off hot chrome – and made his way to the motel. The white-hot street was deserted except for the single figure of a woman who stood stock still. As Johnny approached he wondered what she was doing there, standing still in the afternoon heat, sun striking blue sparks off the huge sequins sewn onto her leisure suit. The fabric was stretched taut over her massive thighs.

'That place is a place of freaks and shamans,' she said, indicating with her head the shanty town bar. Cubes of motel rooms were scattered haphazardly around the building, giving it the appearance of a mother hen pecking in the scabby dirt, her wayward chicks around her.

He blinked once, twice. Then a third time to see if she disappeared. Maybe she was one of those roadside apparitions: the headless horseman; the gallows man; or even one of those saints Johnny had learned about in his Catholic school, conjuring a miracle for the weary traveller. She remained where she was, huge and sparkling. Probably just one of those temperance people who felt it was her duty to turn others towards the paths of righteousness. Johnny inclined his head slightly. It was a gesture that he'd acquired over the years. It might be a movement of deference, of acquiescence even; or it could be a turning away, a withdrawal. Whichever, it seemed to satisfy her and she lumbered slowly off.

He paused in front of the bar and a sick feeling got hold of his throat. Maybe she wasn't even there any more; had drifted away with the sand that blew across the desert. An ancient swinging bench was hooked up from the ceiling on the veranda. For some reason a toy bunny sat in the seat – fluffy and pink, its ears drooped, pink bananas, in the sun.

The woman was just where she'd been before, standing behind the bar, when he'd glimpsed her face as he passed through the town in '97. This was crazy – a one hundred mile detour just to see a woman he didn't know, glimpsed once behind a bar years ago.

Handsome Johnny, with his open respectful manner, his thick brown hair which was slicked back, but when angry or drunk or fucking fell across his eyes so attractively. Handsome dyslexic Johnny, whose clever brain made up for in numbers where it failed with words, never went short of women. Which is why he couldn't admit to himself that the sight of her had followed him. He'd seen her face reflected in the glass when he was drunk; she stared down at him from a full moon. Her face had seemed to multiply in front of his eyes, like a fly's vision. But today, as he'd been driving through and seen the sign for Big Tide, he had kidded himself it was just a place to stop.

Her sleepy eyes were ringed with kohl, gold hoops hung from her ears and her bleach-blonde hair was pushed back greasily from her face. Despite the yellow hair her eyebrows formed full, dark lines over her eyes. The effect was slightly shocking. But underneath the trashy brittle exterior her face shone out like a movie star's or a saint's: her full lips with a little dent in the lower one; her cheekbones strong and delicate; her breasts pouting perfectly in the little black T-shirt across which was written BITCH. Johnny recognised the word.

She asked him with sleepy arrogance what he wanted.

'A beer and a room,' he replied.

When she turned to fetch the beer her walk was measured, loping almost. She handed him the bottle of Bud, the cold of which ran up his arm after the desert heat. His eye caught the diamond sparkle of her ring. Leaning on the bar to talk to her, he was just about to open the conversation, had even opened his mouth to speak, when his eye was caught by the mirror behind her. At first he thought his perceptions had been jumbled up, tricked by the move from the brightness outside to the murky bar. Maybe the window frames were ricocheting metallic light onto the mirror. Then all of a sudden his vision shifted into place. What he could see was actually part of her body – shiny cages of callipers that enclosed each leg. He closed his mouth again in surprise. She shot him a contemptuous look and turned away, her shoulders rising and falling with the effort.

He had a sudden image, almost a hallucination, of taking her from behind, gripping the chrome enclosure around her waist, her opening like a flower behind the metal trellis. Guiltily he covered his lap with his hands. His mind fumbled back, trying to remember whether she'd worn callipers the first time he'd seen her. But he'd only seen her from behind the bar; all he had remembered was her face.

When she emerged into the bar room he couldn't tear his eyes away. It's rude to stare, his mother's voice echoed in his head. But it took his breath away. She hadn't tried to hide herself with long flowing dresses – she wore a tiny skirt which stretched across her behind. The skirt was so short he could see the flash of black stocking tops affixed with buttons and black straps just above the shiny chrome. He felt an obscure tug of shame at his arousal. The sight of her triggered other fractured images: a belt on white skin; the bent chrome of a wrecked car that he had passed days before; the buckle at his waist; the silver Indian head he always wore.

A thud of music and the sound of shouts and whistles came through the window as several cars pulled up, then suddenly the music was choked off. A group swaggered into the bar led by a waspish-looking man, a tiny strip of moustache above his lip. They were carrying guitars, huge amplifiers and mics.

'How you doing, Doll?' the waspish man asked the woman. He stretched his arms around her from behind and thrust his hips suggestively into her back. Johnny averted his eyes. She flung her head back and made a curious purr at the back of her throat: 'Oh, I'm hot tonight, sweetie, I'm so hot.'

The air conditioning in the bar worked, but not too well, managing to cool the air so it was just bearable. It didn't stop anyone from dancing though. Sweat marked their clothes as they moved to the rock and roll the band was belting out on the tiny stage.

The man with the moustache strolled up to talk to Johnny, who was sitting at the bar downing Scotch.

'So what brings you to Big Tide?' he asked.

'Just on my way to somewhere else,' said Johnny. But then felt he was being unfriendly and expanded. 'I'm taking a load of computer software down to the Navajo Nation. They want to update their gambling operation down there and they want all the latest.'

The man seemed impressed enough to offer him his hand and his name. 'Walter,' he said pleasantly. Johnny didn't trust him, he looked pinched and mean, his eyes shifting like storm clouds. A girl, whom Johnny had seen arguing with a big hulk of a boyfriend earlier, hopped up next to him on the bar stool.

'Introduce me to your friend,' she said to Walter.

On the way to his room that night Johnny saw Doll entwined with one of the huge men that had drunk at the bar earlier in the evening. She was humping him shamelessly up against the wall. His large backside thrust in and out and his massive hands cupped her buttocks, lifting her a little way off the ground. She leaned her head against the wall and smiled at Johnny, sphinx-like.

He found it hard to admit that the sight had aroused

him – but as he lay in bed that night just the touch of the sheets against his skin drove him crazy. Her face, that sublime face – he thought she was going to be some kind of angel with a face like that. But if she was, it was a dirty, broken kind of angel. There was a soft knock at his door and he started. It was her, he was sure of it. Despite himself he practically jumped into his jeans and answered the door.

It was the girl from earlier; he thought she might be called Mary. She swayed at the door, a bottle of bourbon dangling from her hand. The single light on the wall outside sparked on the pink glitter of her scarf, which bobbed around her shoulders like little fairy wings.

'Hey, honey, have a drink with me,' she said. She leaned against the door frame and his cock began to harden instinctively.

'I don't think so.' He shook his head. This place was too much. Bad angels and fragile fairies seemed to dog his every step. She pushed her way in, then looked suddenly vulnerable and appealing.

'Just a little one. I get so lonely here.' Tears clouded her eyes. Johnny caught her vanilla smell and her blue eyes widened up at him.

Of course he hadn't been able to resist it, handed over on a plate like that. Her boyfriend was a pig, she told him; fucked her like in two minutes, rolling on and off her like a ram servicing a dumb sheep. Johnny marvelled at how little men keyed into what women wanted; how they regarded them as mere vessels for their cocks.

'Teach me how to come,' she said appealingly, 'I know you can. I felt it as soon as I saw you.'

How could he say no? The weird arousal he'd felt earlier for Doll throbbed and flared. She stripped off her top and stood before him, perky little breasts spilling over her bra, a little pink ribbon between them like she was a present waiting to be unwrapped; her eyes luminous and tearful. He lay her softly on the bed and stilled her hands that sought out his body and slid over his muscled chest, pulling at the Indian buckle on his belt.

'Just take it slow,' he whispered. 'Feel everything down here, focus on it.' He squeezed his fingers between her legs. God she was wet; her juices had soaked her little pink panties. Her body seemed to vibrate underneath his fingers.

'Do you ever touch yourself?' he whispered to her.

Her eyes widened. 'What, down there? Hell, never.' She looked shocked at his suggestion, but then her eyes slanted slyly. 'Well once, us girls were joking around, you know, talking like women do about dildos and stuff. Afterwards I tried, you know, using a hairbrush. But I felt so silly I just quit before I started.'

Her horniness, her soft beauty, her frustrated desire, caught at his throat. She was so young to be mixed up with some Neanderthal man, probably no more than eighteen. He eased her knickers down.

'Go on, touch yourself. Just do it so it feels nice,' Johnny whispered to her.

She put her fingers to her slit experimentally, then stopped all of a sudden. 'I feel so silly.' She laughed.

Johnny smiled. 'Just try again. Lose yourself. It's nothing to be ashamed of; women do it all the time. Sometimes they just take longer to discover it 'cos it's not right smack in front of your eyes like it is with us.'

He watched as she brushed her fingers gently over her sex, tracing the lips upwards and frowning a little in concentration, as if she were trying hard to understand something in class. Her mound was neatly shaved into a bikini line, just a tuft of hair remaining on the peachy bareness. Her breath caught as her fingers touched her clitoris and she gasped, 'Oh, my God.'

Reaching underneath, he unhooked her bra. Shit, she was so juicy, little breasts sitting up to beg like that. He cupped one in his hand and then took her nipple gently between his teeth. She groaned harder and her fingers began to work busily, dancing like fireflies round her button.

'Slowly, slowly,' he urged. Her fingers paused and then started to work again, creaming herself with the wetness that was visibly gleaming in her little slit. Johnny ran his hands expertly up and down her body: the long muscled legs, the flat stomach, slightly concave between her hip bones. A perfect body. American pie.

A flush was beginning to mark her neck and Johnny stilled her restless hands. He shook off his jeans and let his cock lie between her legs, just nudging at her lips. Very slowly he began to move, creaming the bulbous end of his cock so it shone.

'Let it go,' he whispered. 'Just let yourself go.' He ventured in deeper. 'Feel me here,' he said, and pressed his hand just above the blond tuft on her mound. The movements of his cock inside her rose and fell against the flat of his palm.

Grimacing, he bit his lip. The pink glow cast by the bedside lamp lit her rosily. Her soft sugar-blonde hair spread across the pillow and her cheeks burned. He started counting in his head – an easy trick which always worked. She pulled her legs up in abandon and he closed his eyes as he felt the plunge go deeper, enabling his cock to dance and sing against the swell of her cunt, which felt tight and soft at the same time.

Her hands stretched out and tensed, each plum-pink fingernail spreading out as he felt her vibrations underneath him. She let out an abandoned string of curses which seemed incongruous issuing from her bubble-gum-sweetened breath: 'Fuck, fuck, Jesus, fuck.'

She arched her back in climax and then stared at the ceiling for a while, her eyes, as if in shock, unfocused. Johnny let himself rip then, plunging in and out until he felt his balls harden almost unbearably and he buried the hot jet of semen deep inside her.

Maybe it was time to move on. His waking thoughts shifted and moved with the patterns of light that fell through the curtains across his bed the next morning. Already he'd become involved. That Neanderthal boyfriend might just guess something was up next time he made love to his girlfriend with her new-found skills. And Doll, he knew really he'd come here to look at her again. Well, he'd seen her. And now this place felt weird deep down, full of unspoken threats and strangeness.

He opened the door to his motel room. Outside Doll was leaning over a car, soaping the windscreen. She was squeezing the sponge out, her legs stiff in their enclosure as she bent over the hood. From behind, her skirt rose up exposing her little panties, a black triangle between her legs. Johnny felt an ache in his chest. She turned to him.

'Hey, drive with me. I need some help carrying the supplies.' Like she was issuing a command.

'I was thinking of moving on today. It's a long drive to the border,' he said.

She shrugged. Bubbles of soap flecked her T-shirt across which was written FUCK ME. It occurred to Johnny that he had no trouble reading the messages

9

she chose to give out. Maybe a few days wouldn't matter. Give him a chance to rest up before the drive.

'It's Doll, isn't it?' he asked, holding out his hand.

She ignored the outstretched hand and grinned up at him. 'Doll or Dolores,' she said. 'But you can call me anything you want, handsome.'

She drove her specially adapted car fast, far too fast. They rode with the top down and soon the desert sun beat down on them and on the road, sending a curtain of shimmering heat upwards. Several Winnebagos passed them, travelling in the opposite direction.

'Snowbirds,' explained Doll. 'Old people come down here for the winter for the sun. You wouldn't want to be out here in the summer though. One day out here would kill you. They'd find you like a shrivelled up old snakeskin by the road.'

Johnny breathed deep and tried to quell his fear at her crazy driving. His eyes seemed relentlessly pulled down to her legs. Her skirt was even shorter today, if that were possible. Jesus, it was like she was drawing attention to it.

'It's OK, you can look,' she said casually.

'I didn't mean ... you know ... I didn't mean ...' he stammered. She laughed, cutting him short. Her voice assumed a borrowed tenor. 'Oh, Johnny, teach me how to come.' She laughed again, throwing her head back.

'What the fuck, how did you know – ?'

'My boyfriend's just a big pig. Go on, big man, teach me how to come.' She was laughing almost hysterically now. Johnny gripped the car door. Mad bitch. He felt the sting of humiliation. So Mary seduced every stranger like that, did she? With her wide-open eyes and her air of innocence. Christ, weren't people just too much?

Johnny grabbed Doll's arm. 'Stop laughing will you. It isn't that funny,' he said.

Her face composed itself. 'You have to admit it's pretty funny,' she answered.

The sun lit up her face and Johnny almost felt choked by her beauty. It was while he was looking at her, the image burning into his mind, that he saw something else in the corner of his eye. Something seemed to rush at them and he glimpsed a blur of red metal before a deep roaring jolt went through his body.

Doll drove the car – the front a twisted-up mess of metal – off the road. Its wheels rolled silently on the sand.

'Stupid fucks, on the wrong side of the road. They didn't even stop,' she said. She put her forehead to the wheel and her shoulders shook as a dry sob went through her. She leaned back suddenly and her tiny skirt rode up so Johnny could see the crotch of her black panties against the red leather of the seat.

'That was close, Johnny, wasn't it?' she whispered. Her face assumed a new softness.

Still looking at him, she put two fingers down between her legs and squeezed. She gasped at her own touch. Her red nails ran up and down the pout in between her legs, squeezing and kneading hard. The sight made his cock feel uncomfortable and stiff in his jeans. She closed her eyes and thrust her hips forward and the black garters holding up her stockings bit into the flesh at the top of her thighs.

He put a tentative hand out and touched the warm steel of her metal calliper, almost surprised when her eyes didn't widen at his touch – as if the chrome construction was part of her, with its own network of nerve endings and with her blood pumping through them. The soft flesh so close underneath the metal exterior made his heart beat faster. The supports suddenly looked beautiful and obscene, as if Doll had put them on this morning as a tease to flaunt her shapely legs, in the same way that she rolled the stockings up over her thighs, fastening each one with the button and the snippet of ribbon.

Her fingers were inside her knickers now. Johnny could hear the sucking sound they made as they dabbled at her clit. Her eyes were still closed, the heavy lids glamorous with their sweep of dark lashes casting a jagged shadow on her cheek. Her breath quickened.

Suddenly her fingers stopped. As she took them from between her legs Johnny could see the gleam of wetness in the sun. The heat of the sun was making his head feel dizzy. Abruptly he got out of the car and her eyes opened at the clunk of the door.

The desert stretched out as far as the eye could see: dangerous territory, full of rattlesnakes apparently. What was he doing here in this poisonous place, with this crazy woman, out in the middle of nowhere? She swung her legs awkwardly as she got out of the car to examine the damage. The left front side reared up in a twisted grimace of metal. She ran her hands over the wreckage. Her eyes looked unfocused.

'A couple of feet closer . . .' It was almost like she was whispering to herself and a tremor shook her.

She wrenched the back door open and heaved herself inside. Johnny noticed how muscled her arms were. Her biceps stood out in knots as she used her arms to pull herself up to sit on the back of the car. Her legs stretched out stiffly in front of her with her feet resting on the leather seats. She opened up her legs.

'Make me come, Johnny,' she said. 'Make me come.'

He knelt on the back seat in front of her, his knees sliding a little on the leather. She held his head between her hands, her fingers clutching and grabbing at his hair, directing him between her legs. He glanced towards the road. They were still clearly visible if anyone drove by. But there was no telltale blur of rising heat signalling a car approaching in the distance. In fact, everything seemed to have been stilled into quietness which pressed against his ears after the shocking noise of metal ripping metal.

Doll looked like some weird figurehead sitting on the back of the car. He saw her teeth bite into the peachy fullness of her lower lip, leaving a white mark for a second before the blood rushed back and stained it red once more. Tentatively he put his head between her legs and took the silky fabric of her panties between his teeth. The taste of salt played upon his tongue. Tugging the fabric between his lips he sucked at the juice that had gathered there, the fabric heavy with her wetness. Her hands held his head with such force that it hurt. The pain, the heat, the shock of what had happened, and the smell he breathed in great gulps from between her legs, made him feel dizzy.

With one finger – the nail hard and vibrant with red paint – she pulled her tiny panties tight so they bisected her sex, each half of which pouted outwards like a cut fruit. The curls of hair were as dark as her eyebrows. The pinky red of her slit was smooth and gleaming and her long nails tangled with the string she'd made of her panties. She jerked them frantically to one side, clawing at them with her fingers, and he touched her with his tongue experimentally, tasting the flesh between her legs.

She groaned and lay back on the car. Her legs in their bondage tightened around him so he could feel the metal clamping his head, as if it were caught in a vice. Cupping his hands under her buttocks, he drew the moist cunt even closer to himself, so his mouth was buried in it while his fingers clutched deep into the flesh of her behind. Her moaning grew louder and more insistent: 'Jesus Christ, Johnny,' she cried, and the words echoed over the stillness of the desert as she arched her back in climax.

A car had driven up shortly afterwards. Johnny's heart skipped a beat at the thought of how easily they could have been caught, and his own flaring desire temporarily abated. She sat, unconcerned, on the back of the car.

'We'll be fine.' She waved away the help offered by the couple of boys in the other car. Johnny noticed them staring with unabashed curiosity at Doll.

Despite the mangled state of the car she still insisted on driving to the shopping mall to pick up her supplies. They left the car, with its grotesque curls of metal sprouting from the hood like some space age plant, and entered the blissful cool of the air-conditioned mall. In its bright white clean spaces Doll stood out even more than usual, like a renegade from a *Mad Max* movie. Everywhere she went, people looked.

Back in Big Tide again, Johnny helped Doll unload the bags from the car. Mary, who seemed to be a regular at the bar, tottered on her high heels and waved expectantly at him. He stared at her, stony faced.

Most of the stuff in the shopping bags seemed to be cleaning equipment and there was a suspiciously large amount of cans of air freshener, which Johnny guessed took the place of a really good clean in the stuffy little motel rooms. Doll seemed composed, distant almost, despite the afternoon's bizarre twist of events. He watched as she pushed back her white-yellow hair from her face. Dark fuzz sprouted under her arms, like it did with the Italian woman Johnny had once had in New York. It was funny how he remembered her – even now – when all the powdered shaved Marys of this world had merged into one, like puffs of clouds forming into one hazy mass.

'Where d'you live when you're not here?' he asked. The question felt like an intrusion, which, reflected Johnny, was a bit damn strange considering what had happened that afternoon.

'I'm right beside you, sweetie,' she answered after a moment's pause. 'The owners are letting me use the room next to yours while my place gets fixed up, after the fire and everything.'

'What fire?'

'Oh, you know, things happen,' she said vaguely.

The woman in the blue sequins whom Johnny had seen the first day he arrived stood outside the grocery store opposite. Her eyes kept glancing over to them as she spoke to the old girl next to her, similarly resplendent in colourful leisure wear. But he couldn't hear what they were saying.

Johnny lay on his unmade bed. So she was right next door to this room – through that cheap partition papered over with a pattern of palm trees. Stripping off his sweat-soaked shirt he splashed water over his shoulders and arms. His ears picked up a tiny movement from next door and his cock stirred with a life of its own.

She'd given no thought to his desire this afternoon. He'd put it down to the shock of the accident and the untimely arrival of the two boys. But even later, just now as he helped her unload her stuff, she'd acted completely offhand. It was as if this afternoon had never happened; as if she hadn't drawn him between her legs and made him taste the juice that oozed there. He licked his lips. They felt hot and dry and he could still taste the pungent flavour of her in his mouth. His cock felt rampant now and snaked inside his jeans, reaching up to his stomach. He cursed it, then caught another tiny sound from next door and a heat passed over him. God, he needed some relief, if nothing else.

Pulling off his jeans and under-shorts he glimpsed himself in the mirror. Christ, what had that woman done to him? The muscles in his thighs and stomach looked tense and hard and his prick reared out before him, the veins marked out almost painfully. Back at the tap again he splashed more cold water over his face and neck, trying to calm himself down. Several drops cascaded down and fell on his burning cock. He gasped – his sensations were unnaturally intensified, stretched as taut as a wire.

Grabbing a couple of tissues from the box on the rickety table, he circled his prick between his thumb and finger. Oh, the sweet relief – he had to hang on to the basin for a moment for support. His hard-on seemed so huge, it felt as if his prick threatened to engulf him, a wayward impostor that sought control over his body. He rolled his hand up and down the shaft. The action made him groan and sent electric waves of desire running down his legs and up through his stomach.

The image of Doll formed, unbidden, in his mind. It was as if the sight of her, blatantly astride the car, had chased away the memories of every other vanilla-spiced, sweet-faced woman whose flavour he'd ever enjoyed. His balls tensed and hardened at the memory and his buttocks convulsed rhythmically as he stroked himself. That strange sweet mixture of hardness and softness she possessed drove him crazy. He wanted at once to lift her tenderly in his arms and to be crushed by her; to feel muscle and metal squeezing the breath out of his body. That afternoon he had had the sensation of cracking open some strange fruit from a distant island – the hard, spiky exterior opening up to yield moist flesh with a flavour that he'd never tasted before.

His breath began to come in little gasps. He moved his hand frantically now and his cock kept thrusting forward, as if it were trying to fuck the air in front of him. A drop of salty liquid appeared at the tip and splashed onto the cheap carpet and he bundled the tissues up in readiness.

He caught sight of himself again in the mirror: his eyes wild, like those of a horse bucking off its unwanted rider in a rodeo; all his muscles strung and tensed; his whole body straining to that one point, to his cock which jerked wildly in his hand.

He felt a jolt that nearly sent him spinning off his feet and the white fluid, sticky as albumin, shot over the crumpled pink tissue and ran over his hand. He crouched on the floor, panting, and tried to mop up the spilled semen from the carpet. The cracked face of the clock on the wall told him that less than a minute had passed. He dabbed at the sticky mess on his hands. Hell, what was happening to him?

From his position on the floor he suddenly noticed the piece of paper just under his door and he realised with a shock that it must have been pushed under there while he was jerking off.

The words on the note were a patchwork of cut-out letters from magazines, strangely childish in their bright colours. Johnny ran his fingers over the words, as if he might pick up their meaning from touch like a blind man would. If he'd been able to read, the note would have told him:

GIT OUT OF HERE WHILE YOU CAN, THAT CRAZY FUCKING BITCH WILL EAT YOU ALIVE. THIS IS NO PLACE FOR A DECENT PERSON LIK YOU. THAT TWISTED WHORE IS A FREEK AND FUCKS EVERYONE LIKE SHE IS A RABIT.
YOURS
A WEL WISHER WHO ONLY WANTS TO KEP YOU SAFE

Johnny's only guess was that it must be from Mary's boyfriend – that big oaf of a man. Johnny knew that although he was fit and well muscled, he'd be no competition for the sheer size and bulk of him. He folded up the note very small and tucked it into the pocket of his discarded jeans.

Drained, he lay on his bed for a long time. The light started to fade, stretching the shadows across the wall, making squares of light which looked like nebulous doorways to other worlds. Almost without knowing, his eyes closed, and he slept peacefully for a while. When he awoke it had grown darker. As his senses slowly unfurled from sleep he tried to get his bearings. His fuddled mind was agitated at something that was different, that hadn't been there before – a slice of light which fell across the bed, bisecting his leg and ending between the splayed bones of his foot.

The source of the light was a fracture in the panelled wall between the cheap boards. Johnny was surprised he hadn't noticed it before, though he guessed the day he started inspecting the walls of his motel rooms it was time to hand in the towel; before making a mental note to do just that in the next room he rented out.

He applied his eye carefully to the crack where the wallpaper sprouted paper fur at the edges. The sound of his own breath ricocheted off the wall. In the other room Doll stood washing herself at the cracked basin, lit up by the harsh fluorescent strip above, naked except for her callipers. Her warm flesh glowed between the hard, dead metal. She was soaping herself with a big pink sponge which drizzled bubbles over her arms and her stomach. Johnny drank in the sight of her shapely legs, the way the bubbles of soap were caught in her pubic hair and dripped their lather from the curls. Panting, he pulled himself back. Shit, it really was time to leave – this woman was turning him into a pervert.

He packed quickly, gathering up the encrusted tissues and shoving them in his bag – he didn't want to leave anything of himself behind. His mind raged with disordered thoughts. If he'd been able to see her, she must be able to see him; if that was the case then maybe she'd been spying on him with Mary; maybe that was how she'd learned of their conversation which she'd so accurately mimicked. With a flood of shame it occurred to Johnny that if she could see into his room, she may have seen him earlier, jerking off like some wacko, standing in the middle of the room with his prick thrusting in front of him, looking at his own aroused body in the mirror, for God's sake. He groaned, then tried to assess what angle he'd been standing at, and if he'd been visible through the crack in the wall. But it was impossible, so he gave up.

When he left his room he found Doll standing outside, leaning up against the wall and reading, as if she had been waiting for him. The wording on her T-shirt had changed slightly. The one she had on now said simply FUCK YOU .

She jabbed the page with her finger. 'It says here they've found the elixir of life. In some university in Missouri they've been experimenting with rats, feeding them plant extract, and none of them have died yet. Not a single one, and they've been doing it for ten years.' Sometimes Johnny was glad he couldn't read.

He found he couldn't look her in the eye. The easy self assurance which had run through his life like a soft ribbon lay in tatters. The idea that she'd seen him, seen him like that, tugged him back into a tongue-tied state of adolescence.

For the second time he said to her, 'I think I'll be leaving now. I've a long drive ahead of me.'

'Why all of a sudden, like this?' She raised her thick eyebrows. Wordlessly, he handed her the note that had been pushed under his door. He knew that he was being dishonest – the note wasn't the real reason he felt so anxious to flee.

She read the page and snorted dismissively. 'This is just crazy old Edna, you know, the one you've seen hanging around whispering about me. She tried to set fire to my house when she found out I'd been humping her half-wit son. Not that he complained at the time.'

While she spoke, his eyes kept being drawn towards her legs – those beautiful damaged legs in their metal cages. He wanted to reach out and feel the metal, warmed by her body. Reach out to the soft flesh within, like a little boy at the zoo poking his fingers through the bars of a cage, craving the touch of the warm furry flesh of the creature inside.

'It's OK, you can touch, you know,' she said, her eyes fixed on him knowingly.

He reeled back slightly. Had his thoughts been so obvious?

'Go on, touch,' she whispered. 'Touch my legs, touch me.' The words formed an hypnotic incantation. What was it about Doll that made him want to subjugate himself to her; made him willing to be bossed and bruised and dominated? He struggled for the control he usually assumed with women but he found it was only a memory, an attribute that had once belonged to someone else. Mary seemed a hundred years ago.

He fell to his knees onto the dirt and reached out his hands. She thrust her hips out obscenely and her little red mini skirt, fringed with jagged lace reminiscent of lingerie, strained across the top of her thighs. He cradled her legs in his arms. Touching the hardness of the metal gave him the sense that he was embracing some futuristic creature. He kissed the warm flesh between the callipers, the softness at the top of her thighs, and slid his tongue against chrome. The metallic tang sent shivers down his back. Suddenly a car honked in the background. Johnny turned. It was Walter, the man with the thin moustache that Johnny had met that first evening. He was thrusting his hips in and out suggestively.

'Way to go, Doll!' he shouted.

'Up yours, Walter,' she yelled back casually. 'Come on, Johnny,' she commanded. Almost grabbing him by the scruff of the neck, she propelled him through the door of her room.

Johnny had the strange sensation of entering another world, like in sci-fi shows where people popped through a force field and reeled into another dimension. The strip light above flickered into action, bouncing off the mirrors which seemed to be propped against every wall. He noticed her dressing table covered with a weird assortment of objects – bits of bone, twigs and feathers, like cannibalistic cosmetics.

'I like to look at myself,' she said, gesturing towards the mirrors. 'And other people,' she added wickedly.

Johnny felt his cheeks flush. 'I don't know what you saw through that peep hole of yours,' he blustered. He felt his old sense of power return momentarily.

'I know I liked what I saw. You were like some big old stallion without a mare in sight.' She giggled.

The vestiges of self control snapped and Johnny slumped down on a battered chair, his arms hanging loosely by his sides. She came over to him with that strange loping walk that made him catch his breath.

'You looked so fine, Johnny,' she breathed into his ear as she sat on his lap.

The ribs of metal hurt his legs and he felt crushed, despite her dainty weight. Pinned down, he succumbed to her caresses, breathing sharply as she ducked her head and bit his nipple. With a little difficulty she raised herself up using his shoulders as supports, spreading her legs and standing astride him.

His hands moved automatically and fumbled between her legs. Underneath she wore no panties. Her skirt just covered her by a fraction – almost inadequate to cover the heavy lips which protruded from her opening. He held them between finger and thumb. Moist already, the lips hung down so far they almost took on the appearance of a cock. Lifting himself up he took the protuberance in his mouth and sucked. She moaned and held on to his hair for support until after a while she yelled, 'Stop!' He immediately did as he was told.

In the mirror he saw reflected the place in the wall where she must have spied on him and his shame flooded back. Maybe she thought he had known about it, that he had exposed himself like a pervert, putting on a performance for her. Maybe, Johnny suddenly realised, maybe he had. As if reading his thoughts, she grinned at him mischievously.

'Boys used to get a whipping, didn't they, for less than that!' She deftly unhooked his belt with the Indian head buckle from around his waist. 'Stand,' she commanded.

Johnny did as he was told, weak with lust and a sense of strangeness. She roughly pulled his jeans and under-shorts down, caressing his buttocks and letting her palm graze across the hair. Her muscled arm flew out and he felt the sting of his own belt across his behind. His cock jerked and quivered, sticking straight up before him. Thwack, she striped him again. He moaned and his anus tightened with desire. Again, and the stinging action made his prick extend even further. He whimpered and cradled his balls softly in the cup of his hand. The belt hit out at his hand, just missing his cock by a fraction. Like a little boy that had been stung by a bee, he quickly withdrew his hand, a look of hurt surprise on his face.

She laughed. 'Now me,' she ordered, handing him the belt and raising her little skirt above her waist. Her behind peeped cheekily over the metal supports and his cock ached despite himself.

'No, I can't,' he whispered. 'I can't.'

She turned to look at him over her shoulder. 'Like the Nike ad says: just do it,' she almost yelled.

He let fly. The belt snaked across her behind leaving a red stripe.

'And again,' she cried. Once, twice, he lashed out. She groaned in ecstasy, holding on to the back of the chair for support. Johnny caught a sudden glimpse of them both in the mirror – a dream image: the belt lashing out, supports and metal; the red stripes across them both; the subjugated expression on his own face – it was like some netherworld he'd stumbled into. He fell on his knees and began tenderly kissing her buttocks, as if his lips could soothe the red weals away. The lace on her skirt half covered the painful marks, giving them a peek-a-boo eroticism.

Leaning on his shoulder she sat heavily on the bed. He buried his face in her lap, smelling the muskiness of her cunt through her thin skirt. Pulling him up, she squeezed his cock tight in her fist and then drew it between her legs. His sensations were so acute that when she began to play with it, using the purple end to circle and tickle her clit, he cried out. Sweat beaded her upper lip.

'Make me come, Johnny,' she said softly. She motioned him to lie on the floor and then awkwardly straddled him. The weight of the callipers almost crushed his chest as she clambered over him. The metal clanked as she arranged her legs either side of him. She slid her soaking pussy up and down his cock for a few moments before grabbing it in a painful hold and pushing it inside herself. His hips spasmed spontaneously as he felt his prick swallowed up in her soft wetness. The ribbed muscles inside circled him and rubbed with aching softness at his cock.

She was nearly unable to move in that position so he thrust his hips up and down, writhing beneath her. Sweat poured down his forehead as he pumped – each movement felt as if he were being sucked and pulled by a powerful wave. He grabbed the metal enclosure round her waist, his fingers fumbling at the worn leather padding inside.

A flush began marking her neck, darkening with each thrust. He felt her cunt squeeze him deliciously as she arched her back and shouted joyously into the air.

When her eyes regained their focus they fixed on him, watching him with curious intensity.

On either side he felt metal circle his body like a rib-cage, crushing him, squeezing the breath out of him and scoring his skin. He thrust wildly inside her, his buttocks slapping against the cheap carpet. Then, nearly doubling up, he felt the hot jet of semen shoot inside her.

Later, he lay on his stomach, crushed under her weight again as she sat astride him.

'I remember you in '97, Johnny. I cast a spell the day I saw you to make you come back again.' He recalled the jumble of feathers and bones on her dressing table as he felt her diamond ring gouge into his back. 'You'll remember me for ever now,' she said.

As the sun beat down on him the next day, little beads of blood, like red stitching, spelled out DOLL on the back of Johnny's white shirt as he drove the long straight roads towards the New Mexico border.

The English Hotel

I'm not the same as other people. An old lady now (how strange!), I'm alien to those other females of my generation who nod and gossip over their Fortnum's carrier bags full of secret, sugary cakes. With their gardens and grandchildren they would probably regard my moral sense to be as skewed and knotted as the embroidery I laboured over at school, hunched over my desk, mind flying away. Now I wear a patina of respectability like a badly made costume, with just enough conviction to enable me to take part in the chorus.

I may not have the same set of rules as everyone else, but I have my memories, and I'm glad of them now. I take them out like jewels and examine them and they sparkle with remembered light as I turn them over. Those times are so real to me now, it's almost as if it must all still be happening in some not-too-distant place: as if I looked through a telescope I could see my twenty-one-year-old self, still going about her business.

What I can see now is the hotel which was like a luxury ocean liner that had taken to dry land and scoured its way through Amsterdam, finally grinding to a halt, marooned next to the hectic Leidseplein. Before the war it ran like a campaign, to give the rich all the bounty of the west within its four walls. Merchants, diamond dealers, profiteers from the First World War, businessmen and adventurers all came to bathe in its soothing waters of plenty. Wealthy English people made it their first port of call when travelling in Holland – in the way of their fathers annexing another square of earth to call their own. So it became known as The English Hotel.

I had needed to get out of England quickly. The man from the divorce case wanted to see the back of me too and quickly arranged the position of chambermaid through his contacts, English girls being in demand in this little enclave. Chambermaid rankled somewhat, to one with striving ambitions to elevate her social station. But it was a quick, cheap solution – especially for him.

The hotel housekeeper, with her harsh Dutch tones, pronounced my name as Emerlee (my real name is Emily, although my second name was assumed). Her job was to rouse us girls at five in the morning, soft and pliant from sleep, and keep us in order. She soon divined in me the spirit of rebellion and told me that I should know my place. Was I stupid? Couldn't I see how little my superiors had done to earn their place? Was I blind? Didn't she know that I could tell the difference between the cheap decaying lino of the chambermaids' quarters and the deep red pile thickly larded in the guests' bedrooms? I knew my place, all right, but knowing it didn't make me like it.

So perhaps it was whoring. Who knows, who cares? Certainly not the men who stuffed the guilders into my apron. Nor me. Women weren't supposed to lust then, but my libido was like a giant hunger that couldn't be satisfied. It needed constant strange and exciting flavours – sweet and hot, or sour and spiced, strange unheard-of meats with rich sauces and soft exotic vegetables which looked like they'd been grown under the sea.

I built my reputation on being cold and offhand with the other girls; it made it easier to work on my own. After the grim and humiliating task of sorting laundry, we would be dispatched to the guests' bedrooms while they, depending on the time of day, were meant to be breakfasting or to have left the hotel for sightseeing or shopping.

My first was a little over a week after I had arrived at the hotel, bad-tempered with my luck and circumstances. The old man was breakfasting in bed and took my gentle knock at his bedroom door in his pyjamas, promptly inviting me to share his breakfast. He twisted the creamy soft bread of the roll and painted it with butter before offering it to my greedy lips. He shook a little at the sight of my black curls escaping from under the lacy hat and patted the place next to him on the bed.

'Come and sit beside me, there's a good girl.'

He trembled because he thought he was transgressing. What he didn't realise was that my desire probably outweighed his own, so I began a show of innocence seduced.

'I'm still hungry,' I whined. Indeed I was. I'd nearly choked on the thick porridge which was doled out to us at some ungodly hour of the morning.

I sat on his lap, the sheets providing a semblance of distance between us, and wolfed down his breakfast. The sausage was peppery to the tongue and the thick black coffee tasted like heaven. As I ate I could feel his hand under the thin sheet, cradling my fanny, which swelled in response to his restless fingers. His whiskery face was flushed and his sharp brown eyes darted with shame and excitement.

'Are you quite comfortable, my dear?' His voice croaked a little. 'Move a little further up if you're not.'

I shrugged and snuggled further onto his lap so I could feel the hardness pressing against my legs. His breath whistled sharply through his nose as I bounced around on his cock, pretending to find a settled place.

'I can feel something hard underneath me,' I mused innocently, trying to keep a straight face.

'Yes, that's my staff.' Staff! 'It would give me great pleasure if you were to touch it. But perhaps you might be a little bit afraid to grasp something so special?' His eyes were darting in earnest now, his objective within sight.

'Oh, no, Sir, I'm never afraid!' I cried pluckily like some Girl Guide of the Empire.

The black skirt of my uniform spread out around me as I rolled off and sneaked my hand underneath the covers. His cock poked out of the opening in his pyjamas and I touched it softly.

'Like this?' I enquired impishly.

'Grasp it, my dear,' he groaned. 'Be firm with it.'

It may have occurred to him that I wasn't quite as inexperienced as I'd contrived when I expertly circled his prick with finger and thumb, shafting up and down. I love the buried look of pleasure that sex brings to the face and I didn't hurry, letting him fumble with my breasts under their starchy covering of apron. He panted and groaned, finally releasing a spurt which shot over my skirt.

After dabbing my skirt clean with a flannel he pressed a large denomination of the Dutch guilder into my hand. So it began. But I was as unlike those poor creatures who huddled around the old port as Marie Antoinette was to a real shepherdess. My twin desires for sex and money formed into a glorious union. Shame – that instrument of rule over women and the poor – didn't enter my head and I never missed Mass, regarding my confessions as acts of creativity. To have so much to tell! I imagined my adventures to be a welcome change for the priest, among his daily litany of neighbourly jealousies and adolescent soilings of the sheets.

My only regret, if it can be called that, was that that first encounter left me hungry and I vowed never again to leave unsatisfied. That night I drew a deep bath, wiped the steam from the mirror and stood before it, dewy and naked. I admired the tilt of my small, firm breasts and stretched open my sex with the fingers of one hand. The dark curly bush parted softly, revealing the jewel-coloured slit beneath. With the other hand I patted and played, loving myself with abandon. Looking in the mirror made my breath come sharper. It amazed me that men could value their pricks above what I held between my legs. It appeared so big and shiny in the mirror as I lovingly stroked and worried the flushed folds, my fingers dancing round the button of pleasure. The little sucking sound my fingers made as I rubbed thrummed in my ears and I felt the climax gather and then shoot its arrows over my body. A few seconds later some troublesome colleague banged on the door, enquiring archly if I was going to take *all* night...

I became another attraction in that palace of desires – fulfilling the same luxury that the trellised silver, the smell of coffee lingering in the soaring lobby and the heavy liquids in thick bottles behind the bar offered. Despite the want and the talk of war, many prospered.

These men on their business or travelling adventures quickly knew from my approachable manner what bounty could be on offer. They supped at my table, often with their wives out shopping, blithely blessing the Depression for making everything so cheap.

With my petticoats above my head, they'd dip their puckered old pricks in my juicy vibrant little fanny. They'd play with my darling rosebud nipples, panting, 'Hold them up, let me suck at them.' You think that President invented the trick with the cigar? It was a favourite of mine! I liked to think they would light it later in the restaurant, my juices adding to its pungent smoke.

I never forgot that first lesson, though, and made sure my own pleasure came first. I'd sit astride their whiskery faces. 'Stick your tongue right up,' I'd command, the social order momentarily upturned. 'Lick all the juice off the peach.' I took no account of age, but I preferred the older gentlemen. They were slower and more grateful and my uniform seemed to spark memories of youthful long-ago desires for their maids in country houses.

One old darling, who confessed to me that his fortune was made mainly from fraud, loved to wash me. At first it occurred to me he may have not wanted contact with the dirty taint of the lower classes, but he loved the act itself. His pleasure came from soaping my dark pubic curls and watching the lather drip from them, the red of my lips peeking from the creamy embrace of the bubbles. Eventually he persuaded me to let him divest me of these curls. With his shaving brush he lathered me up, using his terrifying open razor to expertly peel away my fuzz. Enchanted, he stroked and cradled it until, almost mad with frustration, I unbuttoned his fly and crouched over him, bouncing on his long thin cock and keeping my new-found bareness within his vision. I was as delighted with my bald little pussy as he and I kept stealing looks at it under the bed covers at night. But when the hair grew back it was scratchy and uncomfortable and I decided that some enthusiasms needed to be restrained.

Before I left their rooms I may have sketchily cleaned the basin or wiped the mirror. But I would say over my shoulder as I left that the room had better be clean, or the housekeeper wouldn't let me stay. With their public school training they would have the rooms sparkling within an hour.

Boredom made me reckless. I had been as confined by the hotel as a nun in her convent, only glimpsing the sunlight from the inside as it poured through coloured glass. Soon I continued in the tradition of escapees by stuffing pillows into my bed at night in a downy replica of my sleeping body. I fled through the darkened humming kitchen and left through a window, or the side door – slippery as one of the eels I would eat later with onions, washed down with acrid gin, or jenever, as it was named, drunk from a thick glass tumbler. Very soon the kitchen porter caught me. But I also caught him, greedily feeding from a joint of beef. So, doubly caught by each other, we became complicit in the need to satisfy our separate desires.

As gluttonous in my own way as the kitchen porter, I tired of the refined international hotel fare of grilled fish and duchess potatoes. I wanted tastes that scorched my palate, and on the Leidseplein I feasted on plates of salty herring in the dark inviting cafes where artists and poets would gather around thickly tapestried tables. I let the pungent liquorice drops bought from market stalls slip down my throat as I wandered, alone and mainly undisturbed. Greedy too for sensation, I would take in the smoke, the hubbub and the music – which came from bars or from loudspeakers playing the radio, strung up like lights across the street – like a transfusion of much needed blood.

I fell for this city of water and reflected light, with its barges and steamers gliding down the canals, their little lamps glowing behind the portholes. But it was the salty atmosphere of Zeedijk that intrigued me most, where in the night clubs I would sit, gin in hand, watching the hectic glamour of men in sequinned tiaras and women with deep voices wearing the apparel of their fathers and brothers.

With the thunder of war in the air, guests in the hotel had become sparser. So I particularly noticed the arrival of a new couple from England as I stood resentfully rubbing at the pared tulips of brass holding aloft the electric lights in the foyer. I would have noticed Mrs Edmondson anyway – how like myself she looked! Except, that is, *her* dark curls were fashionably marcel-waved and her trim figure was hung with expensive tweed and strung with pearls.

Mr Edmondson, who was older than his wife, had high elegant cheekbones and a dashing moustache. He soon informed me that he was acquainted with another gentleman of mine who I remembered had serviced me admirably in the past. Time-consuming preambles were thus brushed conveniently aside and, on the first opportunity, with his wife on some sight-seeing tour, he surprised me while I cleaned his bath, pressing his groin into the folds of my hated uniform.

'How small your waist is!' he remarked, as his trembling hands encircled it. His hands fumbled up my legs to feel my stocking tops and he fell to his knees.

'Let me see your little round bottom,' he begged.

I lifted my skirts obediently and he tugged down my voluminous camiknickers. Arse naked to the air except for suspender straps biting into my cheeks, I leaned over the bath for him to admire the view unrestricted. He groaned and shifted about as he tenderly handled the pink orbs, stretching them apart to reveal the secret mouth within. Then, joy! I felt his heavy breath between my legs as his moustache tickled my sex. His tongue slicked over me and it was my turn to heave a sound of pleasure.

Wanting it all the more because what I was taking was *hers*, I shoved my creamy slit further into his mouth. As he licked he mumbled passionately into my cunt, 'beautiful flower,' and 'dirty slut.' He sat me on the edge of the big enamel bath and, after fumbling about, took his cock from his trousers with the flourish of a magician producing a rabbit from a hat.

'Kiss me,' he pleaded. And, from the way he was extending his thickly veined prick with the palm of his hand, I surmised he didn't mean on the mouth.

I nibbled on the end of his prick, slathering my tongue up the shaft, all the time reaching out for more with my fingers – desperate to feel his stocky legs, his hairy behind and cradle his tight balls in my hand. He shook off the rest of his clothes, revealing a stocky frame like a boxer, and began to tear at the buttons of my uniform.

'Careful,' I cried, 'the housekeeper will think I've been in a street brawl.'

I undid myself for him, peeling away the layers until he was able to rub his tightly shorn curls between my breasts. Craving the velvet rub of his cock inside me, I spread my legs wide, dressed only in my stockings. He guided his prick lovingly to my waiting cunt and began to pump, the action producing the little sucking sound that is the accompaniment to the act. While he groaned and thrust I thought of how he must do it to her; how he must mount her in the dead of night, smuggling his heavy prick into her little slit. Did she enjoy it too? Did she gasp as her climax gathered and swelled, releasing its dammed up waves across her body?

Later that evening, while on some menial errand, I saw her in the restaurant and I spied on her through the kitchen hatch. She wore a fashionable slash of pillar-box lipstick and some diamond jewel glittered from her glossy hair. Her chocolate-coloured eyes seemed to follow me as I passed the open door of the restaurant. I burned in my resentment. So like each other but so unlike: her accident of birth meant that she was buffed and sheened while I was born to scrape away at other peoples' dirt. I was doubly glad then that I was fucking her husband and taking his money.

My resentment seethed and festered and the only balm that soothed it was counting out the money stacking up like building bricks in my overnight bag, with its sturdy lock warning off intruders. When in the Edmondsons' bedroom, I took to playing with her things like a child. It was while I opened and shut the compact with intertwined C's embossed on its lid, listening to its brassy click, that he made the announcement.

'My wife, Nancy, would like to meet you.' He watched me steadily and reclined on the chair, shirt tails ruffled round his legs.

I nearly dropped the compact. 'Then she knows about this?' I was incredulous.

He laughed. 'She likes to meet all my young ladies.'

So that was the secret that burned behind her eyes, that flowed beneath her graceful poise. I said that I would look forward to it and we arranged to meet late so I could be sure of all the dozy girls around me being engulfed by sleep.

All day I was alive with curiosity about the night's adventure. Did she just want to check me over, see that my teeth and hair were sound? Perhaps her husband liked to parade his infidelity before her. It even occurred to me that her pleasure might derive from watching her husband, with his gentleman's face and boxer's body, entwined with another woman, suckling at her breasts and with his cock honeyed by juices that were not her own.

As he instructed I wore my uniform. However much I tried to struggle from its binds, these men would never let me turn loose from it. When I arrived, knocking softly at the door, she wasn't there. At first I thought she may have lost her nerve and packed her bags or be walking the rainy streets in jealous turmoil. But almost as soon as he had set me on his knee, she softly turned the key in the lock and made her entrance. Little drops of rain embossed her hair and coat.

She seemed enthralled, in a state of nervous excitement, and flung herself down on the edge of the bed, her feet in their expensive neatly heeled shoes, pointing elegantly.

'Darling, she looks just like me.' She laughed, as if delighted by her husband's unconventional devotion. 'Is she as pretty underneath?' Her slim neck was craned forward, her dark eyes aglow.

Mr Edmondson snaked his hand under my petticoat ruffles and breathed hard when he discovered my naked bottom underneath. He drew up my skirts.

'Look at Emily's luscious little fanny. It's almost as sweet as your perfect burrow.' I lay back in his arms, the centre of attention, and parted my legs to let her see the fruit he had been tasting.

She was almost bouncing on the bed with excitement. 'Dip your finger in, my love. Let me see you ravish her with your hand.'

So I was right! Her pleasure came from watching her husband with another, witnessing their moist couplings. My slit was creamy and heavy with desire already and, with one hand, I parted it to allow him better access. His fingers stroked my dewy lips before sliding his middle finger up to the knuckle. He slowly pulled it out and then, leaning forward, lovingly painted my juices on his wife's mouth. She licked them off with quick little dabs of her tongue, giving small 'ohs' of excitement.

She began to fidget with the hem of my skirt between her finger and thumb. The swell of my desire grew. I had never experienced the Sapphic delights paraded at the salty clubs around Zeedijk, but they intrigued me as a new journey might. If she would only lean forward a little more she could add her own inquiring fingers to her husband's.

The colour in her cheeks began to redden and her eyes were almost flashing as she knelt down and began to unbutton my dress. I lay back as if in a buoyant sea of lust.

'Would you like me like this?' she breathed heavily to her husband. 'Would you like to take me as a little skivvying slut?'

I recoiled almost as if I had been struck. Despite

our likeness, she had asserted her status without a thought.

'Take it off,' she squealed. 'Let me have your uniform.'

Her eyes had the greedy imperiousness of one used to getting what she wanted. Well, if she wished to wear these threads of oppression she was welcome to them. I decided there and then they had burdened my back for far too long. I stripped quickly and she triumphantly gathered up the garments around my feet. He helped her dress, right down to my stockings which he moulded over her outstretched feet. He finished by tying the little white apron around her slim waist. I saw then by his slavish movements that it was her, not him, who chose and directed their adventures. My discarded outfit fitted her perfectly.

'Look at me.' She was entranced with herself. 'I look like one of those filthy hussies that shakes down our bed.' She was almost dancing about in her excitement. 'Take me like this,' she ordered her husband. 'Do it to me as if I were one of those sluts.'

So the object of her attention had not been me or even him, but my vile uniform. I almost laughed out loud. She leaned over the chair with the skirts almost over her head, as I had done so many times, and from behind it was like watching myself.

'You're a little hussy,' he said severely, his part obviously well rehearsed.

He lovingly smacked her bottom, which bounced with his slaps and her fervour. Her fanny arched up to him like an opened apple and he quickly divested himself of his trousers, his prick extending finely before him.

'You're a dirty little slut,' he crooned, giving her a final slap, his cock bouncing with the exertion.

'Do it to me now, take me roughly,' she squealed.

Soon they were in abandon, his backside working back and forth and his cock working in and out of her juicy opening.

Her discarded clothes were so fine. I slipped on her heavy wool coat and bundled up her exquisite black suit and shoes and stole from the room, leaving them oblivious in their throes of passion.

My bag had to be retrieved. But I did this quickly, scampering upstairs and creeping through my bed-room – the other girls there oblivious also, deeply asleep. On the fifth floor I entered the lift as Emily Parsons, or Emily Protheroe, whichever you wanted to believe. On the ground floor I left as Nancy Edmondson, affluent young wife, elegant in a chic little black suit from Paris. So I shifted into yet another identity, not realising this was the beginning of a lifetime of perso-nas which would dawn and fade like the days.

Thankfully I didn't know the concierge behind the desk. We girls were supposed to be tucked up in our beds long before his duty began. As I left, with a poise and vigour I hadn't previously possessed, he hailed me with a name I didn't answer to at first.

'Mrs Edmondson. Excuse me, but a courier has your order of sterling from the bank. Would you like to sign for it?' It wasn't just the name that was novel to me, it was his tone of voice: deferential.

'Of course.' I shielded myself with the perky little cloche hat as I put some scribble on the page. He didn't even look at it. I was to learn that the rich are never questioned and this made me bold.

'May I have the key to the safe? I want to check something,' I said in an imperious tone – Nancy's voice. I had the package tucked under my arm – Nancy's money.

'Of course.' He inclined his head a little.

Inside the locked box were two small velvet bags. I paused to look inside and the diamond light of Africa shone back. There were other jewels – necklaces and bracelets – but I left her these, a small morsel of comfort. Only an opal ring I took. The sparks of green and red seemed to fly out at me, willing me to slip it on my finger. I'm looking at it now and the colours strike out from its hidden depths as clearly as they did when I first saw it. They say opals are bad luck. But perhaps that means the luck they bring to the wicked can only be good because my opal has been good to me over the years.

And my good-bad opal was to weave its work very soon. For it was the dawn of 1940 when I left that night aboard a cargo ship. In a few short months Amsterdam would be marching to a very different tune to the dance music which jangled through the loud-speakers strung across the streets.

The Puppeteer

Matthew stood on the freezing steps and rang the bell. He strained in the dark to see the writing on the scrap of paper in his hand – flat six. Blowing on his hands for warmth, he looked up at the vast building in front of him for signs of life. The shuttered windows stared mutely back. He rang again. Edinburgh lay around him, stone cold.

At last there was a response. The buzzer sounded loudly and mechanically and he pushed the door open. His hand jolted with cold as he grasped the huge brass doorknob. Flat three, flat four, he passed the closed doors. Damn, it must be at the top of the house. As he ascended the stairs he could sense the carpet's spongy chill, even through his shoes. Right at the end of the corridor was an open door, the room painted red inside. In the dark of the corridor it looked like a vast open mouth.

The heat hit him even before he got to the door, sending gusts of warmth down the hall. He could hear voices and laughing inside but his knock received no response, so he entered. What struck him first was the blazing fire in the grate, licking the whole room with its flames. At first, the scene didn't register in his mind. There were a lot of people around, he thought – it must be a party. Then he realised how many were in a state of half undress. Little groups of two or three were embracing and caressing. On the couch a couple lay on top of each other. The man's buttocks moved rhythmically up and down. Matthew felt numb with shock.

In the centre of the room was a vast wing chair: red satin and wood. Sitting with one heel on a little foot-stool was a tall, slim girl. She wore black net underwear under a long leather coat, her boots reached up to her thighs and she dangled a riding crop from her hand.

'Have you come to join us?' Her voice was guttural with some East European accent.

He straightened his back and resolutely looked her in the eye. 'I'm here to deliver a message to Marzena from the theatre. They phoned but there was no reply.'

As if on cue a telephone began to ring in the background. She flapped the air as if to wave the irritating noise away. 'The machine will get it.'

Matthew felt ridiculous, as if everyone was staring at him, giggling at his discomfort and the way he was conversing as if everything was normal. He handed her the piece of paper. He knew it said: Rehearsal, tomorrow, 3 p.m. She read it, nodded in assent and then threw the paper on the fire.

Next to him the couple were groaning and gasping. A woman got up and went to sit beside them, watching their movements intently. The man raised himself up on his arms and Matthew caught a glimpse of his shining penis as it moved in and out of the woman beneath him.

'I'll be there.' So *this* was Marzena. In the background there was music, the sweet tones of Bobby Vinton: 'she wore blooooue v-e-e-e-lvet.' For some reason it made the hairs on the back of Matthew's neck stand up. Goodbyes seemed superfluous in the situation, so he turned and fled.

* * *

He certainly didn't want to go back there the next day. But he'd been told to by the theatre manager and he guessed it was part of his makeshift job – part handyman, part stagehand – in the tiny, under-funded theatre. Karen had offered to help him pack the boxes of puppets at Marzena's house.

'Do you know what I saw there last night?' He still felt outraged, as if the scene had been constructed to humiliate him. He felt he should warn Karen, in case she should ever stumble into that woman's house, that den of lions.

She looked up at him shyly. 'I was there.' The shock jolted through his stomach.

'Oh Matthew, it's not terrible at all.' She spoke very quickly. 'It's beautiful and decadent, like in the nineteenth century in an opium den or something.' She giggled. 'I saw you there and you looked like you were going to explode.'

The van was broken as usual so they would have to walk. Matthew rooted in the petty cash tin for taxi money. It contained a few coins and a pile of receipts that people were hoping to claim back. Fat chance. They walked through the rain.

'I can't believe you got mixed up in something like that.' He hadn't meant it to sound so bossy, but that's how it came out. Their relationship had always been casual. Matthew had been unable to promise the fidelity that she'd wanted. Now he realised how much store he had set by her own faithfulness.

'I didn't ... didn't *do* anything.' She sounded annoyed. 'I think sex is a beautiful thing and it's selfish to keep it to yourself.' She sounded like an echo of somebody else. 'For God's sake, Matthew, don't sound so ... so disapproving.'

They walked in silence the rest of the way, the rain pattering on their umbrellas.

Marzena answered the door brushing her teeth. Her long brown hair had a morning, bed-rumpled untidiness. Her clothes were a curious mixture: a flowered old-fashioned dress which clung to her body, topped by a little blue and white PVC jacket. On her feet she wore huge men's boots with buckles. All the same, Matthew had to admit that she carried it all with a sense of style. As if any woman looking at her might think, yes, I'll start dressing from Oxfam so I too can look like that. She looked entirely unconcerned when she saw him.

'My puppets are in the studio,' she said. 'Down in the basement.'

The basement was freezing and filthy. Wood shavings scattered the floor and on the workbench dangerous-looking shiny pointed tools lay in a jumble with cold cups of coffee and wood chippings. Pages of magazines were stuck all around the walls. There were photographs of people: running, sitting, lying, posing into the camera. A series of frames from a cartoon ran right around the room. The story seemed to tell of a boy entering a wood and being frightened by a monster who lived there.

'How does she work in this place?' Matthew grumbled. Everything he said sounded petulant today.

He noticed the ripped page from a porno magazine tacked just above her work bench. The woman in the photograph had yellow hair and leather boots. Her pussy shone out wetly from between her legs and she was holding herself open with one finger, teasing the viewer. Matthew looked away quickly.

'Let's get these damned things packed away,' he said.

The puppets were remarkable. Even Matthew had to admit to her talent. Despite the chaos of the rest of the room, they were stacked neatly on a table, their strings looped and tied expertly with little plastic twists, like the ones on sandwich bags. The figures were huge – almost four feet tall. Their faces and bodies were formed from knotted gnarled wood, as if the original tree had transmogrified somehow, assuming human features. He picked up the figure of a girl with piercing blue glass eyes. Its head lolled to one side.

'No, no, never pick them up like that,' Marzena screamed. Matthew hadn't heard her enter the room. She picked the puppet up expertly and tenderly. 'Like this,' she commanded, laying the figure in the box as if she was putting a child to bed.

The packing took forever. Marzena placed each figure in a shroud of bubble wrap before entombing them in cardboard boxes. She issued curt instructions to Matthew and Karen, watching their packing methods like a hawk. When Matthew spoke to her it was through tight, disapproving lips. With a sudden stab of self-awareness he realised how much he wanted her to feel ashamed for last night, for her lewdness, for his humiliation. He would have liked her to cast her eyes down, not to look into his eyes and speak in soft, appeasing tones. On the contrary, she spoke to him in a commanding voice and stood uncomfortably close so he could feel her warm breath on his face.

As she worked she stripped off her jacket. The top couple of buttons of her dress were left casually undone so that her small, rounded breasts could be glimpsed at the neckline. Matthew looked quickly away, as if the two girls might be able to read his thoughts. The image of Marzena's legs spread wide open had been in his thoughts constantly since last night. It had featured in his fantasy as he had masturbated in bed. He had imagined her over and over again, pulling her little knickers to one side to reveal her slit, running the tip of her riding crop slowly up and down it.

Karen had also removed her coat and her cheeks looked pink from the exertion of the work. She chattered to Marzena about how she was trying to find work as an actress while she filled in time helping at the theatre. Her red hair formed a bright spot in the room.

When Karen had told him about her presence last night he knew his feelings of outrage were unjustified. How many women had he been with since he had known her? But he felt something else too – a tingling, excited curiosity. His feelings of relief had mingled with a strange disappointment when Karen admitted to not having participated. As if he could have lived out the scene vicariously through her experience.

They stacked the puppets by the front door, ready for Marzena's friend who was to pick them up. Marzena gave them a stack of leaflets in boxes to hand out to local shops and tourist offices. Matthew picked one up. It started: 'I first learned the incredible art of puppet making from my grandmother in Poland.' (The English was a bit peculiar in places.) 'She was a glorious woman and her talents were spoken of everywhere. I have lived in this great city for six months and now I desire to display these talents, to astound you . . .' Modesty didn't seem to be one of Marzena's attributes, in more ways than one.

* * *

Karen felt curiously light headed as she walked back to the theatre through the rain. Marzena had taught her more about life in a week than she had ever known. About how women should stand their ground, how they shouldn't be ashamed of their sexy thoughts and feelings, that women had been conditioned to think they should stay with one man. These ideas had some-how come to a head last night. Karen had watched the couplings, trembling with fear and desire. Her fanny still felt moist and swollen. How she had longed to take her place among one of the little groups as they licked and fondled each other. It had only been Matthew bursting in like that that had stopped her – though why she should feel any loyalty to him she didn't know.

She glanced sideways at him. As usual his slightly thick-set body and the way the bristles of his hair grew at his neck caused a spasm of longing. She stopped abruptly and put her boxes down to rest her arms. They were nearly at the theatre now, in what had once been the commercial district of Edinburgh – full of grey, small alleys running between warehouses. The arousal that had been implanted last night became almost unbearable, blooming over her thighs and stomach. She pulled Matthew towards her into the darkness of a doorway.

'I feel so hot, Matthew, down here.' She pulled up her skirt for him to see, sliding one of her fingers underneath her knickers. She could feel the wetness that had seeped into the fabric. Matthew's face was a picture! She knew that he expected her to be so timid and loyal. Certainly not exposing herself in this way in the middle of the city. He flushed as he looked down. Karen began to play her fingers across her clit, the movements of her hand clearly visible underneath her knickers. She pulled the fabric further over so he could see clearly the red fuzz that covered her mound. She knew she was showing off now and she inwardly blossomed with pleasure at the effect she was having, of how her performance made Matthew's breath suddenly rasp and quicken.

'What happened last night, it's set me on fire. Oh, you should have stayed, Matthew. You should have seen it. It's like everyone was under a spell; like we were in a different world where normal things didn't matter.' She spoke quickly, almost as if he wasn't there. 'One woman who was near me, she was sucking a man's cock like she was going to swallow it while his girlfriend watched and played with the other woman's breasts.' Her hand stopped abruptly, as if she had been just about to send herself over the edge. Her eyes flew open and focused slowly on him.

Matthew was breathing heavily now, as if he too could picture the scene she had painted so vividly for him. Roughly he undid the buttons of her light-blue blouse. She wore no bra underneath and her pale nipples were puckered into points. His coat grazed against them as he fixed his mouth onto hers. She pulled at the lapels of his coat.

'Kneel down on me,' she whispered. She quickly pulled off her little knickers and threw them on the ground.

As he knelt she lifted up her leg and rested it on one of the boxes. Her hair had come loose from its ponytail and hung about her face. She pulled her skirt right up so that her wet stretched cunt was inches from his face. He groaned and buried his face in the curls of red moist hair, then slicked his tongue between her legs until she pulled him abruptly to his feet by his hair.

She drank in the dazed look of lust on his face. What power she had. She'd never realised before!

Unzipping him, she released his cock which looked squeezed from being jammed inside his trousers. Lifting her leg up further she guided it between her legs, where it quickly found her opening and slithered home. When Matthew began moving inside of her it felt like a new, fresh experience. She tipped her pelvis forward to suck him in further, so that his cock could rub roughly at her clit. He thrust in long, hard jabs, so that her head banged against the door behind her.

Karen felt so hot that she was sure if the rain – which fell like a curtain at the entrance to the doorway – came in contact with her skin, it would bubble and fizz at the heat. Desire shot up her legs and round her pussy, making her moan and pant. She'd never climaxed standing up before and, as her orgasm swelled inside her, it was like a totally new way of fucking. It felt hotter somehow, more urgent and intense.

Matthew put his hand over her mouth as she moaned out loud. As her climax lapped over her she heard the sound of voices close by. She slumped back against the doorway and, in a panic, Matthew withdrew. His prick was wet and painful-looking as he crammed it back inside his boxer shorts.

They emerged to see a group of office workers, standing in the rain under umbrellas to have a cigarette. The group fell silent as Matthew and Karen walked past, carrying their boxes. It must be so obvious, thought Karen, before realising that she didn't care.

The rehearsal had gone badly. Everything seemed to be wrong for Marzena. She stood on the raised platform on the stage, hidden by a screen up to her armpits, and screamed orders.

'Everything is all terrible,' she said dramatically. She shouted up at the lighting man, 'More light, you stupid fuck, do you think I perform in the dark?'

People whispered about Marzena and her temper. But the amazing thing, Karen reflected, was how she managed to purr over and charm them immediately after screaming in their faces. As she left she walked with Karen, putting an arm conspiratorially around her shoulders.

'I'm having a few people over again next week,' she whispered into Karen's ear as if involving her in some girlish conspiracy. 'I'd love you to be there.' She touched Karen's face. 'You're so beautiful, you know.' Karen felt a ridiculous swell of pride in her stomach. Marzena called over her shoulder as they parted, 'Bring Matthew too. I think he needs to loosen up a little!' With a naughty gleam in her eye, she was gone.

Karen was surprised at how little persuasion it had taken for Matthew to agree. She'd almost been thinking she'd rather go on her own. What was happening was an important journey for her and she didn't want Matthew cramping her style. She may want to go further this time.

'At least I'll be able to keep an eye on you.' Matthew's excuse had sounded a bit limp, probably even to himself.

He'd spent several nights at her flat since their unplanned fuck in the shop doorway. Lying in bed, she whispered the torrid details of what had happened that night at Marzena's as she played with his cock, which grew hard beneath her fingers almost at once.

*　*　*

Karen reddened her mouth with lipstick and looped golden gypsy earrings through her lobes. So Matthew must have chickened out. Well, stuff him, she thought. The sense of strange anxiety gathered in her stomach as she got into the waiting taxi. If the taxi driver knew where she was going, would he be shocked? She shivered and settled back into the cold leather seat.

Marzena was wearing a tight, ripped net T-shirt and a short leather skirt when she greeted Karen at the door. She kissed Karen full on the mouth and flicked her tongue quickly inside, once.

'Matthew's not here? Oh well, we'll have fun without him.' Marzena giggled, as if it was all a delightful game, like playing doctors and nurses when you were little.

Karen was so excited she could hardly speak. At first she felt a bit awkward and sat perched on the edge of the sofa with her feet dangling in their tapestried stilettos. What had felt so good about Marzena's last 'happening' was the atmosphere: a kind of excited shame mixed with the sense of moving in a different world – a world which ran alongside normal life, which could be accessed from the humdrum streets through a heavy door leading to a red room. People moved lazily, some fucking, some just kissing or watching. Among them all moved Marzena herself, beautiful and proud, wayward and strange. When she went out of the room it was as if a light went off and people began to seem unsure of themselves. When she returned they relaxed again. She made everyone feel special in her presence.

The wine soon eased the knot in Karen's stomach and made her feel flushed and bright. She talked about theatre with Marzena and a group of her friends. They were a very mixed collection, as if Marzena had scoured the Edinburgh streets for interesting people. There were art dealers, actors, engineers and an investment banker who wore a beautifully cut dark suit. A guy who worked in a sandwich bar – his hair plaited in neat, shining rows and tied into a thick ponytail – took off his shoes and sat Buddah-like on the floor. Karen recognised several people from the theatre who had been there last time and they nodded to each other.

The atmosphere tingled with tension and people's faces took on a different aspect – flushed and tense, as if they were wearing masks. Charlotte, who had played Miss Jean Brodie (always a money-spinner) in the theatre's last production, kicked off her shoes and rested her head on the lap of a man Karen didn't recognise. Some music was put on and the man's face – angular and handsome – pinched with excitement as he played with Charlotte's hair, then with trembling fingers undid the buttons on her blouse. Marzena – with one knee on the sofa, her little leather skirt straining in folds around her bottom – gently parted Charlotte's legs. All eyes were upon them now, as if they were performing on a public stage. Pushing Charlotte's skirt up around her waist so everyone could see, Marzena began to stroke the other woman's slit beneath her little white knickers. Her lips stood out in a swollen pout underneath the fabric.

Karen felt the tense knot of excitement return to her stomach. She felt hot and languorous and ached to be touched. When the guy with the plaits – who had been glancing at her all evening – lay on the floor next to her and traced his fingers over her stomach and her full breasts, she arched her back in pleasure. A wild beat drummed in her ears. He kissed her for a long time. Each kiss set her body on fire, as if her mouth were a sexual organ. His tongue explored the inside of her mouth delicately.

When Karen glanced over to Marzena again, Charlotte's knickers were lying discarded on the floor and Marzena was stroking and pulling at the lips of Charlotte's slit. Charlotte writhed in pleasure and ground her head into the man's lap. Standing behind the sofa the man in the beautiful suit stood watching them. Beads of sweat stood out on his forehead.

Marzena winked at Karen and patted the sofa next to her. Abandoning her newly found partner (who was by now being caressed from behind by a girl with long black plaits), Karen sank into the depths of the huge battered sofa. A stray wisp of horse hair which had burst forth from the base tickled her leg. Marzena put her arm around Karen in a sisterly way and the two sat next to each other, whispering and giggling like naughty children.

'Have you met Ed?' Marzena pulled the suited man over by tugging at his jacket. She hugged Karen drunkenly. 'Karen is my best friend in all Edinburgh,' she told Ed. 'Don't you love her red hair?' Marzena pulled off Karen's hair band and the hair fell around her face. The couple next to them stood up and made their way to the bedroom with their clothes hanging wildly from them.

Ed smiled indulgently as they teased him. His hardened cock was plainly visible inside his trousers and he made no attempt to disguise it.

'Sit on his lap, Karen,' Marzena ordered. Karen felt the hardness under her moist cunt as she bounced and giggled on his suited lap. He smelled delicious and expensive.

'I know what he would like,' said Marzena wickedly as she produced the riding crop from under the cushions of the sofa. 'Kneel down,' she commanded him. There was a wild look in her eyes as she held the crop tight across her body.

In what seemed like an instant Ed was kneeling on the floor with his trousers around his knees. His buttocks were tensed up and Karen gasped when she saw his prick extended out before him, long and thick. Marzena tickled the leather fold on the end of the crop at the crack of his buttocks and then struck him smartly. He flinched and his prick quivered, a tiny drop of milky fluid appearing at the end.

Karen felt a thrill of power. So this was how you made men slavishly adore you: not by being soft and sweet, but by dressing in leather and ordering them about, arousing fear and longing in their eyes.

'You try,' said Marzena, handing her the crop.

Tentatively at first, Karen rapped the crop across his buttocks. Then, gathering confidence, she whacked him soundly, leaving red stripes across the white skin. She felt mad, powerful, possessed, as she striped him again and again. He groaned in pleasure and his balls tightened spasmodically. Marzena smiled approvingly.

Tired out, Karen flung herself on the sofa. Ed lay over her with his fine massive cock rearing from beneath the bottom of his shirt. His smell made her feel dizzy and drunk and she writhed under him. The rest of the room seemed to have blurred almost out of focus.

Suddenly she saw the familiar shape of Matthew standing over her. She saw herself as if looking through Matthew's eyes – exposed and excited, with another man's cock lying heavily on her stomach – and a sense of guilty shame crawled over her.

But she realised Matthew was swaying slightly with

drink. He lay down next to her, kissing her, fondling her tits. 'Oh, my love, my love,' he muttered.

While Matthew murmured to her, Ed stole his prick slowly between her moist folds. He moved lazily inside her while Matthew held her head and stroked her hair.

'I've never seen you so beautiful,' Matthew whispered drunkenly into her hair.

Marzena sat, crouched, watching them like a cat. Slowly she moved into their circle, unbuttoning Matthew's flies and releasing his hardened prick. Checking that Karen was watching, she applied her lips gently to the end, making little sucking noises. Matthew closed his eyes and gripped her hair savagely, forcing her to take more of his length into her lipstick-reddened mouth.

Karen felt a pang of jealousy as she watched him frown and curse in pleasure. So this was how he looked with all those other women, her rivals; they too had transformed his face like that. The jealousy mingled and escalated the rising pleasure. How many times she had imagined what he looked like with those other women. She had fantasised in jealous fury about it when he was absent from her bed, stroking her hot little pussy while she visualised him buried deep inside another woman.

Marzena cradled his balls with her hand while she sucked. Perspiration ran down Matthew's face and his hips thrust forward, cramming more and more of his penis into her mouth. The muscles in his neck twitched spasmodically as Marzena slid her mouth up and down, Matthew obscenely jamming her mouth open to an unnatural width. He began to make short rapid grunts and closed his eyes tight so the sweat ran over his creased eyelids. He leaned over Karen and, with a heave, shot his come into Marzena's mouth, simultaneously fixing his lips over Karen's. A couple of seconds later, Karen felt her own moist pussy contract around Ed's cock. Her muscles fluttered up and down his hardness in a gentle rhythm. His languid, leisurely movements inside her seemed to gather her climax sweetly and slowly and, for what seemed like forever, she felt herself trembling on the edge. Karen glimpsed Marzena kneeling on the floor and swallowing Matthew's sperm greedily. She must have been holding it in her mouth, tasting it. The thought sent Karen tumbling over the edge and the other three watched as she abandoned herself to it, redness marking her pale skin and glowing against her hair.

Matthew's ears thrummed to the swell of applause around him. He had to hand it to Marzena, the performance had been amazing. She had manipulated the puppets expertly, their bodies moving with weird veracity. The story had been a bit dramatic for his taste, involving along the way a two-headed monster who lived in a cave, men swearing undying love to a female puppet with long slender legs, and a double murder. During the murder scene the female puppet had transformed. Knives and scissors had sprung out of secret compartments in her body and her hands had turned into weapons.

The cast of characters were perfectly caught in Marzena's voice. One minute she was the monster roaring from its cave, the next a possessed woman screaming for revenge. It was as though she held all these personalities inside her, waiting to be unleashed. Matthew shifted uncomfortably on his seat and the brushed texture of the fabric set his teeth on edge.

He hung around after the performance, hoping to

bump into Karen. He'd hardly seen her since that night at Marzena's. He sensed she was changing. Every time he saw her she looked happier and more at ease with herself. His body ached for what she used to be, the way she had once belonged to him.

That night of Marzena's last party he'd resolved not to go. He'd sat in a bar downing whiskies on his own. But then a burning curiosity had got the better of him. The images which Karen's whispered words had evoked kept entering his mind and eventually he stumbled off his bar stool and found himself out in the cold dark street, walking quickly towards the area of the city where Marzena lived.

His mind shifted slowly back to the present and he realised most of the audience had left. Karen was talking animatedly to Marzena up on the stage and helping pack up the scenery. The pooled light of the spot above lit up her red hair. The two women looked up, startled at the sound of his footsteps in the dark.

Matthew set about half-heartedly helping them to move crates to one side, ready for the next performance. Marzena had found herself a chair and was sitting on it cross legged, massaging her feet with oil from a little blue bottle which sat next to her. Matthew followed Karen into the wings as she moved something from the stage.

'I've wanted to see you for days. Where have you been?' he whispered. He didn't want Marzena overhearing his desperation.

'I've been around and about. Actually I've been going for loads of auditions,' she went on excitedly. 'I auditioned for Varia in *The Cherry Orchard*. It's only a small production, but the director's really interested. He took me out for a drink afterwards.'

Matthew snorted, a bit too loudly even to his own

ears. A look of anger flushed Karen's face and she strutted off back to the stage.

'It wasn't like that at all, he just wanted to discuss ideas. He's really interested in me, as an actress.' Karen said the word 'actress' very slowly and deliberately.

'Please, I didn't mean it to sound like that. I just wanted to see you.' Matthew felt overwhelmed with longing for her. Her eyes blazed with anger and the new confident stance of her body made him feel even more miserable and desperate for her.

'Why don't you kiss him?' Matthew had almost forgotten Marzena's presence. She was hunched up on her chair, her arms cradled around her knees. She looked like a naughty fidgeting monkey-creature.

Karen smiled, as if caught by an amusing thought. She came close and kissed his face, his lips. His longing increased. He wanted to possess her, to enter her once more to mark her out again as his. He pulled at her arm to try and make her leave.

'No, here, right here,' she said harshly. He groaned and buried his face in her hair. At that moment he would have taken her anywhere: in the middle of a busy shopping centre; in a church, even, sprawled on the pews.

As they tore at each other's clothes, Matthew felt the blood racing in his head making him dizzy. He pulled her skirt right up and tore off her knickers, desperate to feel the sweet, warm wetness within. His finger slid easily inside her. He shook off his shoes and trousers and lay on top of her, entering her quickly with one easy movement.

He glanced up and saw Marzena, a hungry, avaricious look on her face. Her legs were wide open and with one hand she pulled and stretched her sex. With the other she stroked her clit using rapid little movements. Karen's head was turned towards her and their eyes seemed to be locked together. Matthew had the sudden uncomfortable feeling that Marzena was some outlandish obscene stage director and he and Karen were actors. But by now he was beyond caring. At last he was at home, inside that sweet familiar place with her juices coating and soothing his swollen cock. He felt Karen's fingers delve down and flutter against her clit, agitating the little button of pleasure.

Matthew felt bathed in a pool of light from the spot; the heat of it burned on the back of his neck. Almost unwillingly he turned towards Marzena. His penis throbbed when he saw her glazed eyes and her long slender fingers busy at the gaping slit between her legs. Her fingers patted and probed at the crack. Her hips were thrusting up and down in shaky involuntary movements. The spotlight gleamed on the shiny redness of her cunt and caught on the moisture that slicked her dancing fingers.

His forehead furrowed in concentration as he tried to hold on. He turned his head away but Marzena's abandoned animal grunts still penetrated his ears. He came in a rush – furious at being unable to control himself – releasing all the pent-up spunk of the last few weeks. Karen continued to dance her fingers around her clit for a few seconds, until a fiery flush marked her face and neck and her breath came out in little gasps. Lying on top of her, Matthew began to feel his head throb and ache.

Matthew didn't know how long he had been there, in his own bed. The fever swept up and down his body making the sheets damp with sweat. In his heightened state he thought he heard Karen speaking to him, telling him that she had to leave now for her new life.

Then the voice changed to Marzena's and Matthew suddenly realised that it had been her speaking all along through Karen's borrowed voice.

When he recovered he found himself tired and weak. He began to walk the streets to try and strengthen himself and build up the muscle in his wasted legs. His head tumbled with angry thoughts. Karen had got the part in *The Cherry Orchard* and had gone. He knew if it wasn't for Marzena she'd still be here, still be his. It was Marzena who had given her the confidence to strike out on her own. Sweet, loyal Karen, who once would have always stayed by his side.

He found himself in front of the building where Marzena lived and remembered the first night he'd met her; how he'd stood on the cold stone steps waiting to be admitted. Angrily he rang the bell.

Marzena was also leaving; crates and suitcases were scattered around the basement room. He felt a burning resentment towards her. Her hazel eyes glittered with health and life and her long hair went straight down her back in a shining wave. He wanted to accuse her in some way, to show her how she had taken Karen away from him. But he felt suddenly ill again and sat down heavily, closing his eyes.

'You poor thing.' She fussed around. 'Let me make you some camomile tea.'

She was playing at being maternal, Matthew thought with a surge of resentment. How quickly she slipped in and out of roles, finding and abandoning them so quickly that she could be seven different people within an hour.

She perched provocatively on a dining chair, the tops of her stockings peeking out from under her short black dress.

'Karen is happy now,' she was saying. 'You should

be happy for her.' She sat back so that her dress rode up a little more. Matthew had a sudden image of her on that first night with her legs spread wide open. His cock hardened spontaneously and his head throbbed.

He went over and kissed her hard. He wanted to punish her, to bruise her lips. Her legs opened a little more, revealing her naked pussy underneath with the dewy lips peeping out. He squeezed her breasts hard and she slumped back, a smile playing across her lips. For God's sake, he wanted her to hurt, to be punished for his loss. He picked up a coil of rope that lay on the workbench and swiftly fastened her hands together behind the chair, so her arms were locked over the back.

'Matthew, what are you doing?' she whispered in a small, excited voice.

He suddenly felt well and powerful again. As he lashed each ankle to the chair it was as if he was reclaiming himself and asserting his control once more. She sat immobile, unable to move with her legs stretched wide open by the ropes. Burying his face in her hot cunt he roughly tongued her until she went limp and moaned.

He'd show her who was boss. He pulled off his trousers and pointed his cock at her like a weapon. He pushed into her roughly. As his cock withdrew it gleamed from her wetness and she bent her head down to drink in the sight. He clawed and ripped at the tops of her stockings as he pumped. The sucking sounds made by his relentless thrusting echoed round the bare room.

A redness began to mark her neck and face and he pulled at her dress. The buttons flew in all directions and pinged on the cold stone floor. Her small rounded tits spilled out of her black bra and the skin there was patched with redness. She tried to force her hips up to meet him and the chair scraped and knocked on the floor.

'Hold still,' he barked at her. Yes, he was the one in control now. Despite the way she'd made Karen fly off like a bird, despite her conniving, obscene ways, she was now tethered and spread open for him. He grabbed her knees and forced them to open wider. He wanted to split her open with the hardness of his prick, to force himself into every orifice. When he glanced up he saw her watching him intently. He pulled out of her roughly and unwrapped the scarf from around his neck. He couldn't bear the way she was watching him with that little smile on her lips.

He wrapped the scarf around her eyes and tied it at the back of her head to block out her gaze. Guiding his cock towards her mouth he rested the tip against her lips and let her lick at it for a few minutes. When the bulb felt it was about to burst he withdrew it, leaving her gaping like a fish.

He parted her labia and squeezed inside her again. Inside she felt tight and wet and he could feel the muscles in her cunt expanding and contracting. After only a few seconds she came with an arch of her back and the increased wetness slicked against his cock.

The blindfold had slipped off Marzena's face and she looked up at him sideways, her eyes glowing with a satisfied light. It occurred to him suddenly that it was almost as if it had been she who had tied herself up. He had a sudden horrible realisation that as soon as she had heard his voice on the intercom she had darted down to the basement and placed the ropes so conspicuously; that she had mapped out, quickly and carefully, what was going to happen.

With a cry he pulled out of her. He couldn't let her

have his seed, to take it away with her. But it was too late. He cried out as his cock twitched and he pumped out the sticky deposit over the tops of her legs, marking the black of her stockings with the gluey whiteness. Wordlessly he untied her and left.

Karen wrote to him occasionally over the next few months. She was having the time of her life on tour, and had met someone else – quite an important actor whose name was familiar from the television.

One day a small jiffy bag came through his front door. A tiny, carved wooden figure fell out as he opened it – part woman, part monkey. It lay, nut brown wood, in his palm. There was a letter inside from Marzena, she wrote:

'This is something to remind you of me. I think of you still sometimes. Carry this always in your pocket...'

He crumpled up the letter and threw it away.

The next day he caught a train out into the countryside. The sky was clear blue and a cold wind scoured the stony mountains. He walked briskly for a while until he came to some soft earth. He dug feverishly with his fingers until he'd made a little hole. He dropped the wooden creature inside and then stamped back the earth again and again, until the soil was patterned all over from the sole of his shoe.

A Day at the Races

It was a perfect day for the races. Everyone looked keyed up and excited as they climbed out of hot stuffy cars ready for the day's sport. Toffs in green wellies mixed with shady-looking men in shiny suits; large, cheerful women wearing the regulation Driza-Bone hats teamed with strings of pearls around their necks studied the *Racing Times*. Cheeks seemed to glow, whipped into pinkness by gin and excitement. There may as well be a sign outside: come in, roll up, leave the rules and dull old reality outside.

The sky was clear and blue with just a few clouds urged along by the fresh cold breeze that harried and fluttered at the multicoloured flags strung out over the fences. Fiona turned her battered old Land Rover into the car park with a joyous sense of coming home. As she locked the car her nostrils flared with excitement, as if she could catch the scent of the herd on the breeze.

There was plenty of time for a drink before the first race started and Fiona felt the need to bolster her courage for the day's events. She deliberately squeezed through the densest crush of bodies to the bar, aware of hips, thighs, buttocks – and cocks – beneath thick clothing. Men in tweedy suits boomed out orders to the barman, turning to companions and asking, 'Will you have another?' She drained her gin and tonic and felt the Dutch courage run through her veins.

She looked around the room and again pushed

through the crush to another part of the bar. A smile played on her lips as the notion struck her that she had invented a whole new meaning to 'working a room'. She picked out a man in a scratchy brown coat as her first potential frisson of excitement in the sea of bodies. As she passed him she put her hand on his shoulder. She felt the scratchy fabric and he turned and smiled. She smiled back (too old) and carried on. Another man in a leather coat stood with his back to her and she bravely placed a gentle hand on his buttock, cupping and curving around its hardness. He turned, his face open and startled, but she was gone. He peered into the shifting crowd but could see nothing. Back to his friends and a roar of laughter from his group.

The heat of the tightly packed bar seemed to bring out the horsey smells buried in the warp and weft of peoples' clothes. She closed her eyes and breathed deeply. The scent crept with a narcotic effect through her mind. Proper horse smell; not like the pink horses with big blue eyes they sold in the toy shops. Those travesties were usually perfumed with some sickly-sweet scent that was totally unlike the smell of the real animal – straw, leather tack and sweat.

She knew exactly the day that smell began to inflame her senses. It lay on her sexual map like an important city, a landmark patterned with spires and furling banners. It was the day she saw Maggie, her gentle mare, being fitted with the felt shoes that would protect the stallion in case she lashed out. She had spied in trembling excitement as the groom held one of Maggie's forelegs to prevent her from kicking. She'd pressed her legs together as tight as they would go as she watched the long-haired stallion man prepare the beasts for mating. With an easy professionalism he gave the gigantic penis a couple of encouraging strokes before guiding it into the restrained mare. With much snorting and bucking and rolling of eyes, the mare was held in a receptive position while the stallion mated her with long, deep thrusts. Afterwards the stallion quickly slid off its tethered mate and wandered away, his huge cock flopping down to almost reach the grass. That night she had touched herself for the first time.

It had been the smell, the sheer size and the animalistic abandon that had excited her, but something else too: the casual anonymity of the horses' needy coupling had struck her as being some kind of lofty ideal. The realisation that the mare didn't expect to share her stable every night with the stallion for the rest of her life had been a dramatic awakening for Fiona.

The sound of the door opening to admit another group of people made her open her eyes again. It was packed already, but somehow everyone shifted just that bit closer and the new arrivals were swallowed up. The noise in the bar intensified, rising to a clamour so that Fiona could no longer distinguish any individual conversations.

She felt as soothed and supported by the crowd as that mare held by the stable hand, and the gentle stir between her legs bloomed into a needy ache. A hand, trapped by the crowd, pressed against her behind and she deliberately relaxed against it. Heat rose up her body and she could feel moistness seeping out and soaking her strappy thong. Already hot in her carefully chosen outfit of leather coat, high boots and long skirt (thoughtfully split up the back), she felt the room grow dizzyingly hotter. She wondered briefly what the owner of the hand would make of her stolen pleasure, and the thought caused a needle of shame. Did these furtive adventures mean she was like one of those men that rubbed themselves shamelessly against women in the throng of a tube train?

The thought made her lean forward, to give the hand a chance to liberate itself from the crush. When it didn't, her breathing increased tenfold. She felt the strong fingers move a little against the leather of her coat and the roundness of her buttock and a sharp scent of aftershave penetrated her nostrils. The heat gathered between her legs, marking a path up to her stomach and neck. The swell of voices pressed against her ears and she momentarily thought she was going to faint.

The hand on her behind was joined by a leg thrusting between hers, and Fiona felt a surge of joy. It found the split in her coat and the one in her skirt and she felt the rough fabric of his trousers between her knees. The ache spread across her body and knotted the muscles in her stomach. Her breasts suddenly felt hard and heavy, as if they were full of milk.

Fiona felt a nervous excitement pulse through her veins. Could this intimate contact really be accidental? A consequence of the tightly packed room, with people jostling for space, pressed together in enforced familiarity? She moved her legs slightly apart as if to steady herself, or maybe to test the reality of his intentions, not even attempting to turn around. Already an image of him was formulating itself in her head.

He got the message. His hand (it must be his left) moved down and into the slit in her coat and on through the folds to the split in the back of her skirt. She gasped, any doubts swept away, as the unseen stranger's fingers traced the line where her thong bisected her buttocks and continued to move between her legs. He must be feeling how wet I am, she thought, as she closed her eyes and imagined a thick hand, a hairy forearm, a long chestnut mane.

The stranger moved his arm around her hips and cupped and squeezed her swollen sex from the front so she had to bite her lip to stop herself from groaning out loud. Around her the crowd jostled and fidgeted. All at once the throng held her yet swayed in a rippling mass, like wind blowing through a field of wheat, making her place her weight first on one foot and then the other. To keep herself steady she rested her hand on the shoulder of the man in front, who briefly turned and smiled. 'Don't worry, it'll ease off soon,' he said.

She felt the stranger's hips press into her backside and she suppressed a cry again as she felt the unmistakable hardness of an erect cock outlined against her skin. She forced herself to keep her breathing in check, terrified that anyone around her might overhear her excited panting. Fuck me, fuck me – the words echoed in her head so loudly she thought they must be booming round the room.

Abruptly the tannoy crackled into life, announcing that the first race was about to begin. The bar was a sudden swirl of activity with glasses being drained and people gathering up friends. The crowd suddenly thinned. Desperately she glanced behind her but there was only a sea of faces. The door banged open and shut, sending gusts of grass-sweetened air into the stuffy enclosed place. She swayed on her feet as she adjusted to the emptiness that yawned around and inside her. Feeling bereft, she stood trembling with her legs apart and her pants sticking to her wet cunt.

Breathing in gulps of air she tried to calm herself and made a detour to the parade ring. The grounds hummed with human activity. The smells of frying from the fast food stands reminded her of giddy fairground trips: boys' arms clutched tightly round her waist on the

Wurlitzer, hurried fumbles in alleyways, popcorn-flavoured snogs under the multicoloured lights.

It occurred to her to find the toilet and finish herself off, but she dismissed the idea quickly. It seemed such a waste. She stood close to the fence, admiring the horses as they tossed their heads and flared their nostrils in their excitement. Perhaps the stallions could smell her arousal, could pick up the scent of her juices in their quivering nostrils.

As so often before she felt in awe of their beauty – their strong necks arching upwards, the powerful hooves which danced and flicked up sprays of turf. She took a deep breath of horse-scented air, of grass sweetened with furry musk. The sun skimmed over the glossy leather and metal of the tackle that fettered the animals' bodies. As soon as she'd been big enough to actually help with her father's horses, she'd been fascinated by the tackle. Strapping the horses into their restraints made her giddy with pleasure – the warm, breathing, living flesh shaped and restrained by hard, unyielding bondage. Tackle seemed such an inadequate word for the tactile tools that persuaded and cajoled the massive powerful beasts to do her bidding. It was a tangible symbol of the battle for wills: the mastery of a good horseman or woman.

The parade ring was only sparsely dotted with people and the empty space felt like a chasm around her. She roamed on in search of the crowd, the herd, the heat of flesh and fur.

As Fiona wandered towards the stands she sized up the bookies, finally making her choice based on a pair of nice hazel eyes and a sensitive mouth. She studied the horses' names chalked on the board next to him: Poetry in Motion (oh, come on!), Time Out (maybe), Show Time (definitely not), until she finally settled on

Raging Blossom. Raging Blossom – the name had a sweet, swollen blush to it – it sounded like the name for what bloomed between her legs.

She fished out her purse and looked expectantly inside: five ten pound notes and a jumble of silver and coppers. Decisively she drew out all the notes. The bookie dropped them casually into the bulging brown leather bag hanging from his shoulder.

'Number five, look for the pink and yellow colours of the jockey,' he said kindly, obviously surmising that her method of picking a horse was far from clinical. He had very nice eyes indeed. Maybe – an inward chuckle welled up inside her – maybe she would ask him for a drink afterward. With the sun in the right position in the sky, the air scented with horses, grass and summer, every man suddenly became attractive: a nice pair of eyes, a way of walking, a firm hand. She turned away suddenly, as if the bookie might possess psychic abilities.

The stands were packed by the time she joined the crowd and the people looked as hyped up and nervous as the horses in anticipation of the race. Again she pressed her excited body against the limbs and torsos of the crowd as she stood at the back of the throng. There he was – Raging Blossom – high stepping past the crowd, his beautiful chestnut head playfully tossing from side to side as if showing off to his public. Fiona felt a glow of pride in his powerful appearance, as if her own tiny wager bought her into a share of his stallion glory.

The glow increased when the handler tried to load him into the starting stall and he expressed his proud waywardness by refusing. His head bucked from side to side as he approached and he danced backwards on his long elegant legs, determined to be obstinate. Finally he was tempted with a handful of grass held under his nose by the wily handler, who quickly ducked under the gate before the horse had time to kick him for using such underhand tactics.

Fiona leaned on a rail, her senses in thrall to the horses, the sweet, hot day and the thrum of the blood pulsing through her veins. Unconsciously she stuck her bottom out invitingly, her black ponytail hanging down the back of her leather coat, the open vents in the back of her clothing displaying her boots and the backs of her knees.

Just as the horses seemed about to kick their way out, the starting button was pressed and the doors of the stalls swung open. The horses pounded past her, their burnished heads arching proudly forward, eyes wild and orgasmic, muscles straining and rippling as if to burst, their hooves spraying turf in their wake. The crowd pressed against her and seemed to move as one, bodies cleaving together as they leaped and cheered. Fiona stood on the cusp between horses and people, the place she belonged, and cheered with them.

The crowd stirred behind her and she felt a familiar, heavy presence. She caught a whiff of expensive aftershave that sent quivers up and down her body. At last! Her stallion had found her – he must have caught her female aroma as it wafted across the field and followed his nose to seek her out.

Suddenly the brightness of the day felt as if it would overwhelm her: the grass became the blinding colour of a toy village green and the shining acid colours of the jockeys' silks winked in the sunlight. The horses raced past again, thundering and sweating under the burden of the jockeys.

Fiona let out a long juddering sigh as she felt strong

hands encircle her hips and she leaned back. The fleshy presence had a packed muscular solidity behind her. She planted her leather-shod feet firmly onto the packed dry earth as he ground his hips into the soft swell of her buttocks. She could feel the roughness of his coat, scratchy like a hide against the back of her legs. She imagined him as a centaur – half man, half horse, saddled and bridled as he kicked up the dust, his hot breath on her neck.

His hands moved into the vent of the coat, through the folds of her split skirt, around towards her groin and into the crease between thighs and pants. Her pussy was hungry to be touched now and wetness drenched her underwear. When the probing fingers finally made contact, they sent darts of pleasure all over her body. She checked quickly from side to side. The faces of the people around her were twisted into frenzied masks as they bayed for their horses, their eyes fixed on the race.

Fiona could smell horse from the stranger as his fingers sought out her black fuzz and traced a line along her enlarged lips, dipping into her wet cunt and slowly twisting around, before backing up and expertly circling her clit. Panting like a mare, she tried to control her breathing and quell the sound. How easily they could be spotted! What if that woman in front of her, the one waving the copy of the *Racing Times* wildly in the air, just turned slightly? Fiona had a sudden vision of herself, naked and shamed, being paraded by one of the bowler-hatted stewards around the ring, her head restrained by a bridle. The image precipitated another surge of wetness between her legs. Her horseman's fingers felt wide and powerful and they slipped on the gush of excess moisture, slithering wetly over her clit, which now stood out angrily in its arousal.

Standing on tiptoe she raised her backside and pushed it harder into him. Fuck me, she whispered in her head, 'fuck me' – this time the words escaped her lips and were drowned out as the horses thundered by again. Their bodies were tense and straining forward in the heat of the race, their pounding hooves made the dust thicken and the crowd roar (for her?). Abruptly she imagined herself in a field with her own kind. The former image of her shamed self was swept way and replaced by horse-people – playing, running, eating and fucking without a care, without responsibility, without shame.

Her cunt spasmed as his fingers withdrew and her hips thrust backwards as if seeking out the loss. As they retreated, the wetness on his fingers slicked against the inside of her thighs. His hands moved away from her pussy and around to the thread of material separating her buttocks. He flipped it aside and slid a finger around her arsehole. When his thumb briefly poked into the tight opening her muscles involuntarily clenched around the hardness.

At last! She sensed his left hand fumbling with his own zip. The sound of the zip was just audible under the roar of the crowd. Then joy made her heart leap when she felt a thick fleshy prick stealing between her legs. He left it there momentarily, shafting against her moistness. Fiona imagined for a second that she was going to fall over, but he steadied her with a restraining hand on her hip. With the other he plucked the string of her thong aside and abruptly sank his cock into her as the horses took the curve in front of her again.

The thrill went up to the roots of her long black hair. With solid rutting movements he slid slowly in to his full length and then out again, agitating her swollen flesh, then resting for a moment with the swollen tip of his knob at her opening.

The crowd was in a frenzy now, bawling out encouragement as Fiona pushed back so that his prick went deep into her. The race was nearly over and excited waves cascaded up and down her body as the horses rocketed past with the jockeys mounted high, their crops flicking at the toiling flanks. In a state of abandon, Fiona circled her hips to increase the delicious friction. The centaur's face lay close to her ear so she could hear his urgent breath coming in rasps and feel the rough tickle of his long hair on her neck.

Fiona strained forward, the muscles at her throat standing out in rigid knots as the horses approached the finishing line. In desperate urgency she bounced up and down hard on his penis. Chaotic thoughts spun through her mind – she was a beast mounted casually in a field surrounded by her herd, gored by a stranger's fat prick. Their beastly rutting was born of simple need, need so acute that it must be satisfied at once, in spite of the doe-eyed strangers that could turn towards them at any minute. Her cunt tightened and jerked back and forth spasmodically, wanting all of him – all his weight and size – inside of her.

The horses hit the finishing line to a deafening clamour from the crowd. The image of the horses lathered in sweat suddenly fractured into a hundred pieces and she closed her eyes as the orgasm rushed up and down her sweating body like shock waves. As her cunt tightened she heard a grunted 'yeeeees!' breathed into her hair. His cock slammed up hard inside of her, wildly spurting its stallion seed deep into her dark moistness.

As she opened her eyes she saw that the race was over and the glistening horses were being led away.

She felt the stranger withdraw swiftly from between her legs. His animal presence lingered for a tiny moment before she sensed him disappear and melt away behind her without even putting her skirt back into place; she quickly adjusted herself before the crowd turned. The trembling heaviness in her legs rooted her to the spot as the dying embers of her climax scalded her body. She stood as if transfixed with a fiery blush on her face. Sneaking a look behind her, she saw that he had gone – only the trickle running down her thigh proved what had just happened.

The woman who had been shouting madly in front of her turned and noted her flushed, wild-eyed appearance.

'Oh dear, did you have your shirt on that one?' she asked kindly in a plummy accent. Fiona found she could only nod silently.

She had no idea where Raging Blossom had been in the chaotic crush of bodies at the finishing line. But when she made her way back to the handsome bookie he smiled and congratulated her on her win as he counted out fifteen ten pound notes. She smiled back radiantly – not enough to buy her own horse but plenty to bring her back to the race ground another time.

She climbed back into her car, which felt hot and airless after standing all day in the sun. She felt suddenly full and joyous as she started up the throaty engine. As she drove she sang along with the radio at the top of her voice, the sound filling the car: 'I've been through the desert on a horse with no name, it felt good to be out of the rain . . .'

Queen of Brighton

Shirley sat behind her candyfloss stall and looked out over the sea front. Gulls swooped overhead and the bikes rode past her, glinting in the sun, their wheels turning like a child's windmill. Shirley, her name like the fizz of sugary sherbet on the tongue, handed out pink blobs of candyfloss on wooden sticks to children clutching warm coppers in their hands. From the booth on the pier she had a slice of Brighton life, the colours as vivid as a holiday photograph: the girls in their New Look summer dresses, the skirts like down-turned flowers, fluttering layers of stiff petticoats underneath; the stacks of striped deck chairs ready to be hired out to the day-trippers down from London; the handsome boys, defiant with their oily quiffs, probably with a knife or razor secreted within their boot. Sometimes she felt regal from where she stood, as if she were watching her loyal subjects from a makeshift throne – a throne jewelled with bright sweet stuff and coloured soda bottles.

Shirley spooned out more sugar into the whirling candyfloss machine as a man approached her booth. Handsome, she noted, with fine high cheekbones and thick brown hair a shade longer than was considered civilised.

'I'll have one of those sodas,' he said, indicating behind her. He stared pointedly down her body, at her pushed-up breasts and figure-hugging skirt – Shirley favoured the sweater girl look. 'And if you tell me the time you knock off I'll have a drink with you as well.'

She placed the bottle carefully in front of him. 'I finish at five, but I may be busy,' she said archly. Never wise to show you're too keen.

He grinned at her. 'See you at five.' He sounded posh, thought Shirley. Still, that hadn't stopped him goggling at her tits like that, looking her up and down as if she was some prize cow at a show.

She was pulling the shutters down when she saw him again, leaning against Gypsy Rose Lee's booth. The gold tasselling and sequins strung around its edges gave it the look of a giant lampshade.

'Back again?' she asked coolly.

'Like a bad penny.' He grinned at her, displaying well-cared-for teeth, before holding out his hand and introducing himself as Ralph.

Shirley hoped he might take her to one of the grander hotels for tea. Or maybe to a coffee bar where the gleaming Gaggia machine noisily spat cappuccino; where everything from the Pyrex cups to the shining Formica bar seemed to sigh 'America' – that distant, spot-lit world of colour glimpsed in the movies. So when they trailed up to the door of *The Ship*, she felt somewhat disappointed. Beery odours gusted through the doors and mixed with the smell of hot pavement. Inside he led her to the lounge.

'I'll have a port and lemon,' she announced, patting back her newly peroxided hair, which glittered in the late sunlight streaming through the window. The sun marked a passage through the smoke. Ralph drank Guinness thirstily and Shirley wondered what he was after. Probably the usual – well, that might be all right, if she felt that way inclined. He seemed unsure of himself though, his eyes shifting round the pub like a crook casing the joint. She wondered if he might be worried about being taken home to be given the once over by her mother.

'I live with my girl friend,' she explained quickly. 'Couldn't stand it at home, all that prying and nagging, so I cut the old apron strings right off. We've got a lovely little place now. Three whole rooms. We have to cook on the landing, but I don't care. As long as I don't have anyone ordering me about, that's all that matters. I like to do as I please. My girl friend's an unmarried mother,' she added nonchalantly. She like to gauge the shock on people's faces when she told them that. His face remained impassive. 'So what is it that you do?' she asked curiously.

'I'm a photographer,' he explained, 'I take photographs of models for magazines.'

He shelled out for another drink and Shirley began to feel an alcohol bloom on her cheeks.

'Not mucky pictures, I hope?' she teased. She'd once grabbed a much-thumbed copy of *Health and Efficiency* off her brother and locked herself in the lav while he hammered on the door to have it back. The pictures of women looking fresh and outdoorsy in their nakedness (but with the crucial bit between the legs cruelly airbrushed out) had made her tingle all over. She divined a movement in Ralph's eyes.

'They are, aren't they? They're mucky pictures.' She felt an excitement tug at her stomach. 'Go on, tell me about them. Tell me what you do. Do you ever need models?' she asked slyly.

Ralph looked wary. 'Listen, you mustn't tell anyone about this. I might get into trouble. But I am looking for models, blondes actually,' he said, casually glancing at her hair.

The atmosphere between them changed. 'I might be available,' she said archly, 'if the money was right.'

'Oh, the money's good, all right. But I don't know – I could get into trouble,' he repeated.

Afterwards Shirley wondered how he saw it in her, how he'd guessed her hidden nature. She admired the clever way he'd let her do the digging, until she'd excavated his secret. Eventually he agreed to meet her again, tomorrow, on the pier. He seemed anxious about trusting her. 'You seem a game girl, but remember, not a word,' he reminded her before draining his glass and leaving.

He needn't have worried, she reflected. She hadn't been entirely honest about her reasons for leaving home. It was her Mum finding out about Danny that finally did it – although Danny had by no means been the first.

'You're a little tart,' her mother had screamed at her, 'letting him get his wicked way with you.' Her uncle had caught them both out the back, Danny's cock jammed up inside of her. It had wilted pretty quickly inside its rubber sheath at her uncle's indignant shouts.

Actually Danny had been quite reluctant. If there had been a wicked way, it certainly wasn't his. He'd been scared even, and she'd had to bully him a bit. He finally succumbed when she'd pulled her skirt high above her head and leaned against the brick wall of the back alley, bare underneath and saying, 'Look at me, look at me, look at me.'

Shirley arranged for Brenda to take baby Peter along with her the next day and follow them. She wasn't daft; she'd heard about the white slave trade and at least Brenda would clock where Ralph lived. As arranged she found him on the pier by the shooting booth. The green sea swelled beneath them, crashing and falling.

'Win us a prize, then,' she said. He sent five shots spinning accurately over the booth and the stall holder handed Shirley a doll with thick yellow ringlets.

They walked through the streets thronging with good-time seekers until they reached Ralph's lodgings. Shirley had glimpsed Brenda with the pram several times in the background and gave her a wave behind Ralph's back as she went in. The rooms he kept were part of a huge old house, partitioned off for lodgers. She was a bit disappointed by their shabbiness but she admired the large multicoloured painting over the empty fire grate. The painting didn't seem to be *of* anything in particular.

'It looks so modern,' she said.

'A friend of mine painted it.' He disappeared through one of the doors leading off the sitting room and came back carrying a heavy camera.

'Five pounds a time, but no questions asked,' he said steadily, fiddling with the lens.

Five pounds, just for taking off her clothes! She'd often stripped off and admired herself in front of the mirror – pulled her skirt up and looked at her own naked fanny from behind, framed by suspender straps either side, her excitement growing as each little private piece was exposed. A born tart her mother always called her. It was true – anything that was hidden fascinated her. You weren't supposed to talk about it but it went on all right: behind closed doors, up back alleys, always whispered about. Shirley never whispered about it. She loved the words; liked to say them right out loud to herself – cock, prick, cunt, fuck. Their hard sounds made her tingle all over.

Ralph looked so handsome today with his jacket hanging loosely across his broad shoulders and a little curl of brown hair falling over his forehead. She'd liked him as soon as she'd seen him. When he'd asked her for a soda that first time, she'd known right away he was a real bit of class. She wondered what his heavy shoulders looked like under his jacket and shirt. She undid a few of the pearly buttons on her blouse, showing a creamy peek of breast. He squinted through the lens and Shirley felt a heaviness between her legs at the undivided attention.

'Where do these pictures go?' she asked curiously.

'I said, don't ask any questions,' he replied firmly. 'Now, do you think you could do it bit by bit, like a strip?' His tone was businesslike.

She leaned back against the settee with just a few buttons undone, pointing her legs prettily. The flash-bulb went off and momentarily drained everything of colour. Ralph changed it, handling the hot, dead bulb quickly and expertly. She undid the rest of the little pearl buttons that fastened her blouse and sat in her brassière, her full, round breasts shapely in their lacy cones. Ralph focused his eye on the lens and a hot wave of pleasure swept across her body. Her breasts felt hard and heavy as she removed the brassière. The sight of her own nipples glowing rosily sent waves of pleasure up and down her body. She stretched it across her body coquettishly so that her tits spilled over the top and Ralph captured the image.

Without being asked she squeezed her breasts together with her hands and her skin tingled to her own touch. She pointed her nipples at the large eye of the camera. He seemed different now, as if this was just work to him. Maybe when he finished with his photographs ... Shirley imagined them both bouncing on the settee together, his muscled back working up and down. Her nipples stood out in hard peaks as he murmured thoughtless encouragements – 'Lovely, beautiful, that's it' – to her. His cultured tones sounded like cream slipping down the throat.

Soon she was down to her suspender belt and stockings. As she bared her little pussy she felt a thrill of guilty excitement. She'd felt the same lifting her skirt to show Danny the full glory of her cunt – the little gold-brown hairs curling so prettily around the opening. It made her feel hot and dirty when men looked at her like this. Her sister had told her then that even her husband hadn't seen her that way, in broad daylight and everything. More fool them, thought Shirley, as she opened her legs wide for Ralph to get his picture, the shiny lips inside spreading open. She loved to be looked at: opening her legs so trembling boys could examine her and seeing the hectic, nervous excitement in their eyes. She relished the guilty look on men's faces when they saw down there – it just made her want to make them look more, to put it right up close to them and make them touch it.

Shirley was startled out of her reverie by the scrape of a key in the door and she began to struggle back into her clothes.

'It's fine, it'll just be Jack – he shares the rooms with me,' Ralph said quickly as another man entered the room.

Boy, if she'd thought Ralph was good-looking Jack really put him in the shade. He took her breath away. He put Shirley in mind of a film star: a cross between the elegance of Cary Grant with a bit of Rock Hudson's roughness thrown in. His thick black hair was Brylcreemed smoothly back, his dark eyes fringed with black lashes and his jacket suggested the hard clean lines of his body underneath. He was dressed better than Ralph too – in his fine summer suit he looked like he'd just walked out of some expensive London tailor's. Which is why it surprised her when he opened his mouth and spoke in an accent very like her own.

'Got a lady in.' He winked at Ralph. 'D'you want some tea?' he asked Shirley casually – which, reflected Shirley afterwards, was a bit damn strange considering she was standing there with her tits all out and on display.

Shirley stomped home afterwards, her pointed shoes with their brittle heels ringing out on the pavement. What right had Jack to go and treat her like she was a bit of dirt! He'd sprawled over the settee in a proprietary fashion with his copy of the *Daily Post*, saying, 'Poor old Ralph, he only has to do this since his dad cut him off without a penny.' Pretending he was all posh like Ralph, when Shirley knew – even if he did try and make his voice all la di dah – that the inside of some bare grubby terrace would be as familiar to him as it was to her.

As usual, Brenda placated her. She switched off the bare bulb overhead so the room was lit only by the glow of the fringed pink shade of the table lamp.

'Let's put some music on. Peter's asleep,' said Brenda, leaping up.

The Dansette record player was on the sideboard, displayed like some rare ornament. It was the only thing, apart from the clothes she'd stood up in, that Shirley had rescued before she'd fled home. Shirley shuffled through all the shiny record sleeves. The names – *Columbia*, *HMV*, *London*, *Parlophone* and *Decca* – had a soothing familiarity to her, a litany to a fresh new age. Brenda clunked on the automatic feeder on the Dansette and the black vinyl spun out the crooning tones of Johnny Ray. His voice seemed to reach out and fill all the tiny spaces in the corners of the room.

'Come on, let's dance,' said Brenda, grabbing Shirley's hand to shake her out of her sulk. They often danced together on the square of carpet in the middle of the room. Brenda's big, puffed-out skirt, splashed with squiggles of blue roses, rustled against both their legs. It had been a difficult job finding a landlady willing to house a scarlet unmarried mother. Now after a few short months of living here, this place felt more like home to Shirley than her mother's ever had.

In the next few sessions, Ralph grew familiar with Shirley and asked her to do more and more risqué poses. Shirley found playing to the camera came naturally to her, but her desire for attention grew stronger at Ralph's refusal to look at her except through the lens of a camera. Sitting on an open-top bus one day, the wind blew up her full skirt and she saw the man over the aisle look at her all agog. Deliberately, she let the next gust of wind fly her skirt up around her waist so that he could see the black lacy suspenders and the triangle of satin between her legs. The layers of crisp petticoats fluttered around her throat. It thrilled her to see his eyes pop and stare like that and she longed to have the same effect on Ralph.

She exposed herself again and again to Ralph, but all he ever did was ask her to raise her tight straight skirt up higher so her stocking tops peeped out underneath, or cast her eyes up to the camera. When she posed with her legs astride the arm of the settee, the hard, nubbed fabric chafed against her, sending her mad with desire. She crouched down with her legs wide apart, so that her fanny spread and opened, nearly touching the carpet, her lips shining wetly as they hung down. She had the urge to touch herself in his presence, to rub her pussy and squeeze her nipples between her fingers. But if she did this the only thing Ralph would do was tell her to move her hand a bit so the camera could see.

Every time she returned from his place she experienced the same pent-up frustration. In the bath she soaped and fondled her breasts to ease the ache and, with a familiar guilty thrill, she'd take the shower head off the rubber apparatus she used to rinse her hair, leaving just a pipe. Fiddling with the taps until the temperature was pleasantly warm she pointed the jet of water between her legs. Its soothing warmth ran between the folds of her fanny with a delicious liquid touch. She sighed and lay back in the bath, imagining it was Ralph's fingers caressing between her legs. Squeezing the sponge out she watched the lather of bubbles slipping over her fanny, the creamy whiteness contrasting with the swollen red folds. What was it that made the sight of her nakedness so resistible to Ralph? The sight of her own sex always excited her to a frenzy. Almost as if she was looking at someone else – at the juicy, tanned girls in her brother's magazine.

Parting herself with one hand, she pointed the rubber nozzle, letting the water play around her clitoris. She imagined Ralph's head between her legs, the silky touch of the water to be his tongue, slicking over the folds and grooves of her slit. She squeezed her nipple as she felt the climax approaching, cupping her full breast and drawing it up to her lips, flicking her tongue back and forth on the very tip. The bath water lapped in a tide to her movements as the orgasm ripped through her body.

Ralph might have remained impervious to her charms in his vague, uppercrust way, but the proceeds of posing for him sure beat working on a candyfloss stall; so Shirley continued turning up at his lodgings on her days off. The desire and frustration she felt grew day by day and she took to wearing nothing underneath so she could feel the cool breeze tickling her fanny. A secret thrill welled up inside her at the thought of what people would make of her nakedness underneath. She had the urge to lift her skirt up in the street and imagined a crowd gathering around, admiring her little pussy. Sometimes the urge became a pressing need. Once, in the bakery, the middle-aged shopkeeper gave her the wrong change. When she complained he tried to bully her until, caught by a sudden hilarious desire, she lifted her skirt at him, bearing herself. His eyes stretched and goggled at the sight, his hands trembling, a huge bulge clearly visible in his trousers. He threw the money down on the counter. 'Get out,' he spat, and Shirley had run laughing all down the street.

That afternoon Ralph casually told her that he was looking for something special.

'I've got a collector interested. He's willing to pay quite a bit, you know, to see two girls together.'

'Brenda'll do it,' said Shirley after a moment's hesitation.

Shirley knew she'd jump at the chance. Brenda loved to hear every detail of what went on when Shirley was posing and regarded the crisp notes admiringly as Shirley spread them out on their rickety dining table.

She pressed her legs together tightly in excitement as Shirley described what she had done that day: how she had stuck her arse up to the camera so Ralph could snap her rude bits from behind as they bulged obscenely between her legs, or how she held up her tits as if offering them to the camera.

Brenda was a bundle of nerves as the girls climbed the stairs to Ralph's threadbare rooms. Shirley warned her about the broken banister that had been there ever since Shirley had clapped eyes on the place. At the top she had to grab Brenda's hand and practically heave her up. 'Just think of the money,' she hissed.

They were a bit early. Ralph answered their knock looking slightly ruffled and with his feet bare. When Jack appeared close behind, Shirley's lip curled. She'd grown more and more resentful of the offhand way that Jack treated her, flitting in and out when she was posing as if she wasn't there. It seemed to Shirley that he sat around on his backside all day while she and Ralph did all the work. The way Jack ordered Ralph around as well was shocking: it was all 'make me some tea,' and, 'lend us some money'. She'd once noticed Ralph's intent stare at the hard, clean lines of Jack's muscled throat and jealousy had tugged at her stomach, alongside something else – an intense curious thrill.

Ralph ran his fingers through his untidy-looking hair. 'Oh well, now you're here, we'd best get started,' he said, a touch testily.

Brenda was practically shaking with nerves and, judging by the telltale way she pressed her legs together, also with excitement. The women giggled together as they took off their dresses and carefully laid them over the backs of chairs, feeling like two naughty schoolgirls. They stood, shivering slightly, in their satiny underwear, ribbon straps holding up their best silky nylons. Ralph directed them like a harassed headmaster.

'Now, close together, that's it. Relax. Now kiss each other, just pretend you're film stars in a movie.'

They both giggled and then fell silent when Ralph snapped at them to shut up. Shirley took Brenda's face in her hands and fastened her lips onto her friend's. As she felt Brenda's soft pink lips on her own, a huge, unexpected thrill of desire shot up her body. She opened her eyes and Brenda's own soft blue eyes were looking at her wonderingly. Curious to know if Brenda had also experienced this strange electricity, Shirley kissed her again. Shirley felt Brenda's soft body yield against her own. A whirring sound and a blinding flash of light told them that Ralph had captured the image.

Without being directed, Shirley reached behind Brenda and undid the row of metal hooks. Brenda's large round breasts swung free. Shirley cupped one in her hand. It felt soft and delicate, so unlike the hard musculature of a man. Squeezing the pink, hard nipple she saw a tiny quiver run down Brenda's curving, firm body. Ralph clicked away, only pausing between each shot to yank out the dead bulb from the flash and insert a new one. Balancing on her knees Shirley took Brenda's nipple in her mouth, tasting it experimentally. She heard Brenda repress a sigh. She suckled there for a moment and a slow dreamy feeling enveloped her body.

Her body ached for Brenda: for her softness, her sweet prettiness. My God, thought Shirley, I'm really beyond the pale now. She knew what she was longing for was the darkest, the dirtiest secret of all the secrets there were. She wondered about Brenda: her body felt so warm and responsive under her fingers – did she have this secret dirty feeling too? She guessed that Ralph, in his usual laconically bored mood when taking photographs, hadn't noticed the real tremors that passed between the two women. Shirley's fingers slid across the pink satin elastic of Brenda's girdle. She dug her fingers under the waistband and peeled it off. Brenda stood before her, looking shy and uncertain, a puff of golden hair between her legs.

'Right, this collector has asked for a certain thing,' said Ralph, sounding world-weary. 'He wants to see girls licking each other, you know, between the legs.'

Shirley positioned herself so she would be caught in the camera lens, and slowly parted Brenda's labia with her fingers. It was like touching some strange forbidden flower. Shirley nearly stopped breathing when she felt wet honey on her fingers. Her tongue slid between Brenda's wet folds and she felt her friend tremble. The fuzz of golden hair tickled her top lip like a moustache as she experimentally moved her tongue, tasting the saltiness of Brenda's juice. The trembling she detected in Brenda's legs, the clenching and unclenching of her buttocks vibrated through Shirley's hands. Shirley felt suddenly strong and powerful like a man. She wanted to lie on top of her friend and grind kisses onto her lips, push something hard inside the pink folds between her legs. Ralph turned away to fetch another box of bulbs from the mantelpiece and Brenda abruptly shivered from head to toe. Shirley could feel the rapid vibrations of her friend's climax through her own tongue, her hands.

Ralph swore as a knocking sound emanated from downstairs. 'That bloody landlord, he really picks his times. I suppose he must have finally decided to mend that banister.'

The noise seemed to wrench Brenda from her daze.

She looked at the clock above the mantelpiece and squawked.

'Peter,' she shrieked, 'I said I'd pick him up from the babysitter half an hour ago.'

With that, she struggled into her clothes and fled without a backward glance. The door slammed loudly behind her.

As Ralph disappeared into the tiny kitchenette, Shirley stood silent and trembling. The waves of ecstasy that had rolled up and down her body when she touched Brenda seemed to echo and taunt her. She suddenly realised she was on her own in this room for the first time. She tiptoed over to one of the doors leading off the main room and silently opened the door. Black paper was tacked over the windows. Sneaking in her bare feet, she opened the other door. Two single beds were pushed together, made up neatly with a blue candlewick bedspread. A Westclox alarm clock ticked loudly on the bedside table, giving time to the thumping of her heart.

She jumped as she heard Jack's loud voice from the kitchenette. 'So the two tarts have left at last, have they?'

Anger flared at his words. Who the hell did he think he was? Jack came into the room, gnawing on the corner of a piece of toast, to find Shirley fully dressed, sitting with her legs crossed on the sofa.

'Oh, you're still here,' he said rudely.

The untapped desire still thrummed through her body and mingled with her flaring anger.

'I bet your landlord would like to know what's going on here,' she said spitefully, 'in *and* out of the bedroom.'

Ralph appeared behind Jack, his face set in a look of petulant annoyance. 'Now look here . . .' he began.

Jack cut in. 'No, let her carry on, Ralph. Little fool, prancing around and flirting with you all the time. He's not interested, dear,' he said nastily.

It suddenly occurred to Shirley that he was jealous! Jealous of the attention Ralph gave her, even if it was only down the lens of a camera. There was a high colour in Jack's face and his eyes flashed. 'See, dear, this is what he likes.' He grabbed Ralph and kissed him soundly.

Shirley almost stopped breathing at the sight of the two men entwined. As Jack kissed Ralph deeply and passionately, she could see his tongue moving in and out of Ralph's mouth. They looked like two magnificent stags with antlers crossed. Ralph tried to pull away but Jack held him, squeezing the bulge already visible at Ralph's groin. 'He likes that too,' said Jack. 'See, he's not interested in your little pussy.'

The image of the two men together burned indelibly into Shirley's mind, like a photographic negative.

'Go on,' she said wildly, 'go on or I'll scream so that landlord can hear and I'll tell him what goes on here and how you've been forcing me to pose in the nude.'

Ralph spluttered in indignation and Shirley felt a deep sense of satisfaction at his discomfort – this would punish him for resisting her for so long. Now the tables were turned and it was her turn to issue the commands.

'Kiss him again, Jack. I want to see what you boys get up to in your spare time,' she ordered.

Ralph began to splutter again but Jack simply laughed. 'Let's give the silly little tart what she wants; the shock'll probably kill her.'

He kissed Ralph again, using his fingers to trace the outline of Ralph's cock which jutted forcefully under his trousers. Ralph groaned and fell against Jack's strong arm which was wrapped around his waist.

Shirley curled her legs up underneath her. As she bounced in excitement on the settee, she could feel her heels pressing into the swell of her sex. Jack seemed to be thoroughly enjoying himself now, showing off, even – Ralph was *his* man and he was going to prove it. With one hand he divested a weakly protesting Ralph of his belt then efficiently stripped him of his trousers and underwear. Ralph's erect prick jutted rudely from beneath his shirt, the purple head looking as if it was about to burst. Jack cupped the other man's tight balls in his muscular hand and, with a sly glance over to Shirley, dropped to his knees and stretched his mouth over Ralph's cock. Ralph groaned and tangled his fingers into Jack's thick hair to steady himself.

Shirley could hardly contain herself at the sight of Jack gobbling away at the other man's dick. She'd heard rumours, of course, but these rumours had always been a bit vague about what they actually did, men like this. She pressed her thighs together tightly and felt a hot flush creep up her neck. Her earlier experience with Brenda had been soft, as gentle as butterfly wings. In contrast, the muscled force of the scene in front of her seemed so powerful, brutal almost, it made her shudder with terror and excitement.

Jack slowly withdrew his mouth from the swollen cock, kissing the end gently. His mouth looked red and taut from where it had been stretched. 'Seen enough?' he asked in a mocking tone. Shirley shook her head dumbly.

He shook off his own clothes and Shirley gasped at the sight of his muscular body. His beauty was like that of a Roman gladiator just about to enter the arena, with his broad, powerful shoulders and strong chest

dark with hair. Shirley had read somewhere how glad-
iators had sometimes wrestled naked and the image of
how they might look – their cocks half erect as they
locked together in combat, sweat shining on their
knotted muscles – had formed so powerfully in her
mind. Now it was as if the fantasy had been made
flesh before her.

'Take your shirt off,' Jack commanded the other man
curtly.

Ralph was utterly passive now and appeared totally
under Jack's rule. He closed his eyes tightly as Jack ran
his tongue over his body, tracing the hard clean lines
of his muscles and slicking down the fine hair that ran
in a line down from his belly.

'This'll give you something to think about,' said Jack
slyly to Shirley. His voice had assumed its natural
roughness. Sure of himself now, any pretension of
strangulated, high class vowels had disappeared.

He reached over to the heavy old-fashioned desk
and extracted a jar of Vaseline from the drawer. Shirley's eyes nearly popped out of their sockets as he
larded his finger with the grease and then used it to
smear over his cock until it stood out proud, hard and
shiny. With a flourish, like a conjuror about to perform
a trick, he gouged out another fingerful of grease and
parted Ralph's buttocks gently. The anus winked up at
them as Jack smeared the Vaseline liberally around the
puckered opening.

Shirley rammed her fists down between her legs and
joggled back and forth on the hard ridges of her knuckles. Her mouth dropped open in an O shape. What they
were doing wasn't only the sort of thing that would
probably get them beaten up by men like her father
and her uncles, they could probably even be arrested.
The thought made her excited beyond belief and her

own brand of wickedness paled into insignificance compared with this sweaty, rough intimacy. She heard the landlord whistling and the sound of wood being sawn. My God, she thought, he'd drop down dead if he could see through walls!

Using his hands to stretch Ralph's buttocks apart, Jack slowly inserted his stiff cock into the puckered opening. Ralph tensed and started swearing roughly, 'Fuck, fuck, fuck me, fuck me.' He seemed lost in his own world now, oblivious to her presence. Jack moved slowly back and forth, his buttocks tensing and relaxing. The two men looked as if they were locked in some violent, brutal street brawl rather than an act of love.

Ralph's prick, which extended finely out, bounced up and down with Jack's movements. Jack gripped him firmly around the waist with his strong arms and began to thrust harder. Shirley could see a milky drop of liquid appearing at the tip of Ralph's cock. It hung for a moment like a drop of water clinging to a stem, and then fell to the carpet. Jack was heaving and panting with his exertions. He paused to reach down and grasp the other man's prick, making Ralph groan deeply. With his strong, large hand he gave Ralph's twitching cock a couple of firm strokes. It was all he seemed to need – a jet of milky semen shot out in front of him and plopped onto the carpet at his feet. Almost immediately Jack covered his own mouth with his hand, to quell the noise. He held Ralph up, who was now as limp as a rag doll, with his other arm and thrust his hips vigorously. The muscles on his neck and legs stood out in knots as he pumped his semen inside the other man.

It was dark as Shirley made her way home. The carnival glare from the coloured lights strung across the sea front illuminated peeling, tatty posters which advertised the cheap, good times to be had in Brighton – dances, whist drives, gala shows. Shirley breathed in the air scented by candyfloss, fish and chips and the tangy salt of the sea as if for the first time. Her body felt as if it were engulfed in flame. The sight of the two men fucking, like sailors caught in unnatural acts, kept returning unbidden to her mind. All she wanted now was to see Brenda, to see if she was all right.

Brenda was wide awake in bed when Shirley returned. Her big gentle eyes brimmed with tears as she stared up over the sheet.

'You think I'm disgusting now, don't you?' Her tears spilled onto the sheet. 'I must be so dirty, to have felt like that. For it to ... you know, make that happen.'

Shirley sat down on the bed and took off her shoes, easing the ache of feet trapped inside the pointed heels. 'What would everyone say?' Brenda carried on weeping. Shirley pulled off her sweater and skirt and rolled down her stockings. She slipped into the single bed alongside her friend. 'Ssh, ssh,' she murmured soothingly as she stroked Brenda's hair.

Tenderness bloomed inside of her. Brenda looked so sweet and pale lying there in her little white ribboned night gown. Shirley felt down and put her hand up the nightie, brushing against Brenda's pubic hair with her hand. She squeezed her finger between the other woman's folds. Inside she felt wet and warm. Brenda stopped crying abruptly and gasped.

As Shirley pulled the garment over her friend's head, Brenda held up her arms like an obedient child being undressed. The ache returned with a vengeance between Shirley's legs as she felt the softness of Brenda's curves. The two hard points of Brenda's nipples bumped against her own. They kissed tenderly before Shirley pushed the bed covers aside and opened her own legs wide and leaned back. She wanted Brenda desperately now, more than she'd ever craved Danny or any of those men she'd ever encountered, even Ralph.

Brenda crouched between her friend's legs. The touch of her cat-like tongue sent sparks of pleasure dancing over Shirley's body, in sweet aching relief. Brenda lapped between her legs, pausing only to kiss the fluff of hair on her mound. Each slick of Brenda's tongue sent Shirley spinning further and further to the edge and the soft, dreamy feeling returned with a vengeance. Brenda's pale yellow hair brushed against the inside of Shirley's thighs as she felt the heat gather between her legs, rising upwards, making her nipples stand out hot and hard and her back arch.

She held Brenda tightly for a while, then watched tenderly as she fell asleep in her arms. Her soft pink and gold friend. Her very own sugar-spun Queen of Brighton. Her wife.

An Open and Shut Case

'I did it,' he said, leaning back in the chair.

Sophie peered at his file which lay open on her desk. Defendants usually wriggled a bit more than this. She put her finger on a line of print. 'It says here, on the 18th of January 2002 you –' she began.

'Well, I did. I did everything it says. Probably a bit more besides. I wanted a night out. I stole the money. It was stupid. I'm sorry, I need to be punished.' His short, staccato sentences indicated just how quickly he wanted the whole procedure over and done with.

Sophie shifted in her chair as she crossed her legs, feeling the expensive silk of the underwear Scott had bought her. She was glad of the big, heavy desk, the way it kept her clients at arm's length. It wasn't so much a desk between them, she thought, more a yawning chasm – thank God. His curly hair looked like it hadn't been washed in a while and he kept pulling at the frayed collar of his shirt. His eyes, flecked with bits of green and brown, settled on her breasts which pointed prettily under her silk blouse. She stood up and went to look out of the window. Far down below, tiny cars moved up and down the street.

'I take it you know about bail conditions from previous experience,' Sophie said coolly, turning back to him. She tucked her honey-coloured hair behind her ears. Legal aid cases always made her feel a bit on edge though, of course, like Scott said, it was their duty to take them on.

After he left, Sophie threw open a window before noticing a scuffed leather wallet under the chair where he'd been sitting. She sat on her desk, holding it in her hand. Too nosy for her own good, her mother always said. Well, that's what made her a good lawyer, wasn't it? Like a pickpocket she dipped her fingers into the wallet. Old bus tickets were mixed up with stubs of coloured cardboard, like the kind they gave you in night clubs. Sophie noted how little money the wallet contained: just a jumble of coppers and silver and a disgusting, old five-pound note. Something else too. She pulled at the corner of the photo with her fingertips.

Dizziness and nausea suddenly clutched at her throat. The garish fairground colours of the Polaroid showed Michael Shannon rammed up inside a small dark pretty woman. My God, you could see everything. The woman sat on the sofa, legs wide apart, laughing up at the camera, with Michael's cock sunk deep inside her. Her extravagant dark bush curled around the deep red of her vagina, the flash of the camera catching the gleam of wetness around her gaping lips. Michael was turning slightly, his arm extended towards the picture and his hand disappearing from the frame as he reached to press the button. Sophie could feel her cheeks burning. She dropped the picture quickly, as if it had suddenly caught fire in her hands.

Sophie felt a curious mixture of smugness and fear as she watched the children below from her viewpoint on the filthy terrace. At least when she had kids they wouldn't have to play on a filthy estate like this. They were kicking broken bottles around, cheering loudly when one smashed against the wall. She shuddered and drew herself further inside her coat, as if it possessed magical powers of protection.

Impatiently she rang the doorbell again. One of the glass panels in the door was gone, replaced with a flimsy piece of plywood. It occurred to Sophie that the bell might not actually be working so she hammered on the door. She was just worrying about the wisdom of leaving her gleaming sporty silver Jag parked downstairs when Michael answered the door, barefoot and wearing only jeans.

She hadn't intended to set foot in the grotty flat but he wordlessly turned and disappeared into the gloom, leaving the door wide open. Sophie wrinkled up her nose as she went in; the place smelled of dirt and shut-up windows. The sitting room was as bare as a monk's cell except for a huge, expensive-looking wide-screen television in the corner, and a battered old red sofa and chair. She recognised the sofa straight away as the one in the photograph.

'I didn't know legal aid extended to home visits,' said Michael, a touch sardonically.

'No, it's nothing to do with the case, it's...' She ground to a halt as she looked to an open door off the main room. As her eyes adjusted to the gloom of the flat she could make out a bed in the room beyond, the sheets all tangled up and half on the floor. Suddenly her brain went blank. What was it she was here for? Her mind groped around for the reason she might be in this horrible little place, with this awful man grinning at her. Oh yes, that was it. Her hand went to her bag.

'You left this in my office yesterday,' she said, her composure momentarily recovered. She handed the wallet over. Its secret contents made the leather feel hot in her hand.

He smiled at her thoughtfully. 'This is beyond the call of duty. You could have just given me a ring.'

The ingratitude! 'That's quite all right,' she said crisply. 'Now I'd better get back to the car.' Before it gets scratched by one of the yobs outside, she added mentally.

'I hope you haven't been peeking.'

'What?' she said, aghast.

'You heard. I said I hope you haven't been peeking inside.'

'I don't know what you're talking about.' She tried to sound offhand and cool, but the telltale colour flared in her cheeks. Damn that blush, it had plagued her ever since she was a teenager, blazing out her true emotions and hidden thoughts.

'It's wrong to look at other people's property without their permission,' he said sternly.

He, lecture *her* on what was right or wrong! The bloody cheek of it. 'Well, that's all right because I haven't.' She tried to make the words final, but he carried on.

'Oh, but I think you have. Your face is glowing like a beacon.' He came up close. 'I think you looked at the naughty picture inside, didn't you?'

'I don't know what you're talking about,' she stammered, her blush intensifying.

'Did you like looking at it? Did it make you feel hot to see Kim all full up like that?' He was so close now she could feel his breath.

'No, I didn't. I thought it was disgusting,' she burst out, before turning to the door to flee.

Bastards! One of the windscreen wipers had been torn off and now it lay broken and twisted on the ground. The complete mindless vandalism infuriated her. She slid into the driver's seat and tried to calm herself down before she took to the road. How had he guessed that she hadn't been able to resist looking? She vowed to keep her curiosity in check in the future.

She heard the sound of footsteps approaching. The car door opened and Michael peered in. Perversely, he'd put on a shirt but his feet were still bare.

'Look, I'm sorry,' he said. 'I don't care what you saw, I didn't mean to upset you like that.'

'I'm not upset,' snapped Sophie, in a tight, upset voice.

'Come back in and have a drink. Look, you're shaking, and they've messed with your car as well, haven't they?' He stood up and yelled over to the kids, 'If I catch anyone trashing this car, I'll fucking strangle them.' He sounded genuinely frightening and the kids all cast their eyes down and put their hands in their pockets. She let herself be led back to the flat. Christ, today was turning out weird.

'D'you want a drink? I've got some lager in the fridge,' he said. Lager! Why on earth was he offering her lager at one o'clock in the afternoon?

'No, thank you,' she said primly.

'OK, I'll make you a cup of tea then.'

The mug was chipped and a bit smeary round the edges. Her mouth felt dry as dust and she sipped the tea while trying to make as little contact with the mug as possible.

'Look,' he said, rolling a cigarette, 'I was just getting you back for being so snotty yesterday. I don't blame you for having a look. I would have done exactly the same. But I'd have probably nicked the fiver as well.'

'Snotty? I was not snotty. I'm never snotty,' she said, outraged.

'Oh, come off it. All that look at me, but don't touch.

Being all cold and formal and then patting your hair and swaying over to the window so I can have a look at your bum all done up in that tight little skirt of yours. I'm not blaming you, it's a nice arse. I'm just saying, that's all.'

He slung one grubby foot over the arm of the chair and stared at her, eyeing her tits up. Despite herself, his gaze ignited a warm heat between her legs. Then she suddenly realised that she was sitting exactly where that slut in the photograph had been. She had a sudden image of the photo, only this time the naked woman's body had her own face superimposed upon it. She shuddered. Sophie knew from her work how dangerous photographs could be – hard, indisputable evidence – you never knew whose hands an image of that nature might fall into.

He stubbed out his cigarette abruptly as if he'd reached a decision. He stood over her with a speculative look on his face. His body was tall and slim in his scruffy jeans and creased blue shirt which hung loosely round his hips. As she looked up from where she sat, his legs seemed to go on for ever.

'Perhaps you'd better go now,' he said, 'unless you want to tell me how hot it really made you feel, seeing me and Kim like that.' His words made her flush again but she said nothing. Her tongue felt too heavy to move.

He seemed to take her silence as mute acquiescence and dropped to his knees in an easy, lithe movement. Parting her knees he slid one hand boldly between her legs. His breath drew in a little as his fingertips touched the roughness of the lace at the top of her hold-up stockings. Thank goodness she'd just happened to choose such nice underwear this morning, she thought.

Then, with a sudden rush of self-awareness, she realised how really it hadn't been chance at all. None of it had been chance: the dropped wallet; the picture; her unorthodox visit today. He'd intrigued her from the moment she'd seen him.

She started trembling all over as Michael's fingers fumbled under her skirt. 'Go on, tell me,' he whispered, 'did you look at the photo for a long time?' She nodded dumbly as he squeezed between her legs, his fingers pawing at the delicate fabric of her knickers.

'What did it make you feel, seeing me all inside that horny little slut? Did you get wet?' Sophie nodded again.

It was true. She'd retrieved the photo she'd flung on the floor and studied it for a long time, examining the girl's full tits, her laughing face, Michael's cock stretching her cunt wide open like that. As she looked she'd pressed the corner of the desk where she sat hard between her legs.

Michael opened her legs up a little further so he could see the tops of her stockings and a peek of her filmy black knickers, the fabric sprinkled with little pink flowers. He pulled the crotch to one side and groaned at the sight of her pussy, her bush clipped neatly in its bikini line to a tuft in the middle. She watched as he ran his finger, with its torn fingernail, up and down her slit.

'What a pretty cunt,' he mused, before sinking his finger between her folds. 'You're completely soaked.' His voice sounded as if the muscles in his throat had suddenly become taut and stretched.

Sophie could feel her breath quickening into little gasps. She ached to be touched all over, on every inch of her skin. His rough fingers, moistened by her juice, pulled open the buttons on her blouse. With his lithe hands he cupped her neat little breasts, squeezing the soft skin. She moaned and lay back.

His voice whispered rapidly in her ear, 'You're just as horny as all the others, aren't you? Playing that high and mighty ice queen, when all the time your cunt's drenching your little designer knickers.' He pulled her blouse off roughly and his hand snaked around behind her, unclasping her bra. Her firm little tits bounced out from their restraints. Her nipples, sticking out rudely, felt hot and swollen.

She whimpered, desperate to feel the touch of his fingers between her legs.

'I want you right up inside me just like with the girl in the picture,' she said. It was as if someone else had formed the words.

He leaned over and kissed her hard, before abruptly standing. She felt completely exposed as he went over to the other side of the room. What the hell was she doing, sitting here in this filthy flat with her top off and her pussy all wide open and revealed? She really ought to leave before this went any further. But then Michael fished around on a cluttered shelf and a thrill flooded right up to the roots of her hair when she saw him retrieving the Polaroid camera. She watched him silently as he placed it carefully on top of the TV. Her stomach contracted as he pulled his clothes off. His slim body was delicately muscled like a dancer's. Her eyes ran down the line of hair that circled his belly button and marked a passage to his cock, which looked bruised and red in its hardness.

Her body was throbbing now and her legs trembled involuntarily, her high heels making little knocking sounds on the bare wooden floor.

'This was just how she was sitting,' crooned Michael

as he pulled off Sophie's knickers and then rubbed her clit into a state of delicious agitation with his thumb. She panted and reached out almost blindly until she felt the hardness of his cock in her hand, guiding it hungrily towards her. He chuckled slightly at her impatience before sinking inside her, filling her up. Each thrust made her more juicy, until Michael's knob seemed to slide in and out on a tide of wetness.

He grinned at her. 'A little memento for me,' he said, before reaching out behind him towards the camera, shifting his legs slightly to reveal the intimate sight to the lens. A blinding flash of light dropped over them both like a white sheet as he pressed the button.

'You can't do that,' she shouted.

He ignored her and began thrusting his cock again, deeper inside her this time, the tip of it caressing her G-spot. With the light still dancing in front of her eyes, Sophie felt her climax well up inside her until her hips thrust back and forth involuntarily, drawing him in even deeper. As the last few movements died away she felt his cock tremble inside her and he came with a loud shout of pleasure.

Before leaving Michael's flat she deftly palmed the photograph and slipped it inside her bag.

The photograph seemed to burn a hole in the sleek leather of her handbag as she turned the key to her house and let herself in. The sweet, clean smells of wood polish and freshly washed linen greeted her and she breathed them in deeply. The relief of being on familiar territory flooded through her: the immaculately painted walls, sparkling tiles and neatly displayed possessions all sung their reassuring hymn to affluence and order.

Fishing the photo out of her bag, she wondered what

to do with it. She studied her own face on the verge of climax: her expensive, tweed skirt up around her waist; the rough, grubby man deep inside her. The picture was almost a reproduction of the other one – the photograph must have been taken from exactly the same place, with the camera positioned on top of the TV. Except, of course, this time it was her own image so starkly illuminated by the flash.

She stripped off and ran the shower until the water was steaming hot and then soaped herself with the strongest-smelling shower gel she could find. What had she been playing at? Michael was a client, for Christ's sake; she could be struck off for this. She groaned and slumped against the tiled wall of the cubicle, wracked by confusion and sheer gut-churning terror. Her mind groped back for the sequence of events that led up to her being photographed while Michael Shannon fucked her. She remembered standing at his door. She'd been feeling curious – excited even, if she was truthful with herself. She supposed she'd just wanted to see him once more before the long wait until his court appearance. To see exactly what kind of person carried a picture like that around.

The front door slammed and made her jump. A few seconds later Scott opened the door of the bathroom.

'Christ, are you having a sauna in here or something? And what the hell's happened to the car, there's a wiper missing,' he added crossly.

'Oh, just kids. I didn't get a look at them properly.' She held her breath.

'Well, you'll have to take it to the garage tomorrow, I'm busy.'

Sophie reflected that for a lawyer he was pretty damn trusting, before guiltily realising he really had nothing to be distrustful about. Shit, the photo. Scott wasn't in the habit of going in her bag but paranoia made her practically leap out of the shower. She wrapped herself in a huge fluffy bath towel which smelled sweetly of the special expensive lavender fabric conditioner she always used.

She carried her handbag through to the bedroom and took out the picture once again. Really she ought to throw it away. 'I'm around next Thursday morning,' Michael had said loftily as she left. Yeah, like she was going to go back for seconds with that oik. Carefully, she slipped the photo between the pages of her diary and then buried it in her underwear drawer beneath the neatly sorted knickers.

Every time Sophie thought of Michael through the week her cheeks flared and wetness instantly stained her knickers. Sometimes it felt as if what had happened had just been a dream, a secret, guilty dream to be carried off by the fresh morning wind and forgotten by the time the office was reached. Sophie had to sneak the photo out from its hiding place to remind herself what had really happened. The shock of seeing herself like that didn't diminish as the days went on but in a curious way it seemed to intensify. The image appeared more extreme every time she looked at it.

In fact, if she didn't have that damn picture, she reflected, she might just have been able to put the incident down to experience. She certainly wouldn't be negotiating these rubbish-strewn streets again in her immaculate shiny car. She parked well around the corner this time, in a busy street. A car like hers in the same place a second time might attract more unwanted attention. Who knows? The police might get involved this time. She shuddered at the possible consequences.

Anxious to be let in before anyone saw her, she hammered loudly on the door. She could hardly believe it when mute silence greeted her knocking. For him to have asked her here, for her to have actually turned up only to find him out – it was preposterous! She hung around for about five minutes. This was ridiculous, she thought, standing about on some filthy concrete terrace.

She was just about to turn around and leave when Michael appeared from the corner. He grinned when he saw her. Loping next to him was another man in a long torn coat. He looked like a modern-day character from a Dickens novel. Inexplicably they both carried armfuls of fruit.

'I'll let you in,' Michael said casually. His mate leered at her, taking in her tailored suit and expensively tinted hair. As Michael fumbled for the keys in his pocket, the fruit slipped from his arms. Melons rolled away down the concrete floor, like spinning yellow suns against the grey.

'Amazing what you can find when you get up early,' Michael said cheerfully, retrieving his bounty before opening the door. His mate gave Sophie a final leer and disappeared.

The smell hit her again as soon as she stepped into the shabby hallway. In one way it made her want to gag, but in another curious sense it sparked something buried in her imagination. The smell reminded her of everything that was hidden and bad: it was fucking in the middle of the day with someone you hardly knew; it was sluttish girls with red gaping slits and cheap black tarty underwear, greedily offering themselves up for sex. And now – the thought caused a trembling uneasiness in her stomach – now the smell was her. Her own juicy odour must be mixed with all those other smells, lingering on the sheets and on his clothes.

Michael led her over to the bedroom and she sat down heavily on the rumpled bed. She looked down. It reminded her of that woman artist's bed: dirty and dishevelled, streaked with stains and smelling of bodies. Michael went off to the kitchen and she could hear him whistling and filling a kettle. She was just wondering what it was that drove her to jeopardise her whole life – a life that had seemed more than perfect until Michael came along – when her eye was caught by a shiny gleam of colour half hidden by the bed.

Nosily, she stuck her hand under the bed. It was a magazine – no, several magazines. A woman with bright peroxided hair stared back at her from the cover of the one on top. Her wide-open legs were encased in tarty fishnet stockings and she was pulling provocatively at her tiny lacy black knickers, so that her lips furled wetly around the string of fabric. There was a lot of garishly coloured writing on the cover; Sophie quickly recognised it as being Dutch.

She trembled all over. How absolutely cheesy and gross. She opened the magazine to the first page, gasping in shock at the first image. A man leaned up against the wall, his eyes closed. His huge, erect penis shafted forward and there, on her hands and knees, was a woman with her bright lipsticked mouth clamped around it. One of her hands was reaching up to cup his tight, hairy balls. The next photograph depicted the same woman on all fours, sticking her bum up in the air. The man was behind her now on his knees, his cock half buried inside the woman's pouting slit. She turned the page. The pictures must run in sequence, she thought inconsequentially. Sophie pressed her legs tightly together as she flicked over the page. He'd pulled out of her now and was doubled up, his lips drawn back over his teeth. A shining spatter of white semen dripped off the woman's back.

She turned the pages quickly. The settings all looked incredibly normal: there were fleeting glimpses of bedroom furniture in the background, flowered curtains and patterned duvet covers. There was a man with short blond hair, his cock jammed inside a woman crouched over him, her fanny lips pink and curling around his prick. Sophie flicked again, her breath coming in little gasps. Now there was another woman greedily sucking a man's cock while another man entered her from behind. The glossy pages shone with pinks and reds and dark patches of hair. Now two women were entwined, one with her tongue snaking inside the other's slit, their pussies cleanly shaved . . .

'It'll make you go blind.' Michael was standing in the doorway, holding out a mug in his hand.

Sophie jumped at the sound of his voice and the magazines fell to the ground, fanning away from her. He set the chipped mugs down on the bedside table and sat next to her on the bed. Shame burned in Sophie's cheeks. He always seemed to be catching her at something.

'Did you like looking at those?' he asked softly.

'Absolutely not,' she said in a high tight voice. 'I think that sort of thing is revolting!'

His hand delved between her legs. 'Let's see if you're telling the truth this time,' he teased. She tried to squeeze her legs together to block the exploring hand, but he firmly but gently parted her knees with his other hand. His breath drew in sharply as his fingers touched the soft wet fabric between her legs.

'I think you've been telling lies again,' he said with mock severity as he fingered her drenched knickers.

Gently he began unbuttoning her blouse. 'You're a real juicy slut underneath, aren't you? I knew it as soon as I saw you, sitting behind that desk, being all Miss Prim and Proper.'

Wordlessly she allowed him to lay her on the bed and slowly pull her knickers down. He left them so they tangled around her knees. She curled up on her side, drawing her knees towards her forehead, her skirt up around her waist, leaving her pussy exposed from behind. Her flaring desire mingled with shame. To have been so aroused by those images, those pervy pictures in his dirty little magazine! He selected one of the magazines and opened it next to her. The page depicted a scene of a woman standing in a hot tub. The bubbles on the water skimmed and frothed over her sex, like a delicate covering of lace. Three men cavorted around her, one deep inside her from behind, the other two both fondling their own pricks lovingly as they looked on.

A trembling ache spread from inside her to the tops of her thighs and fluttered round her arsehole, making the opening feel tight and puckered. The ache became almost painful when Michael knelt on the floor beside her and put his head between her legs, his tongue grazing against her pussy, which pouted rudely from behind.

The pillow smelled musty and grey light squeezed through the dirty, curtainless window. The filthy room gave her the strange feeling that she was playing a character in some sleazy movie. The feeling of being someone else heightened all her senses, as if she could see everything that was happening from a distance.

Michael moved his tongue slickly and expertly over

her slit. He nipped the swollen lips gently with his teeth and then parted her buttocks and flickered his tongue around her puckered anus, soaking it with his saliva. His tongue moved round and round until she suddenly felt it enter the tight space. Feebly, she thought of protesting – this intimacy seemed too much somehow. But the ache became even tighter, reaching to the pit of her stomach. She tried to move her legs but her knickers seemed to have bound them, trussing her knees together tightly.

She kept glimpsing the image in the magazine spread out before her. Each time she looked, shock contracted her stomach at the sheer filthiness of it. The pink and black flesh tones shone on the glossy page and Sophie's eyes felt inexorably drawn to the point between the woman's legs – to the cock pushed up inside her so crudely. She felt Michael's probing thumb circle her slippery ring then slide inside the tight hole. The thumb stayed, unmoving, making her feel more stretched out and exposed than she'd ever felt before. She closed her eyes but the image of the photograph before her seemed to be printed on the back of her eyelids. Michael began sliding his tongue in long sweeps up and down her pussy. She shuddered deeply in response. Heat coursed all over her body and her anus contracted sharply around his broad thumb as she came with a high-pitched moan.

She lay for a long time on the musty-smelling bed. Again she pictured herself from a distance, as if she were hovering in an out-of-body experience. Her astral self surveyed the scene: the grey, wrinkled sheets; her semi-naked body, still dressed in her spiky heels and open blouse; the knickers stretched tight around her knees; the dirty magazine laid out beside her; the jumble of dirty mugs and crumpled tissues on the rickety table next to the bed. She wanted to picture every sordid detail, to illustrate to herself how low she had really sunk. Her mouth felt dry and sticky as she swallowed.

The climax had ripped through her, leaving her feeling washed out and limp. It was the most intense she'd ever experienced, she reflected, as she coasted on the dying tremors. Quickly, as if in punishment for the thought, she gave herself another dose of the sleazy sight of herself as from above. But this time the effect was a restless stirring between her legs. Not again, she thought with a groan. This time was meant to be the last. Just a means of getting it all out of her system.

Michael had left the room and she could hear him again in the kitchen. He returned with some cut-up melon, the neat pale yellow slices fanned out over the plate. He fed her some of the juicy flesh as she lay immobile on the bed. The heavy sweetness of it slipped down her throat like liquid, slaking her thirst. Stolen melon, she thought with an inward giggle.

As she struggled out of her knickers her hand touched a damp patch on the other side of the bed.

'Yuck, what's that?' she asked, wrinkling up her nose.

'Oh, that's where I jerked off this morning,' he said cheerfully. Her eyes widened in response to his openness. Didn't this man have any shame?

He began unbuttoning his shirt and rolled towards her. 'Actually I was looking at the same picture as you were just now. I know how hot it made *me* feel.' He stripped off his shirt revealing his slim torso. Her eyes feasted on the line of hair snaking up above his jeans.

'You make me hot too, Sophie, you know that, don't you?' he said.

The bulge in his jeans was like an exclamation mark,

his cock straining against the denim. She looked at the spattered traces of his semen on the sheet and had the sudden urge to strip naked and to roll in it, to film her body with the wetness. She felt suddenly sleazy and preposterous, like a girl from a sexy cartoon strip in a red-top newspaper, all pointing tits and pouting mouth. She kneeled in front of him, her skirt straining around her wide-apart legs, and took off her bra as slowly as in a striptease. His eyes fixed on her small round tits and she cupped them both in her hands, lifting them up and squeezing them together. Her nipples with their hardened peaks pointed rudely towards him. His breath quickened, making his stomach rise and fall. Like a panther she prowled over to him and roughly undid his jeans, pulling them off with one swift movement. 'Stand up!' she growled.

He stood on the bed, steadying himself with one hand on the wall, his prick arching in front of him. She bounced a little on the bed in her excitement and the movement rippled through her breasts. His penis looked tight and hard, shafting towards her face, the veins bulging up towards the tip, like one of the pictures from the magazine made flesh. As she grasped it in one hand he nearly doubled up at the touch, groaning in what sounded like relief. With a grunt he thrust his hips forward so his cock shafted within her fist. The smooth helmet appeared, blazing purple, from within her clutch. Slowly she squeezed him up and down, cupping his balls with her other hand. He thrust his hips forward again, this time in small, rapid movements to hasten his pleasuring. A small drop of milky liquid appeared at the end of his knob. She smiled and stroked him harder, watching his face screw up in pleasure. His legs tensed up even more and she felt a wild surge of excitement as he made a series of short involuntary grunts.

'Go on, come,' she ordered. 'I want your come all over me.'

She held her face up towards him as he gave a final heaving gasp and his spunk looped down in an arc, showering her face and dripping down her throat to her skirt. Exhausted, he fell back against the wall as she put up her hands and smeared his semen over her face, dabbling her fingers in it and staining her breasts and stomach with the sticky secretion.

As she drove back to the office, she could still feel the tight dryness across her body where she had painted his semen. With one hand she picked at a crust of whiteness that marked her tweedy skirt, the other hand steering the purring car. What was happening to her? Making love with Scott had always been fine. But somehow it lacked the heady, narcotic buzz she felt with Michael. Up until now she'd always regarded sex as wholesome clean fun, a healthy part of a relationship, good for the mind and the body – a bit like playing tennis in fact.

Every time she saw Michael, she swore it would be the last. His court case was creeping ever closer and she knew how potentially dangerous their relationship was. When she tried to visualise standing up in court to defend him, her mind fell blank.

But somehow a week usually didn't go by without a visit to his horrible flat. Her stomach churned for hours before she was actually due to meet him. Fear of being caught dogged her waking moments – which is why she found it so hard to understand why, when he asked her what she wanted to do that day, she responded, 'Fuck outside.' Without hesitation.

'Get your coat,' he said quickly, and before she knew it they were walking side by side in the direction of the Heath. People passed them walking their dogs or just out for a stroll. Sophie cast her eyes down and turned her head away, terrified in case she bumped into anyone she knew.

They went into the dark wooded part of the Heath. Sophie looked behind her uncertainly; she could still clearly see people up by the path.

'It doesn't seem very hidden here,' she said.

He shrugged. 'Everyone knows what goes on here, so they stay away. Unless they want to watch, of course.'

She felt a stab of fear clutching at her stomach. 'I need to pee,' she said suddenly.

'Well, go on, then. I'll watch,' he said. He fell to his knees.

Sophie giggled nervously. 'I can't in front of you. I mean you really can't be saying you like seeing that, for goodness' sakes.'

'I want to see you pee.' She looked at him. His heavy lids half covered his eyes, his bony, elegant face looked set, and he seemed deadly serious. A thrill suddenly ran up her body.

She pulled up her skirt and coat and bunched them around her waist. Underneath she wore long, elegant boots that came up to the knee. Michael slipped her knickers off, threading them over her boots. She lifted one foot then another up for him.

'Spread your legs apart,' he said. His face looked tense and expectant.

She did as she was told and tried to empty her tight bladder. 'I can't, I just can't,' she protested.

'Just relax, try again,' he commanded. His eyes were

fixed on the point between her legs. She closed her eyes in concentration and a few drops of golden liquid scattered down. A high colour marked Michael's cheeks as he held her hips either side. Sophie's legs shook. The whole situation seemed so outrageous, so filthy, it sent her senses reeling. A breeze tickled her sex and Michael tugged at the tuft of hair that ran in a line up her otherwise bald pussy. The action made her clit pout forward. She suddenly let go and a golden stream ran to the ground. Michael breathed in sharply at the sight. A few wisps of steam rose from the liquid before it sank into the earth. He dabbled his fingers at her pussy, liberating the last few drops.

He smiled up at her, his eyes slanting. 'Who'd have thought it,' he said, 'on that first day we met, with you in your power suit? Now you're taking a piss in front of me.' He seemed wilder, more keyed up than usual. Sophie felt a little thrill of fear.

Roughly he pulled at her coat until it fell in a heap on the ground.

'What are you doing?' Her voice trembled a little.

'I want to show you, Sophie, what it feels like to be out of control.'

He flicked open the button at the side of her skirt and it slithered to the ground, leaving her lower body naked to the cold air. His eyes glittered, making her tremble with fearful excitement. Why was it she felt like this with this man who treated her, to all intents and purposes, as if she was just another of his sluts?

If she was caught, here and now, she risked losing everything. Everything – for a brief, dirty fuck with this unwashed criminal. The tabloid descriptions for his kind sprung from her subconscious and echoed through her mind: low life, scum, trash, filth. But despite her turmoil she knew with a sudden certainty that standing naked from the waist down in these filthy little woods excited her beyond anything she'd ever experienced. All the candlelit dinners, soft music and carefully chosen gifts from Scott paled into romantic parody compared to *this*.

He pushed her face-forward against a tree and unbuckled his belt. 'The first time I saw you I knew I'd have you.' The belt flicked against her buttocks, making them bounce and sending a deep ache rocketing between her legs. She dug the heels of her boots into the ground to steady herself.

'I know you thought you were better than everyone else.' He'd come up close to her, grinding his hips in their jeans against her bare buttocks, the fabric scraping painfully against her tender skin. 'But look at you now, being fucked against a tree in the roughest part of the Heath by one of your nasty little crims.' Triumph pervaded his voice.

Abruptly he moved around the tree and pulled her hands together so her arms circled it. His face looked set and determined as he looped the worn and twisted belt around her wrists, fastening them together. He stood back to admire his handiwork. Sophie could hear his movements but all she could see was the rough bark of the tree against which her face was pressed painfully.

He came close again, moving his hand between her legs, seeking out her clit. Shooting stars of desire exploded over her when he touched her little button. His breath was hot against her hair as he rubbed away. 'What do you want?' He leered at her.

'Fuck me,' she whispered, 'fuck me, fuck me, fuck me.'

'Are you sure?' His voice was teasing.

'Yes, I'm sure,' she spat, riled by his mocking tone.

She heard the sound of a zip then felt the hardness of his cock nestling between her legs. With a heave, he sank inside her with one movement. Her breath gathered pace as he thrust deeply inside her.

'You never know,' he whispered in her ear, 'who may be around. People prowl around this part of the Heath. Perhaps someone is watching us now.'

The bark scraped her cheek as she twisted her face around. From the dark enclosure of the trees she could see through the web of branches to the bright clothes of a jogger in the distance. The man pounded joylessly down the path.

Michael's prick felt huge inside her as he thrust; she could feel it pumping away at her womb. Her muscles tightened around him in fear and pleasure. The colours of the jogger's clothes liquefied as her climax approached and she abandoned herself to whatever might happen first – her orgasm or being discovered. She could hear Michael's breath coming in jagged blasts until he gave a sudden heave and shot his climax inside her. Desperately she thrust her hips backward and forward on his dying orgasm until her legs buckled beneath her and she felt the tide of her own climax ebb and flow over her body.

Still shaking, she watched the jogging man take a right fork in the path so he veered away from them, eventually becoming a small, bright spot in the distance.

Three months! Sophie felt a pang of guilt at her sense of relief.

Of course, his previous convictions hadn't helped. Michael had seemed calm and resigned sitting in the dock but his eyes remained fixed on her throughout the whole proceedings. They hadn't seen each other for a few weeks. The incident on the Heath had shaken her in its intensity, and she had felt she needed a while to calm herself before standing up in court to defend him. All the same, a knot of anxiety had gripped her stomach the whole time as she sat in the court room, as if everyone would be able to guess their dirty secret. His eyes seemed to burn into her as she addressed the court with her mitigation speech. Little good that it had done though. The judge looked in a thoroughly disagreeable mood; maybe his lunch had been served up cold or something.

Sophie stripped off her scratchy wig as she made her way down the narrow little steps to the murky warren of corridors and cells behind the courtroom. She consoled herself with the knowledge that she'd done the best she could for him. But at the same time the relief of feeling back in control was intense.

'I need some time with my client,' she told the uniformed guard imperiously. The guard showed her into the cell where Michael was held.

'I'll just be outside, Miss,' he said. She nodded at him quickly.

'Michael, I'm sorry. There was nothing I could do. That judge had it in for you as soon as he clapped eyes on you.'

His eyes stared out at her. His hands trembled a little. 'My God, you looked so hot,' he said unexpectedly.

She looked at him aghast. 'Michael, you've just been sentenced to three months . . .'

He cut in, 'Would you mind, I mean, d'you think you could, you know, put your wig back on?'

The appeasing tone he used was new to her. She shrugged and sat on the corner of the table and carefully arranged the wig over her head. His eyes widened.

She swung her foot in its black heel back and forth. She'd never seen him so meek and acquiescent and she was rather enjoying it. She could see a bulge appearing in the trousers of his rather tatty grey suit. He swallowed hard.

'Do you think you could, maybe, just pull your skirt up a little?' he asked quietly.

She pressed her fingertips together and looked at him sternly under her wig. 'D'you really think that's a good idea?'

He nodded, swallowing again.

'Well, you do it,' she commanded harshly.

With tentative fingers he pushed her clinging black skirt up a fraction – so that her knees were exposed. She was acutely conscious of the guard and the tiny eye of the spy hole in the door. Her heart pounded as adrenaline rushed through her veins. Impatiently she pulled her skirt right up so the tops of her stockings and her little black knickers were exposed.

'Be very, very quiet,' she whispered sternly.

She hooked a finger through the flimsy material of her knickers. His eyes opened wide as she pulled them to one side. Her exposed sex looked doubly obscene next to the arcane uniform of gown and wig. He reached out his trembling fingers and dabbled them at her cunt.

'Harder,' she commanded. Obviously anxious to please, he did as he was told and began rubbing her clit earnestly, agitating it so that her lips folded back and forth with the movement. With a small cry he lurched forward and applied his mouth to the juicy feast before him. She let him lap there for a few moments.

'I said be quiet,' she repeated in a stern voice. 'Now get up and take your cock out.'

She relished the way he now sprang to her commands, responding to the authority of her uniform and quickly unzipping himself as she'd instructed. Sophie quaked inside, one eye on the door – this was a hell of a risk. But the sight of her own pussy, open wetly on the table, made her stomach lurch with desire.

'Come on, hurry, hurry,' she whispered impatiently, until she felt the sweet hardness of his cock filling her up.

His hands roved all over her as he thrust wildly, touching the tops of her thighs and the swell of her breasts under her gown. 'Faster!' she ordered, looking at the door. He pumped in double-time as she reached down and felt for her clit. A surge of electricity went over her as her fingers found the fleshy mound. She rubbed, breathlessly watching the door. As his cock flew in and out it made sucking noises in the cradle of her pussy. The noise seemed to echo so loudly around the bleak little room that she could hardly believe the guard would be unable to hear. Almost in panic she creamed herself with her fingers which tangled with his darting prick.

Looking down at his shining cock as it flashed in and out of her made her muscles begin to contract in climax. She let out a deep quiet moan as she came that filled the barren cell. Michael's eyes were wide and staring now, drinking in the sight of her. His face grimaced in an effort to restrain the sounds of his orgasm. He let out a series of short, smothered grunts as he spunked inside her, his eyes roving over her in half-terrified desire.

She quickly adjusted her clothing, took a deep breath and opened the door.

'We don't need any more time,' she told the guard.

* * *

She found the door to Michael's flat open. It looked as if it had been kicked in, the door frame had been reduced to jagged splinters of wood. She'd had a vague notion that he might be back now his sentence had passed, but the flat was cold and empty. The TV and sofa were gone and only a jumble of clothes and boxes remained in the corner. She felt surprisingly relieved, as if her life had taken a weird detour and all that was left of it were these few battered relics. Things had changed though; she was putting some of the lessons learned from Michael into practice with Scott, who was turning out to be an unexpectedly good pupil. Eager to learn, in fact!

She wandered into the bedroom. The sheets she had once lain on were in an untidy heap by the window. She picked them up and examined them by the grey light filtering through the window. They hadn't even been washed. She held them to her face and breathed deeply. They smelled strongly of sex. Sophie swore she could still detect her own odour lingering in the weave. She took out her nail scissors from her bag. The tiny blades winked as they hacked into the fabric and she snipped away until she had a rumpled cotton square. Folding her trophy neatly, she slipped it inside her bag and left, pulling the bedroom door closed as she went.

Painted Lady

Brazen Hussy. Stella had to put her glasses on to read the tiny lettering stamped at the bottom of the tube of lipstick. She painted a thick layer over her lips. All that was visible in the mirror of the compact was a huge scarlet mouth, reflecting back at her.

The lipstick must have been left by one of her students. Stella had found it under a chair after a group tutorial. It wasn't her, she decided. It revealed too much somehow, announcing her buried nature like a bleating siren.

Stella smoothed her neat brown bob which she wore like a disguise. She was suddenly struck by the notion that you lived a life according to what you looked like. Stella didn't feel like Professor Fanshawe on the inside; on the inside she was a vamp with an armature of predatory fangs and long, curving nails.

There was a tentative knock on the door.

'Come in, Andrew,' she called.

Andrew peeked round the door, clutching his paper on gender relations in seventeenth-century Dutch art. His eyes widened in surprise.

'Professor Fanshawe. You've got lipstick on!' The words were out of his mouth before he could stop them.

She took a tissue out of her briefcase and wiped it firmly off.

'I expect you have a very good explanation, Andrew,

as to why your paper is three days late,' she responded sternly, staring at him over her glasses.

Andrew shut the door quietly after he'd delivered his paper. He liked Professor Fanshawe but he always felt a bit uncomfortable in her presence. He couldn't quite put his finger on it but she always inspired at least the ghost of an erection in him. It was something about her confidence, the way she looked at him with her greeny-brown eyes, her glasses down on her nose. He was sure that she didn't intend to have this effect on him, probably nothing was further from her mind. That's why his arousal in her presence felt so shameful. It was just ... just a feeling that emanated from her. He could imagine her wearing black suspenders and stockings under those tweedy skirts, taking her glasses off ... Why, Professor Fanshawe, you're beautiful without your glasses!

Andrew had shagged a couple of his fellow female students since he'd arrived at university, losing his virginity around the second week after he'd arrived. But college life was hardly turning out to be the orgy of hedonism he had hoped for. The sex had been vaguely unsatisfying: drunken, furtive encounters in dark bedrooms at parties. He despised the fact that at the age of nineteen he still hadn't seen a naked woman properly, in the light and everything. Christ, life was passing him by; he'd be too old for it soon.

His cock felt hard and awkward as he walked to the main door. There was nothing for it – the thought of her had made his semi-erection bloom into a full hard on. He slipped into the men's toilets and secreted himself in a cubicle. His cock felt heavy in his hand as he released it.

Leaning against the side of the cubicle he fantasised

about Professor Fanshawe down on her hands and knees in front of him. He imagined the tight clutch of his own hand to be her mouth locked around his prick. If she only knew what he was thinking and doing right now she'd probably drop down dead. What *would* she do? Andrew had a sudden vision of himself, his trousers around his knees as Professor Fanshawe smacked his buttocks with the flat of her hand. The idea made his knob jerk in his hand, as if it had an independent life of its own.

He rubbed at himself, paying special attention to the sensitive bulb at the end. He tried to keep his muffled grunts in check, hoping to God that no one else came in to overhear him.

Images of his tutor tumbled through his mind, splayed out in all sorts of filthy positions. One moment she sat in front of him on the desk, her legs spread wide; the next she was on all fours, pushing her slit up towards him. With his free hand he grabbed some sheets of loo paper off the roll. He imagined her (in his fantasy she entered the men's loos by accident, somehow no longer able to read the sign on the door) opening the door of his cubicle, discovering him red-faced and with his huge erection barking for attention like a naughty puppy between them. His shame and her look of horror in his imagination was too much. Little jets of spunk burst forth from him and shot into the crumpled tissues in his hand. He stood, leaning against the wall and panting for a while, trying to recover.

Andrew really was too sweet to get seriously annoyed with, Stella reflected as she gathered up her papers and packed them away in her briefcase. He had the looks and the cute awkwardness of Prince William about him which brought out the hidden temptress in her. She looked forward with some anticipation to their tutorial session tomorrow. She'd had her eye on him for a couple of months now. Every time they were alone together she would deliberately lean back in her chair, parting her legs a little. Stella wondered if he ever caught a trace of the juicy odour which exuded from her whenever she was with him. Perhaps he could sense it, like an animal smelling the female of the species on heat – she certainly hoped so.

She took her coat from where it hung neatly on its hanger. She'd have to be careful, though, the situation with her last 'cute' student had very nearly exploded in her face. The only reason the parents hadn't taken it any further was that she'd opened a bottle of whisky and got the father steaming drunk. Dad had ended up by saying he thought his son was a 'lucky chap'. The mother hadn't been so easy – all that weeping and wailing over her son's lost innocence. Though if she'd known with what eagerness her little darling relinquished that innocence she mightn't have made so much fuss, reflected Stella.

It was growing dark as Stella left the Institute. She headed out into the soft gloom, looking forward to the hot bath and the whisky that awaited in her little warm flat.

She'd almost decided against taking things any further with Andrew when he arrived for his tutorial the next day. But he looked so young and fresh from his bike ride in the soft rain that Stella could feel the skin at her throat flush with excitement. It *was* that touch of the Prince William about him that really got to her, she reflected, with his large, blue eyes and full pouting mouth.

She'd been laying the ground slowly over the last few months – softly, softly catchee monkey, she always told herself. But part of the excitement was never being quite sure of how they would react. Most of the boys she'd had over the years yielded quickly to her. She thought it must be something in her schoolmarmish appearance which excited unfulfilled fantasies about their nannies in these educated boarding school boys.

Stella skipped through his paper as Andrew unwound his scarf from his neck and sat beside her. He played nervously with the hem of his sweat shirt.

'Not bad,' she said, indicating the paper in front of her. Whatever their attractions she was always scrupulously genuine about their work. 'You've just missed a few points.'

She went to the cabinet which housed the hundreds of drawings and prints that were held at the Institute. That was what was so great about teaching art history here: you could pull out an original drawing to illustrate a point, or take the student down to the airy spacious gallery and talk about paintings while you were surrounded by them. There was nothing quite like spending time in the presence of original artworks. Stella carefully extracted a drawing covered with a sheet of protective tissue paper from one of the drawers. It might not be a Vermeer, but the combined collection here was valuable enough to have necessitated an expensive new security system.

She lifted the sheet, exposing a drawing of a woman pouring liquid from a jug. The artist had lovingly rendered the sensuous tilt of her arm and neck.

'This was done by one of the apprentice artists in seventeenth-century Holland,' explained Stella. She studied the drawing closely. It still thrilled her to see for real the actual pencil strokes put down so confidently hundreds of years ago.

'See how the place of woman is illustrated. She is a quiet, domestic creature. As much a possession of her husband as the table or the jug.'

Stella brushed her hand against Andrew's leg. He jumped slightly, but didn't move his leg away. Stella took this to be a good sign.

'This was probably the preparatory work for a commissioned oil painting. When a man looked at this he could think with satisfaction that he owned everything represented.'

Andrew leaned towards her, ostensibly to study the drawing closer. Stella worked her hand further up his young muscular thigh which trembled under the table. It was almost too easy really. He was like a cherry which hung ripe and ready on the tree.

'See how the artist has so eloquently depicted the girl's neck and bosom, playing on her sexuality,' said Stella in a quiet soothing voice. She felt like the snake in *Jungle Book*: trust in me, trussssst in me.

Andrew blushed deeply as her hand alighted on his cock – which was already hard and heavy in his jeans – as if his arousal was a guilty secret which she'd just uncovered. Stella made her voice soft and gentle as she explained the drawing to him, kneading his erection under the table. Any minute, she thought, and my eyes will have those hypnotic rings around them and my forked tongue will whip out to lash him.

Andrew shook all over as she stroked him harder and his breath began heaving in long telltale sighs.

'Professor Fanshawe,' he said shakily.

'Yeees,' she replied in an abstracted fashion, busy with his zip.

'I've always thought you are a very attractive woman.'

'Thank you, Andrew,' she replied briskly as her hand plunged inside his jeans, her fingers seeking out the hardness. 'I've always thought you're attractive too,' she added, as her hand grasped his cock, snuggled tightly inside his briefs. The action made him wince with pleasure.

She held his balls firmly in her hand. 'Of course, you must never tell anyone about this,' she said, making her voice threatening this time.

He shook his head quickly. 'Oh no, honestly I won't.'

'Good, because if you do, I'll simply deny it,' she said. She amazed herself how ruthless she could be in the pursuit of firm young flesh.

After a few firm strokes of his cock, Andrew was blushing and shaking all over. Stella could see that this one wouldn't last for long.

'Lie on the floor,' she ordered.

He lifted his head and stared at her. 'What . . .?'

'Go on, lie down. I promise you'll like it.' Stella took care to form her voice into a gentle tone again.

She stripped off her sensible tweedy skirt to reveal wispy purple panties with a butterfly embroidered on the front. Its position made it appear as if it was emerging from between her legs, poised to fly free. She chose all her underwear from a smart, expensive catalogue. If she had to look respectable on the outside she was damned well going to give herself free rein underneath. She whisked off her panties and let them flutter down from her fingers; they landed on Andrew's stomach.

He grabbed the filmy piece of fabric with shaking fingers while his eyes travelled from the knickers and fixed on Stella's naked pussy. A strangulated sound escaped his lips at the sight of the hair forming a dark patch between her legs, like a mysterious shadow at the entrance to a secret, enticing place.

Her heels made little clicking sounds on the parquet floor as she stepped astride him, naked from the waist down. Deliberately she placed one foot either side of his head. His big blue eyes rounded as he looked up into the crease between her legs. His sweet face with its firm pink cheeks looked up at her, his eyes caught between lust and fear. Oh, how she'd love to see his young, muscular body bound up beneath her, helpless, unmoving, his cock sticking up like a sapling emerging from the earth. Her eyes glazed over at the fantasy. Careful, careful, she told herself. He might be eager but she didn't want him to run crying to mummy if things got out of hand.

She lowered herself slowly so that the dewy lips between her legs nearly touched his. She crouched for a few seconds, her pussy just inches from his mouth.

'Taste it, Andrew,' she said softly.

He stuck out his pink tongue and experimentally touched the tip on her folds. Although the touch was light and uncertain it resonated through her body. He looked suddenly unsure of himself.

'Was ... was that all right?' he asked shakily.

'It's OK,' she said soothingly, 'taste me again, I like it when you do that.'

This time he gained confidence and tangled the tip of his tongue between her folds. When, almost by accident, his tongue smoothed over her clit she flung back her head and groaned loudly, her mouth pulling back from her teeth. He grinned in satisfaction at the effect he'd managed to have on her and went back to his licking with renewed confidence. The pleasure she felt in her little button began to overtake her. Abruptly she climbed off.

'What's the matter?' he asked, looking a bit crestfallen, as if he'd done something wrong.

'Nothing, nothing, sweet William,' she said softly.

He jerked his head up quickly. 'My name's Andrew,' he said quickly, a note of panic in his voice.

'Yes, yes, of course it is,' she soothed. She bit her lip; she was letting her imagination run away with her.

To take his attention away from her faux pas she began to unbutton her shirt as she stood over him. His cheeks flushed red and his eyes bulged as she slipped the shirt from her shoulders. His eyes goggled at the huge red nipples which flushed through the sheer purple fabric of her bra.

'OK, now you show me yours,' she said with a little giggle.

Andrew hesitated for a moment, terrified that her simple gaze on his throbbing erection would be enough to make him come.

'What if someone comes in?' he asked, his voice quavering slightly.

Stella walked over to the door in just her high heels and bra. Her lithe buttocks bounced a little as she walked and Andrew's eyes slavishly followed her progress. She locked the door and brandished the key at him.

'There, absolutely no one can see us now. Anyway,' she added, 'everyone will have gone home long ago.'

Crouching so that her glistening pussy was stretched out near his face, she pulled at his jeans. She could sense his eyes fixed on the feast set out before him. He lifted up his behind obediently to enable her to ease the jeans over his hips. Stella licked her lips as she looked down. Andrew's cock was crammed inside his tight white briefs – the fabric looked as if it might split open at any minute.

As she traced her fingers over the hard shape, Andrew's whole body twitched and jerked in response. She hooked her fingers under the elastic and his cock sprang upwards, the tip peeking out over the waistband, looking almost bruised and sore.

Sweat began to flow from Andrew's face as she slipped the briefs down, and again he lifted his bottom obligingly. Her mouth went dry as she looked at him lying naked on the wooden floor. His eyes were closed tight shut, almost as if expecting a blow. She wondered if she dared take his prick into her mouth and the thought prompted a rush of saliva. No, she didn't want to take him too far – she wanted to save that sweet hardness as much as possible.

She straddled his hips and her pussy gaped wetly as she parted her legs. Andrew opened his eyes and gasped at the sight of his professor spreadeagled over him. He looked longingly at her breasts.

'Please . . .' he said, touching her bra.

'You want to see my tits?' she asked, smiling down at him indulgently.

'Please,' he said again, in a polite voice.

Stella reached behind her back and unhooked her bra. Her tits jiggled and bounced as she threw her bra onto the floor. Stella could see him practically drool at the sight of her huge inflamed nipples.

'Touch them if you want,' she said magnanimously.

He cupped them in his hands, marvelling at the sight, and a shudder ran down Stella's spine. His face was bright red now, and when she looked down she could see his cock protruding from underneath her dark thatch of pubes. Already the tip looked shiny and wet.

Stella grabbed his knob and pushed it between her legs, desperate to catch him before it was too late. Taken by surprise, he writhed and twisted underneath her. His hips jerked upward spasmodically as he entered the moist, delicious place, thrusting his whole length deep inside her.

Boy, he wouldn't last for two seconds if he carried on like that. 'Keep still,' she muttered, and his body slumped back to the floor. His face twisted in a desperate grimace as she began to ease herself up and down, her wetness slicking his shaft.

His pubic hair tickled her as she bounced on him madly. She could see from his face that he was desperately holding on, and the muscles on his neck were standing out in hard ridges. Her fingers flew down to between her legs and she nuzzled her clit with her finger. He groaned deeply and she worked her finger harder, grinding it over her clit. He gave a deep, low howl and his hips thrust upward again. Sweat poured from his brow as he shot his semen deep inside her. Frantically she rubbed her finger round and round, the muscles of her cunt squeezing his wilting erection. She felt a tingling tightness round her anus which gathered and spread through her sex. The tightness moved upwards, clutching at her stomach and moving over her breasts. Just as the feeling became unbearable, it cracked and broke and she came with a series of loud, short pants. 'You beautiful, beautiful boy,' she moaned as she slumped forwards over his sweat-drenched body.

Lee lifted the corner of limp white bread on his sandwich. Salami again! He grabbed the Mars bar instead and bit a huge chunk off the end. He didn't know how many times he'd told Beccy he didn't like salami. He didn't know why she was even making him sand-wiches anyway, he'd certainly never asked her to.

The buttons on the console winked back at him under the lights, almost as if they were taunting him. Really he didn't have a damn clue about how the new system worked. When his boss had run through it he'd smiled and nodded knowledgeably but the old guy may as well have been talking gobbledegook. Biting another chunk off the Mars bar he pressed the buttons randomly. Black and white images flicked on and off the bank of screens before him: the empty foyer; the gallery with that valuable painting, Lee couldn't remember who it was by; the empty tutorial rooms – Christ, what was that? The image had only appeared for a second as he punched the buttons. He began pressing them again quickly. Which one had it been? Images of empty rooms appeared and flickered on the screens as he tried all the buttons again.

There, there it was, he hadn't been imagining things. Lee gawped at the screen. Was that . . . it couldn't be . . . it was, it was Professor Fanshawe. Lee could hardly believe his eyes – the prof straddled over some young student, sitting on his face. He craned forward to get a better look. Lee was struck by her firm, long legs either side of the boy's head. Actually her body wasn't half bad underneath those frumpy clothes she wore.

Unthinkingly he shovelled the rest of the sticky chocolate in his mouth and chomped on it. Who would have thought it – the prof. Lee often said goodnight to her when it was his turn to cover the main door. She always seemed to be the last to leave the building – well, now he knew why. She always said goodnight back in a slightly abstracted fashion, as if she had her mind on higher things. Lee snorted and then goggled at the screen again. She was standing up now with her back to the camera and Lee could see her bottom peeking underneath the hem of her shirt.

His knob felt uncomfortable as it swelled inside his trousers. The dirty cow – she had stripped off her shirt and was divesting the boy of his underpants. Her bottom reared towards the camera. Lee quickly unzipped himself. What a floor show ... this was certainly brightening up a dull evening! He grasped his cock with one hand as he watched the professor climb aboard the boy and start pumping up and down. 'Take your bra off,' he said under his breath. A few seconds later, almost as if she'd heard his muttered command, she stripped off her bra. Lee gripped himself with renewed enthusiasm as her tits joggled in time to her thrusting.

Lee's hand flew up and down so quickly it almost formed a blur. Christ, he'd felt horny enough when he'd arrived at work that evening: not only did Beccy give him crap sandwiches and make threatening noises about moving in, he seemed to be getting less and less these days. Now this. After only a couple of minutes Lee could feel the spunk gathering in his balls. A tissue, quick! Lee looked wildly on the desk – there wasn't a tissue in sight. Oh well, he'd just have to improvise. He grabbed the cling film that his sandwiches had been wrapped in. It would have to do. He wrapped it round the tip of his knob which showed through the plastic, moist and red.

The two figures writhed around on the little screen like puppets being jerked about on invisible strings. The prof was really going for it now, her head thrown back in pleasure. Lee's cock thrust forward in his hand as if it had a life of its own, and he could feel the jet of spunk making its ascent. He let out a strangulated cry and the semen pumped out in a glutinous mass. When the tremors had faded he wiped the sticky deposit off the end of his cock and parcelled it neatly into the cling film. He stuck the whole thing inside the discarded Mars bar wrapper and aimed it at the bin. When he looked up, he saw the two figures had disappeared, leaving him staring at the empty room on the flickering screen.

Stella looked up as the security guard entered the room. She frowned at him; he could have at least knocked.

'I thought it was about time you looked at the new security system, Professor Fanshawe,' he said.

'Oh, yes ... that,' she replied. She'd been away while it had been installed and the whole thing had slipped her mind.

'Now would be a good time,' said the security guard.

Stella frowned again. The man seemed to be leering at her in the most peculiar fashion. It flitted through her mind that he could be considered quite handsome, despite his closely shorn blond hair and his nose bent to one side. Not really her type though – too old. She sighed. She supposed now *would* be as good a time as any, she'd never get round to it otherwise. She pushed the pile of marking to one side.

'All right, Mr, er . . .?' she said, groping for his name.

'Call me Lee.' Honestly, he was acting in a most familiar manner. She'd have to nip that in the bud.

Lee led the way and she had trouble keeping up with his long strides as she followed him up to the fifth floor where the main security room was housed.

When they were in the stuffy little room, Lee gestured proudly towards the bank of screens.

'Quarter of a million quid this cost,' he said.

'Yes, there are some very valuable works in the collection.' Stella pushed her glasses back on her nose, wondering how long this was going to take.

Lee extracted a video tape from his rucksack hanging on a peg. 'Of course, there are now cameras in nearly every room of the building. Except the lavs, that is. People don't want to be watched having a widdle.'

A sick feeling gripped her stomach. 'Every room?' she stammered. It struck her all of a sudden, the possible reason for his peculiar leering manner.

He grinned at her. 'You see the strangest things of an evening, up here, all on your own. Take this example, that got picked up by the cameras last week.'

He slotted the video tape inside the player and fiddled with the button until the screen jumped into life. Stella's jaw dropped open as she saw herself lit up on the screen – locking the door to the tutorial room, naked from the waist down. As she swung round to confront him she noticed the huge lump in his uniform trousers.

'Of course, I could hand this in to the Dean. I'm sure he'd be very interested,' said Lee.

Her eyes drifted back to the screen. Waves of horror washed over her – oh Christ, she was sitting on the boy's face now. She wondered how many times Lee had watched this particular piece of tape. She guessed it was probably nearly worn out by now.

His light-blue eyes mocked her discomfort. His cap sat at an untidy angle on his head. To her horror she saw him unzipping the trousers to his blue uniform.

'I really don't think . . .' she stammered.

'Don't think what, Professor Fanshawe?' he asked, coming up close behind her.

He pushed her roughly so she was bent over the desk, the tape playing out obscenely right in front of her face. There was the sound of a zipper again, only this time she realised it was her own. Her skirt fell to the floor.

'Nice underwear,' he leered.

She looked down and her cheeks burned. Typical, she'd chosen the tiniest red briefs to wear today. Her dark bush glowed underneath the see-through red lace at the front of the tarty knickers. It looked like this man was uncovering all her dirty secrets.

Suddenly her knickers were around her thighs and Lee was pulling at her long lips between his fingers. She could hear him panting behind her.

'Boy, you've got a gorgeous cunt,' he said, his voice heavy with desire.

'For God's sake get it over and done with,' she said curtly.

The thick material of his uniform scratched her skin as he unceremoniously sank his prick inside her folds. He slid in quite easily – she could hardly believe it, the situation was actually making her wet!

Lee panted like a dog as he thrust in and out of her. She could almost imagine him behind her with his tongue lolling out, salivating. To take her mind off the horrible vision she focused on the screen. Andrew still looked beautiful, even in the grainy black and white image. She admired his supine young flesh. Even she had to admit that the tape was pretty hot. No wonder this – what was his name? – Lee, no wonder he'd got so fired up by it. She noted with some pride how long and lean her legs appeared as she crouched over Andrew.

A sudden flow of moisture flooded between her legs. Had she really made Andrew writhe about in such ecstasy? She smuggled her finger between her legs. When she touched her clit it sent shock waves through her, making her muscles clench and tighten. Lee groaned in appreciation, thrusting harder. Her finger glided over her clit. Wow, she could see how close Andrew was on the tape now, his face all screwed up as if he was in pain. Her finger worked busily, occasionally knocking against Lee's hard cock.

On the glowing screen she could see Andrew's hips thrust upwards in desperation and the sight made her cunt muscles tighten another notch. Lee was making little grunts now, his hot breath gusting on her neck.

'Hold on, hold on,' she said, panicking that he would come any second now.

Lee stopped thrusting and held still. He leaned forward and grabbed at Stella's tits, squeezing them in his big hands. Her finger made little sucking noises as it moved. She could feel her pussy clench and unclench around Lee's wide tool, which held her open.

In the grainy picture she watched Andrew as his face twisted. His mouth opened and gave silent cries of pleasure. Her climax roared through her body in sync with Andrew's silent orgasm.

As she slumped forward, Lee cackled obscenely behind her.

'Enjoy that, Professor?' he asked, before thrusting wildly inside her. After only a few strokes he let out a yell and, with a final pump, he came inside her.

She gathered up her skirt and stepped back into it. She had to get hold of that tape, she decided. No way was she going to leave such incriminating evidence in Lee's hands – he'd probably hold it over her for ever. Their quick shag had been nice enough, but she had no desire to repeat the experience. That was OK – she'd engage Lee in some unchallenging conversation, perhaps send him out for a drink of water while she nicked the tape. She could stick it under the waistband of her skirt. Actually, she reflected, she wouldn't mind viewing it again – in private this time.

Stella glanced at the screen furtively out of the corner of her eye to see if it was close to rewinding and her mouth dropped open. She had left the frame now: all she could see was Andrew as he dressed himself. Bare-chested, he was doing up his jeans, looking for all the world like he'd just stepped out of a Levis commercial when – no, she hadn't imagined it, she was sure – he looked up cockily in the direction of the camera and gave a lascivious wink. And despite the blur of the footage, Stella could swear she could see his eyes shining in triumph.

Greed is Good

'Sex sells,' said the young man sitting at table three in the corner.

Barbara put the plate of linguini studded with mussels down in front of him carefully – so as not to spill any of the precious sauce pooled around the edges of the plate – and looked at the open page of the magazine he had indicated. A woman in a plastic bikini sprawled over a very ordinary-looking car. Barbara noted her plucked bikini line and the hip bones which jutted out beneath her skin.

'She doesn't sell anything to me,' she said with great certainty. The man laughed, looking at Barbara's breasts that bulged out over the top of her cook's white jacket. On her way back to the kitchen she wondered idly what it would be like to take him. He looked starved, poor love, his eyes glued to her tits like that. She'd give him milk if she had any; draw his head to her nipple and let him sleepily suckle there, his hands kneading the full white skin like cat's paws. She sighed. Sometimes it just seemed like the whole world was hungry.

People came to her restaurant for the spirit that seemed to hover around her, like warm honey. They also came for the food, a south European fusion – Italian sun with a dash of Spanish heat. Food was good, Barbara knew that in her heart. She couldn't understand why some women turned it into an enemy, choking back their little crudités of celery and carrot as if they were taking vitamin pills. She loved gluttons, even loved the word.

Ian was rattling pots and pans in the kitchen – fussing around, checking the bookings for tonight, ordering wine.

'Has he only just started?' he said irascibly, looking at his watch. 'You shouldn't have served anyone this late.'

'Oh, leave him,' she replied, 'he's starving.'

The man took ages over his food and they could still hear the scrape of cutlery on china some twenty minutes later. Barbara sliced mushrooms carefully in the kitchen, revealing their meaty insides, and doused them in white wine ready for the sauce later that day. Ian was on the phone talking to the wine merchant: his voice was becoming loud and impatient.

'No, I said two cases of the Australian, not one, and one case of Claret, not two. Jesus Christ.'

Barbara felt suddenly empty inside and nibbled on a breadstick dipped in a smoky red pepper sauce. The sunburnt taste of Spanish pimentos awoke her senses. Boy, did Ian have a temper! He was scrawling angrily on his notepad and she could hear the wine merchant's appeasing tones down the line. She knew she'd made the right decision when she employed Ian as manager. His hectoring manner kept everything running smoothly. The deliveries of cream and milk now arrived punctually; the boxes of vegetables were always the freshest, the aubergines ripe and plump next to swelling rounds of tomatoes. Everything was newly picked and beaded with cold. It left her to concentrate on what she loved most – the cooking.

His temper made his eyes blaze and she studied him: his heavy frame, the way his mouth curved in clean lines and the hair that grew at the nape of his neck. They often shagged casually in the kitchen, in between lunch time and evening opening. Ian would lean against her as she peeled, sautéed or sliced, squeezing her generous buttocks and stealing his prick in between her legs. The sense of emptiness Barbara felt suddenly yawned and roared.

She hopped onto the steel counter in front of him and began to kiss his neck. 'What reds do you have in stock at the moment?' A tremulous note had entered his voice.

She reached down and unbuttoned his trousers. His cock was beginning to harden responsively. She squeezed and rolled it and he covered the mouthpiece of the phone as he groaned gently. She kicked off her clogs and they fell with a dull bump, bump, onto the tiles.

A bottle of olive oil sat next to her on the counter. She poured a little of the heavy green liquid into her palm, feeling the dense slickness of it in her hand. She touched it with her tongue: this was good oil, the fruits of southern Italy had an especially peppery quality. Rubbing it over her palms she used the fluid to slide over his cock, squeezing as she went. He closed his eyes and leaned back against the wall.

'Tell me all about the region it's from. Have you been there?' Ian just managed to croak down the phone. She could hear the distant voice of the seller – he wouldn't be used to such a friendly, quiet tone from Ian. The poor guy probably thinks he's got a massive sale on his hands, thought Barbara with a smile.

Ian was breathing heavily and silently. She loved to make him hot like this, when he was least expecting it. When she drew up her skirt under her white apron she could feel the cold steel of the counter against her naked, white thighs. She slicked herself with the precious oil until her lips stood out shiny and swollen.

The fluid lent a velvety feeling to her own touch and she lingered for a while, pleasuring herself. A tiny drop of oil beaded onto a curl of dark brown hair.

With the phone clamped to his ear Ian grasped his cock with his other hand and rubbed it tenderly around her clit before sinking inside her. She squeezed her knees around his waist and her pussy tightened. He nearly groaned out loud this time and she just managed to cover his mouth with her palm in time. Mustering all his self control he said firmly down the phone, 'Give me all the prices on that line, I'm writing it all down,' before he began thrusting, his hips making tiny movements.

If she bent her head down she could see his cock emerge from underneath her fuzz of hair, glossed with oil and her own juices. The action made little sucking sounds which filled her ears – she found it hard to believe the man jabbering on the other end of the line couldn't hear it. His cock felt smooth and slippery from the oil and her cunt began to warm up and quiver inside. He leaned over and whispered, 'You dirty bitch,' softly into her ear before the waves of heat began to spread over her body. They gathered in intensity until she felt those few seconds of quietness, like looking over a cliff, before the climax undulated through her body, making her back arch like a cat's.

A few seconds later they heard a knocking on the counter out in the restaurant. The young man called out, 'Hello, can I pay?' Barbara threw back her head and laughed, tickled by the idea of the stray diner's unwitting presence. 'I'd forgotten our hungry man,' she said.

A small knot of excitement always gathered in the pit of her stomach at this time of the evening. The little coloured lights strung up at the window reappeared in miniature on the polished glasses and silver cutlery. The smell of garlic, warm oil and baking bread curled out from the kitchen and Barbara felt, as always, that the scene was set for the evening. She looked out to the rainy night, the twilight gathering already, knowing what an oasis of food and wine and warmth she had created here inside.

Ian whistled, calmed and happy from their impromptu fuck, and patted her arse soundly as he passed.

'You're a bad girl.' His light-blue eyes teased her. God, he was handsome, not in a conventional sense, but his wide shoulders and strong cheekbones still thrilled her.

'Bad is good,' she said, looping her brown curls into a knot and skewering them with a clip.

The restaurant was tiny and soon crowded out, even though not quite twenty people had arrived. She gathered her thoughts: cooking took complete focus for her, almost an act of meditation. She became strong and authoritative in the kitchen, issuing quiet orders to Ian, who assisted her. Here she was a head of state, the kitchen an ordered country that she ran with a firm hand. She stirred minted cream into the fresh pea soup and the cream melted, leaving behind fragrant flecks of mint. Soon the colour in her cheeks burned as she worked with a quiet intensity.

The waiter, Jake, arrived, shaking the drops of rain from his hair.

'Where the fuck have you been?' Ian exploded at him.

'As I told you, I've been to pick up my mate Thomas, who agreed to step in after you abused that girl in front of everyone. God, honestly, I only stay in this place for Barbara.'

Jake looked at her with a wink. He didn't mean it. He got on well with Ian, didn't take his moods personally – unlike the last waitress who had yelled at Ian 'Go fuck yourself' in front of all the startled diners before storming out. Jake's mate stood shyly behind them, wondering what den of lions he had entered. Barbara frowned and shut out the drama from her head as it exploded around her, and sprinkled thick crystals of sea salt over a glossy leg of lamb.

The swell of voices was punctuated with the clink of glasses and cutlery and the sound seemed to roll in waves through the open kitchen door. She arched her back to ease the low ache. Everything was now nicely simmering, roasting or cooling. She made her way out to the restaurant. Barbara always liked to see her customers, so it didn't feel like she was feeding one huge anonymous mouth that lay beyond the kitchen door. She loved to see people enjoying her food, their cheeks flushed with wine as they offered a piled forkful – 'Here, try this' – to their partners, whose ready, open mouths looked like baby birds.

Only one chair was empty, at the largest table which seated some kind of office gathering. Barbara had an inkling they were solicitors. The door pushed open and a dark attractive girl entered. Rain frosted her Afro-style hair in a fine mist. Jake took her coat, glancing slyly at her curving figure, and she went to join the others. The young man sitting next to the empty chair stood up as she approached. They shook hands as they were introduced and his eyes unconsciously flicked up and down her body.

As the evening went on, the heat in the kitchen became intense, emanating from the ovens and the bright blue gas flames. Barbara loosened the top couple of buttons of the stiff white shirt with its square mandarin collar and wandered out into the relative cool of the restaurant. Her eyes were drawn to the woman who had arrived late, now leaning over to the man seated next to her – she was laughing and slanting her eyes at him provocatively. The girl stood up, slightly unsteady on her feet. Her red dress clung to her body, outlining her slim waist and the gentle, sexy curve outwards of her stomach. She brushed her fingers against her companion's neck as she passed on her way to the loo. Roughly a minute later he also stood, furtively checking the rest of the table to see if they had noticed. Barbara doubted very much if they had – they all seemed drunk and engrossed in their own conversations. Empty wine bottles log-jammed the middle of the table. As if drawn by an invisible string, Barbara followed them.

She hesitated in front of the toilet door and then removed her clogs. She padded on bare feet into the tiled space. A huge bowl of rose petals sat by the wash basin, scenting the whole room with rose and vanilla oil; Barbara couldn't bear synthetic smells. Pinkish light glowed from a beaded lamp set on a shelf. Lighting was so important. She wanted every woman who reapplied her lipstick in the mirror to be flattered by her reflection. One of the cubicle doors was firmly shut. Soundlessly she smuggled herself into the adjoining cubicle, pushing the door closed with her fingertips.

Smothered pants and moans emanated from the space next to her. Barbara wrapped her arms around her body, all ears, as the sounds grew more abandoned. She felt like a furtive intruder, frozen in vicarious excitement, caught up in their moment. Suddenly there was a deep collective groan, male and female, and Barbara could almost feel the man's prick entering her own moist space. She was hardly breathing. God, how she missed this. Fleeting memories of her own encounters with strangers spun through her head – chancy, exhilarating moments which still burned in her memory.

The adjoining partition began to vibrate with a steady rhythm, muffled 'oh's' were punctuated with the man groaning 'fuck, fuck'. Barbara sat completely still, her heart knocking, it seemed, in time with the beat that drummed on the partition wall. She felt a heat stealing up her neck, tingling her cheeks, reaching downwards, making her breasts feel full and heavy. She could almost smell the woman's wild excitement and the man's furtive joy as his prick was enclosed sweetly by the moist cunt.

The banging on the wall grew louder. They didn't care any more; Barbara knew they were beyond the fear of being discovered. A deep sigh filled the room, echoing off the cold tiles, and Barbara felt a vicarious warmth spread between her own legs. Then she heard the man grunt. The sound was heavy, animal.

There was much whispering and giggling and Barbara heard the main door open and fall shut. There was a sound of taps turning on and a splashing of water before the others left, probably trying to assume a casual expression on their faces before joining their companions. Barbara wondered if they had noticed her cubicle door shut or seen her clogs where she'd kicked them off. She unbolted the door and splashed water on her burning cheeks, curiously shaken by the longing that had awoken in her. How long was it since she'd been swept away like that – felt the nervous thrill of meeting someone new, whose face and hands spoke such irresistible messages that the only choice was to fall into their arms.

The dining room lay bare. Jake and Thomas had stripped the tables of all the plates and cutlery, efficiently folding up the table cloths so the scattered breadcrumbs, spilled salt and crumbled candlewax was enveloped inside. Barbara lit the tea light under the incense burner and shook some drops of oil into the little ceramic well over the flame. It was lemongrass, to clear the air and dispel the chattering ghosts of conversations which had risen upwards and still seemed to bubble and fizz around the ceiling. The hectic spirits fled out into the night, whooshing down the dark street, calling to each other in brittle voices as they went.

As usual, her staff had gathered around the largest table in the centre of the room. Collars were loosened and aching feet rested as Ian poured them all a glass of wine. Holding the plate with both hands, Barbara carried in the cake she had made with sleepy concentration that morning. She'd still been in her pyjamas as she'd studied the recipe book, whisking cream while she read. She'd never made this cake before and she wanted to unveil it to the others and get their opinion before she added it to the menu. It was a Leaning Tower of Pisa cake: layers of meringue glued together with whipped cream. A sticky orange sauce spilled over the top and ran in rivulets down the sides. The Seville oranges which she had simmered slowly with sugar and water provided a bitter antidote to the sweetness. The meringue cracked as she sliced it, sending a small, sweet cloud of icing sugar, pouf, up into the air.

Thomas took a forkful from the slab in front of him and tasted it delicately, his hazel eyes glassing slightly with the sugar rush. Barbara admired his slow appreciation, suddenly realising how attractive he was: his quiet movements, languid and sensual, sure of himself within his skin; his dark hair bristling on his head like an animal's.

'This is sublime,' he pronounced. 'We made one a bit like this in college, only my meringue disintegrated in the oven.' He laughed, a smear of cream on his bottom lip.

With the air of utmost seriousness, as if she was explaining the solution to world peace, Barbara expounded the art of meringue making: the slow oven, barely lit; the long cooking as the froth of egg whites harden and form a crust.

The wine was making her limbs feel heavy and voluptuous. Jake was quiet and relaxed beside her, his leg resting lightly against hers. She was flirting with Thomas, she knew – not with words, but with her eyes and the way her hand kept touching her hair. Her body still felt awake to the sounds she'd heard earlier of the couple making love. As if in some subconscious way they could sense her arousal, Jake and Thomas leaned towards her. Was this so bad? she thought to herself. She had a sudden longing for newness, strangeness. It was as if the witnessed encounter that evening had blown away the contentment of her life with Ian. She felt a craving for different flavours and textures: the touch of a chilli on the tongue, almost painful; the sour, saliva-sucking taste of bitter tamarind.

Ian began fussing around. He hadn't touched his cake yet. He was still hyped up from the evening and flittered about, stacking menus and rearranging the bottles on the shelves so the labels could be seen. God, he was irritating her, like an annoying moth that was batting round their circle of warmth and light.

Jake's leg grew warm against her own and she thought she felt the brush of his fingertips against the cotton of her skirt. It occurred to her to move away but somehow her limbs felt too heavy and languid to shift. Ian was carrying a box of vegetables from the cellar to the kitchen. He brandished a carrot in his fingertips.

'Something for later, Babs?' The comedy lift of his eyebrows irritated her.

'Fucking with vegetables is just so ... so passé,' she said witheringly. The carrot seemed to droop visibly in his fingertips. Why was she being so mean? she thought to herself as he retreated to the kitchen, the straightness of his back belying his hurt. Thomas was talking about his time in India.

'It was the bread that really got to me, there's so many different kinds ...'

Under the table Jake began to stroke her leg, his touch tentative at first, then becoming bolder as she didn't retreat.

'They make it out in the streets with little fires under metal plates. The smell goes right to your guts,' Thomas went on.

What was happening? Had Jake sensed her arousal through the evening? She had to admit to herself she had been flirting with him outrageously tonight, catching his eye, leaning towards him, flicking a stray dark curl away from his forehead lightly with her fingers. At one point she had felt him lean over her from behind, as if to secretly smell her hair. She was so sure he'd been about to touch her, she could feel the ghost movement of his fingertips on her behind. Then Ian had rushed in, fulminating about some awkward customer, and they had broken apart quickly. Probably too quickly because she'd seen Ian looking at her thoughtfully after that.

She felt Jake's hand pinch the cotton skirt she was wearing and pull it upwards. The fabric slid softly on her skin. Her cunt felt moist and hot between her legs

– just one touch, one touch of his fingers against her naked slit and she'd come, she was sure. His hand delved between her legs and brushed against her knickers, the swell of her lips beneath. How dare he! she thought in excited indignation – with Ian just beyond the kitchen door and his friend sitting across the table.

She looked at Thomas as he spoke. She hardly dared breathe in case her breath betrayed her. Thomas's long fingers played with his fork as he spoke. God, could it be? Did he know what was happening? She felt a craving for his touch too. For him to sit on her other side and graze his lips across her ear, to feel crushed between them both as he slipped a hand inside her shirt and cupped her breast. Greedy for the unknown: for new scents, new tastes, greedy for more – not one but two! Jake's probing finger slipped underneath her knickers and stroked up and down the slippery wetness. She didn't dare move now and she felt rooted to her chair as she felt his finger gently enter her. It was immediately encircled by her wet folds. Her cunt pulsed around the intruding finger.

The kitchen door clunked as Ian reappeared and Jake's finger withdrew, as if in respect of his presence. He picked up his plate and shovelled some cake into his mouth.

'It's missing something,' he mused. 'Chocolate, it needs the accent of chocolate,' he said firmly.

'Well, make it your bloody self next time,' she stormed at him, and rushed from the table, tipping up the chair as she went.

The next day the restaurant stayed shut. Barbara always closed on a Wednesday: a day to gather her thoughts, to experiment with new dishes and to think about colours and flavours. But she wasn't in the mood for cooking today. Food needed calm concentration and a clear head. Cooking with a bad temper curdled the milk, made the sauce lumpy, burned the cakes.

Last night she'd lain with her back turned to Ian in bed, the tension like a taut chain between them. She knew he must have sensed something when he came back into the dining room and seen the three of them together in the pooled candlelight.

She had no secrets from Ian. He knew her history and her appetites before they met: the men casually met and fucked on trains; lovers dropped after a few wild nights; her thirst for newness. She'd imagined taking both of them last night, Thomas and Jake. Not one but two. Was that so greedy?

The cards would clear her head and tell her what to do. Cards and cooking. She smiled to herself. When she'd read *Chocolat* she'd been struck by the similarities between herself and the heroine of the book, Vianne Rocher.

She took the pack of tarot cards from the soft velvet bag and lit the incense burner – rosemary this time, for focus and divination. Closing her eyes, she began to shuffle until she began to feel a calmness. Three rows of three: the past first ... a man who's trying to get her attention. She snorted; as ever, the cards telling her what she knew already. Her eyes turned to the present. There he was again, the hanged man – he often turned up in her present, which made sense as she always turned to the cards at times of indecision. The dangling figure represented nothing sinister, just that she was swinging in the wind, waiting for something to happen. Now for the future, the best bit – there was always a little tremor of excitement in looking at the future.

She was startled by the rap of knuckles. Thomas's

face peered through the glass door. His beautiful wiry hair was combed back and stubble marked his chin. She let him in.

'I was just passing.'

She smiled, a likely story. His eyes took in the cards spread out on the counter, each one a bright patch of colour.

'I didn't know you were into all this,' he exclaimed. 'I had my fortune told in India, by this little wizened old man. He told me I'd always be travelling, only setting down in one place for a few years at a time. Perhaps he was right. It's scary really.'

Thomas stood close to her as he spoke. His hand brushed her breast as he reached over to pick one of the cards up for a closer look. It was the page of cups.

Barbara started to breathe faster. Could it be? Could Jake have told him about their furtive encounter last night and was he now coming by for some of the same? But he just looked eager and a bit awkward, bowled over but a bit in awe of her. God, he was as tempting as Jake. Barbara imagined taking him in her mouth – gobbling on his stiffened prick, her mouth jammed open, satiated. It seemed temptation was everywhere, as if the furtive sounds of the couple's lovemaking last night had set something loose in her so that she wanted everything she cast her eyes on.

'Ian's asked me and Jake out for a drink tonight.' That was the first she'd heard of it. She shrugged. 'Well, have a good time then.' So that was what Ian was up to – flattening the opposition before they had a chance to oust him. She crossly pulled the bolts on the door to let Thomas out.

Barbara spent the evening in the kitchen emptying all the bottles and packets out of cupboards, trying to calm herself by sluicing everything out with soapy water and counting out herbs and spices. She felt at odds with herself. She'd thought she loved Ian, did love him in fact. But how could she settle down with this greedy longing for the touch of other men plaguing her? All she needed was one last monumental fling, one last exploration into unknown territory to purge herself of these cravings. Ian was probably marking his turf right now, telling the two men to back off. A bottle of wine slipped from her trembling fingers and smashed, spreading out in a red carpet on the kitchen floor.

When they arrived back she felt calmer, decisive. She was going to tell Ian she needed a break – maybe six months, maybe a year – so that she could taste a few final fruits. The decision terrified her. Perhaps in a year he wouldn't want her back. And would it be worth it? Those fruits might leave a bitter taste in her mouth.

The three men's noise filled the quiet space, their faces flushed with cold and drink.

'So what did you get up to?' Barbara asked, trying to be pleasant.

'I took the boys to that lap dancing place,' said Ian.

The statement left her speechless. The action was completely out of character for Ian and she wondered what the hell he was up to. But she felt intrigued, despite herself. So perhaps that accounted for the high colour in their cheeks. Barbara could almost see the images imprinted on their minds from their evening out. She'd seen these places on television: girls with bikini-waxed pussies, the little tufts of hair rude against the naked skin, swaying close to the seated men (look but don't touch!); the firm tits jiggling with the motion of the dance, just inches from the men's faces. She felt a surprising stir between her legs at her thoughts. She wished she could have spied on them and seen the hunger on their faces.

She was just about to ask Ian what he'd been playing at, taking *her* staff to a place like that, when he disappeared into the kitchen. After much banging and crashing he emerged with plates and bottles stacked in his arms.

'Food,' he said wildly. 'Let's all eat.' He spread out a feast on the table: a ripe Camembert, its thick white crust enclosing the soft ripeness within; huge purple grapes, each globe with its pearly sheen; bread; Parma ham; salami with globs of white studding its pinkish insides; cake; olives; breadsticks; stuffed vine leaves. Enough to make anyone burst.

The three men seemed keyed up, giggly almost. Ian sat next to Barbara and lifted a thin slice of ham to her lips with his fingers. 'Eat, my lovely,' he crooned in her ear. The tender meat slid down her throat.

'Jake, you feed her,' Ian ordered. 'Give her one of these.' The black olive passed from one man's fingers to the other. Jake sat the other side of her and fed her the olive. Thomas looked on, nervously sipping wine.

Ian looked wild tonight, his beautiful mouth curved into a deep sensuality. He played the host with passion, urging everyone to eat, to have more, help themselves. He took off his jacket and loosened his shirt, filling and refilling his glass. Pulling the long tangle of curls away from Barbara's face, he kissed her neck.

'Feed her more,' he said to Jake. 'Give her some Camembert.'

Tension cracked the air as Jake fed her some of the ripe cheese from his fingertips and as Ian caressed her throat. Barbara allowed them to stroke and feed her – her employees ministering to her wants as if she were a needy goddess.

She felt hot with excitement. What did Ian imagine she would allow him to do? To shag her in front of the others to demonstrate she was his? Was he testing her with temptation only to confront her and ask who her choice was? The last couple of days had felt like the time before a storm, just before it breaks. Well, something was breaking now and the unknown outcome made Barbara tense with nerves and excitement. To question too much would break the spell and change the outcome.

Ian had pulled her dress off one shoulder and was kissing her there, slowly and intimately. 'She tastes so beautiful. Jake, you taste her too,' he murmured.

Jake leaned over and ran his tongue delicately down her neck. Thomas took the seat opposite them and watched.

Barbara glanced uncertainly towards Ian, but he smiled down at her, wine and generosity lighting up his eyes. So that was it! He was giving her to Jake, handing her over on a plate and pre-empting an affair before it happened. Ian stood up and went to draw down the blinds. The atmosphere changed and thickened.

The warmth of the two men enclosed her when he sat down next to her again. Ian began stroking her tits as Jake kissed her deeply, making her feel like a goddess again, being placated by her minions. She opened her eyes, half expecting Thomas to have got up and left in embarrassment. But he was still there, his throat working nervously.

Ian called to him across the table. 'She's got the most beautiful big tits. Just as good as anything you saw tonight.' He started unbuttoning her dress. 'Would you like to see them?' Thomas nodded once, then nervously again.

Barbara felt a small stab of shame as Thomas undid her dress and pulled out a large creamy breast, cupping it in his hand. Exposing her like this to the other men, to her employees, for God's sake. The shame mingled with desire as Jake began to run his fingers up the inside of her thighs. Ian rolled her naked tit in his hand. 'Taste her,' he said to Thomas. 'She tastes of milk and butter.'

Thomas didn't need to be asked twice. When he stood up the bulge in his trousers looked huge and painful. Thomas crouched down before her and took the proffered nipple in his mouth. He sucked delicately with his lips rounding childishly on the puckered teat. How obvious her fantasies must have been – Ian had read her like a book. Now she was letting Ian give her away as he might offer to share a meal. She felt swept away, overwhelmed by the fingers and mouths as they touched and probed. Thomas licked and sucked at her breast, breaking away only to say to Ian dreamily, 'She does; she tastes of milk and unsalted butter.'

Ian knelt in front of her and lifted her dress up slowly. Automatically her hands flew down to stop him. The idea of her naked cunt, shining moistly for all to see, made her feel hot with embarrassment. Insistently he drew up her dress again, over her pale thighs, until it was hitched up in folds around her waist. Her lacy blue knickers stretched over her swollen sex and Ian stroked the damp fabric between her legs. With his large hands he reached up and began to pull them off. They fell around her ankles. Her cunt looked exposed, shocking even to herself, the generous dark hair with the bright red lips peeping rudely from below.

'Look,' said Ian, 'see what a gorgeous cunt she has.'

Barbara's hands again moved unconsciously to cover herself, but Ian pulled them firmly away. Jake looked down, his blue eyes shining and his curly hair wild. All three men admired her pussy. She felt like a toy in a shop window – with eyes staring wistfully in desire at a much longed-for object so close in proximity.

Ian looked up to her face. 'I want you to feel full,' he said before burying his tongue in the hot space between her legs. Artfully circling her clit with his mouth he gently sucked there until rivulets of desire ran up and down her body.

Her legs felt weak as Ian pulled her up. Pushing the plates out of the way he spread her face-first over the edge of the table. She saw Jake quickly shake off his clothes and his prick stood out rigid and proud in front of him. Ian lifted her skirt over her behind with the action of someone unveiling a painting. He kneaded her bare arse and ran his finger up and down her soaking slit.

'Who wants her first?' he whispered. 'Thomas, I think it should be you.'

If she had the will she'd protest, Barbara thought: showing her off like this, handing her round like a plate of vol au vents. But somehow no words would form in her mouth, and she watched Thomas quickly undress until only his shirt was left on, fascinated by his full muscled legs and his short thick cock. She felt herself opening up as he played around, pushing his prick in slightly then pulling back out again, letting the end of his cock tease her. Slowly he entered her up the to hilt and she sighed, a deep, gushing sound. Unhurriedly he pulsed inside her, his wideness opening her out to the full.

'Who's next, who's next?' said Ian wildly. He turned to Jake. 'I'll wrestle you for her.'

They were both quite drunk now. As they play-wrestled on the floor their outstretched pricks bounced with the exertion. When Barbara saw them rolling naked and laughing, their swollen dicks brushing against each other's bodies, her pussy heaved and tightened. Jake, the victor, sat astride Ian, his penis rearing over the hair on Ian's stomach. Ian lay drunk and laughing underneath.

Thomas withdrew, leaving her suddenly bereft. She turned over and stretched out across the table. She felt abandoned to what was happening now, every orifice open and available, spread out like a feast. Jake grabbed her by the hips and quickly pushed his cock inside her. He felt so different to Thomas: he was thinner but longer, and seemed to reach up inside her, nestling in her pussy. Thomas's prick looked swollen almost to the point of pain, red and ridged from being inside her.

'Let Barbara take you in her mouth, she's good at that,' Ian said wickedly. Naked and flushed, he looked like a lord of revelry.

To soothe his aching prick, Thomas held it near her lips from the other side of the table. She licked and sucked it, taking it into her mouth as much as she dared. With her mouth stretched out she sucked hard. She had a desperate desire to be filled up, satiated – any unfilled orifice felt like a gaping hole. Thomas's face looked tense and wired and his hips gave short, involuntary thrusts outwards. The two men's cocks felt warm and heavy inside her. Tasting a salty drop from Thomas, she thrust her hips upwards to meet Jake. Thomas stared over at Jake, watching as his shining prick emerged and then disappeared between her legs. He groaned wildly and his cock seemed to swell inside her mouth before she tasted the salty come. She swallowed greedily and the liquid slipped down her throat.

Ian cradled her head. 'Oh, baby, my baby,' he crooned. He lay next to her on the table, fondling her and then turned her over onto her side like a roll of pastry. Manoeuvring himself expertly, Jake kept his penis inside and moved with her. With his head propped up on his arm she stared closely into his blue eyes as he continued to stroke in and out.

She felt Ian part her buttocks from behind and rest his cock against her arsehole. Oh, to be completely full, to have the greedy hunger assuaged.

'Relax, my darling,' he whispered, 'relax into it.' Slowly, stopping every few seconds, he began pushing his cock inside her arsehole. The passage felt tense and dry. He jumped off the table and grabbed a pat of butter from the side table. She felt his fingers slathering the butter around her tight opening, working it all around. He applied some of the grease around his own knob before resting his tip against the puckered hole.

Barbara breathed slowly in and out as she relaxed her muscles one by one and welcomed him in. Now she was full, completely full as never before. She felt overwhelmed. What a wicked, greedy woman she must be – not one, not two, but three. But bad was good, she remembered, greed was good.

Ian didn't move, he just stayed in that most intimate space. She could feel the weight and expanse of him as Jake continued to carefully slide up and down. She wondered if they could feel each other inside of her; feel the weight and presence of each other's dicks. Her arsehole tightened further around Ian's cock as her climax began to gather and rise. When it ripped through her whole body it felt as if the three of them were suddenly meshed together by the force of it, like lightning melting metal.

Barbara felt replete when she fell into bed with Ian that night. She realised how he must have planned this: decided to share what was on his plate, perversely giving away what was his so that he could hang on to it.

'I never want to share you again,' he murmured, before he went to sleep. In her heart she knew that was fine. She felt full to bursting.

'Those bastards.' Ian slammed the restaurant door shut, making the glasses shift and tinkle on the tables. 'Jake and Thomas, do you know what they're doing? Only opening their own place a couple of streets away.'

Ian stared angrily out into the road, as if he could zap all the buildings in his fury like an ancient god, bricks and mortar crumbling before his eyes. He ripped down the blinds to shut out the offence.

Barbara carried on calmly clearing tables. In truth she felt a bit relieved. There had only been a slight awkwardness between them all in the few intervening days since that evening, but she was glad to be rid of it, to move on. That night had been a kind of gluttonous binge before a diet. But what a glorious diet. She drank him in: that heavy brow; the thick straight hair falling down his neck; his eyes flashing with anger, with feeling.

She smiled. 'What does it matter? The world is full of hungry people.' Her soothing words seemed to calm Ian and he ceased pacing the floor and sat down heavily.

Feeding – that's what he needed. She picked up the jug of cream by her side and sat on the table opening her legs wide. She was naked underneath, and the cream made stripes of white against the red as she poured it down her wide open sex.

She leaned back on her elbows and thrust out her pussy.

'Eat me,' she said.

Mad About the Boy

Cannes, 1962

Jane emerged from the sea feeling purged by its salty cleanliness. She lay for a minute on the sand and let the intense bleaching sun suck the water from her body, leaving dry caked crystals of salt on her skin.

'Honey, we thought that picture was great. What was it called again?' She was startled by an American voice above her. She looked up to see a plump, middle-aged couple nodding and smiling at her.

'I said to Brett, your part should have been much bigger. Why, we hardly saw you, honey. But you were great, and that was a great picture.' The woman's enthusiasm made her flowered beach gown shake with excitement.

Jane smiled despite herself. People often didn't know how to handle it. It was as if a ghost had stepped right off the cinema screen and stood before them. It always surprised her to be recognised but in this instance she guessed it made sense. She looked pretty wild – hair clotted with sand and water dripping from her body – and in the movie she had played a goddess who had emerged from the sea and screamed at a load of monsters. The sea creatures had strange crenellated lizard heads with human eyes recognisable beneath, staring out.

In the end she discovered that the couple came from a town very close to home in Maine. When she heard the familiar place names she felt a sudden warmth for the big cheerful couple in their ridiculous clothes, and walked along the beach with them, back towards her villa.

The French had a good word for it: *ennui*. The feeling seemed to flutter down on the little group of Americans like dust the next day as they sat around the pool. The sun had increased in intensity and the rays sparked off the chrome on the Bolex camera that David always kept by his side. The smell of chlorine hung heavily in the air and burned in Jane's nostrils. She had been watching the painters as they clattered their ladders against the walls of the villa to take her mind off the fitful, tired conversation.

When Simone had said languorously, 'So, who's fucking who these days?', nobody quite got round to answering, as if the heat had taken away their power of speech.

The painters worked stripped to the waist, shouting in rapid French to each other as they painted over the pink walls of the villa. The new colour was an intense umber which seemed to throb and bake in the sun. Jane sat up as one of the workmen splashed water over another's back. The water shone in a bright sheen across his broad shoulders. He responded by tipping the entire bucket of water they used to clean their brushes over his work mate. The drenched boy stood mouthing what she assumed were French profanities as the water tinted his body with umber, like tribal paint.

How must they see us? Jane wondered. She had a vision of themselves from the outside: movie people, bloated by money, lying around drinking and bitching all day.

'D'you think people think we're strange?' she said suddenly.

The question hung unanswered in the air and Jane closed her eyes. Sparks and loops of light flashed behind her eyelids like the end of a tape roll on a lit-up screen. She attempted to control the swirling lights and turn them into pictures: a jellyfish illuminated and pulsing its way through the water; a shower of fireworks lighting up a blood-red night sky. She gave up and swung to her feet abruptly. The baking tiles scorched her feet as she pulled on her shorts and a little crochet top.

'Where you going, honey?' David asked. Under his white straw hat little rivulets of sweat ran into the grooves around his eyes.

'Maybe for a walk,' she answered sullenly. She stood before him with her arms crossed over her boyish body, the couple more in the attitude of father and daughter than husband and wife.

The group of workmen were taking a break now with their legs sprawled out. The woody smell of French cigarettes enveloped her as she passed them, and they looked up indolently at her, saying nothing. Their wooden ladders were propped untidily against the wall, bruising the scented geraniums on the sills, which responded by releasing their peppery sweetness.

The woods were cool and still. She lay on a soft bed of pine needles and let the distant sound of the sea thrum over her. She felt the desperate urge to slough off the artifice, the commercial atmosphere she had been breathing for days. She felt trapped by David's presence, and gagged by Simone's chalky sweet face powder, her long nails and heavily set hair. For God's sake, women didn't have to wear gloopy red lipstick, push-up bras and girdles any more. She slipped her shorts off and then, after checking quickly around, defiantly removed her crochet vest and bikini top.

The sun made dapples on her body through the trees. Her breasts almost disappeared as she lay down, just her brown sheeny nipples poked upwards to the sky. The bitter scent of pine needles acted like an anaesthetic and she fell into a half-waking dream. Something about swimming out to sea and drinking the froth, great gulps of foaming water. She was thirsty beyond belief and this seemed like the most refreshing drink she'd ever had. The sound of the ocean filled her head. She frowned in her sleep. Just audible under the swelling of the sea was another sound – a tiny, human sound. Her dreaming self tried to figure it out as the sound became more persistent, like a small percussive note in a large orchestra. She awoke with a start and raised her head.

Perched up in the tree was the painter who had been drenched earlier in the day. The dark umber colour still marked his already sunbronzed body. He was balanced half sitting with one leg outstretched on a branch to steady himself. Jane's eyes travelled down from his appalled face and drew her breath in shock as she realised the reason for his agonised expression. Pushed down around his thighs were his shorts. One hand was wrapped around a branch to steady himself while the other was clamped around his erect cock. The purple end bulged over the top of his hand.

The fraction of a second that they stared at each other seemed to last for ages. The image seemed monstrous, too much to take in: his dark thighs with that thing between them. My God, he had been jerking off over her! Not only that, but she seemed to have caught him at the moment of climax. The muscles on his neck were stretched and taut and the expression on his face almost one of pain.

Despite his anguish at being discovered he was obviously unable to stop himself and, before Jane could say anything, he came. He tried to catch the spunk as it came out in little jets and dribbles between his fingers, but it was as fluid and tricky as mercury. His other hand lost its grip on the branch and he swung out on one foot, nearly losing his balance. The sperm thudded softly onto her stomach with little plops, like sap falling. With a horrified expression he jumped to the ground with agile grace and ran off, pulling his shorts up as he went. All this happened in seconds, but each moment seemed to elongate, Jane reflected afterwards, like in a slow-mo sequence.

'You want to keep an eye on that wife of yours.' Simone had been addressing David but her eyes were narrowed at Jane. 'She looks wilder every day.'

Simone dressed up even for dinner. Her white-blonde hair was piled on top of her head in a hard lacquered twist and her tits formed conical points under her pink shirt which was tied with starchy folds around her midriff. Jane started at the comment.

'I like to dress sloppy,' Jane answered defiantly. Her creased, open white shirt contrasted with the tan at the base of her neck. It was a real bore being the youngest here – everyone commenting and picking at you, like little ants snipping away at a leaf.

'Perhaps you're spending too much time in the sun, honey.' David was examining her like a side of beef. 'You don't want to be too brown for when your next picture comes along.' He studied the freckles that the sun had caused to bloom across her face and arms.

'Nonsense, tanned is good now,' Simone cut in. 'Tanned is natural.' It was as if she wasn't there.

Jane found herself trembling. She hated the distant way Simone and David spoke about her, as if they were her parents rather than her husband and a 'family friend'. Her secret experience burned inside of her. She felt strangely tearful and ecstatic at the same time. She kept thinking, how dare he? As if the French boy's intrusion had shattered a pane of glass which had kept her safe for a long time. She could almost sense the shards around her bare feet. The image of the semi-dressed boy jacking off kept flashing uninvited into her mind, like a dirty picture in her pocket that she felt impelled to keep peeking at. God, what would happen if they knew? David would probably use his connections or something to have the boy pushed over a cliff. Jane couldn't fathom her sense of terrified excitement.

But the real secret was not what had happened, though that was bad enough. The real secret, Jane realised, was that it had left her in this state of trembling, tearful excitement. The arousal she had felt ever since was almost unbearable. Every touch of the smooth cotton shirt on her bare breasts sent shudders of pleasure across her body and her white panties felt soaked under her jeans.

David was already asleep when Jane climbed beside him into bed that night. She sighed and turned over. The picture of the boy replayed in her mind, this time almost in close-up – just his hand with the sperm dribbling through his fingers. Pulling the cold white sheet between her legs she bunched it up, rocking her cunt against it.

She used to do this with her teddy bear, lying in her bed, the pictures of teenage idols snipped from magazines around her. Elvis had smiled down at her approvingly as she'd rubbed the rough fur between her legs. But she always felt a stirring of guilt afterwards. Surely this wasn't something her female friends did? Her mother even – God, what a thought!

Knotting the sheet up harder she rocked against it, coating it with the honey that flowed from between her legs. Her imagination spun the experience out with the French boy. This time she played the scene from before she awoke. He must have climbed the tree, furtively pulling his shorts down as he stood on a branch. Perhaps he got bolder when she seemed so soundly asleep. He probably leaned out to get a better look at her smooth tiny breasts, the nipples rising and falling as she slept. Maybe he focused his eyes on the way the thin fabric of her bikini shorts stretched over her mound; the cleft shape must have been clear under the puckered fabric which folded in a sharp crease between her legs. He must have felt the sweet sensation of relief as he circled his hand over his aching prick, pumping as hard as he could while keeping the sounds of his gasps in check as much as possible. How must he have felt when she woke, just at his point of climax? Just when it was too late, when he was helpless and exposed, the climax had come, bursting out from between his fingers ... With a deep sigh Jane felt the orgasm rocket through her own body. Minutes later she was in a deep exhausted sleep, her husband oblivious beside her.

Jane sat on the stone steps which led from the pool to the garden, alternately taking mouthfuls of coffee and water, swirling the scalding coffee around her mouth, then letting the fresh cold water purge the dark burnt flavour. The morning sun already had bite to it and the cracked dry stone grew warm beneath her as she pondered what would happen now. Probably in his shame he just wouldn't turn up again, letting the others finish the work – cat calling and teasing each other as they clothed the walls of the villa with the colours of the earth. If he did come he would probably be subdued and withdrawn, averting his brown eyes away from her whenever they met, casting down his head with that sleek, dark hair which yesterday had been damp with sweat in his desire.

She was just trying to push the idea out of her head that his reticence might bother her in any way, when she heard someone running over the other side of the wall. The sound of plimsolls slapped on the dusty stone and approached. He appeared at the bottom of the steps and looked her full in the eye. In a swift motion he ran to where she was sitting and placed a loosely tied bunch of leaves and flowers beside her.

'*Je suis désolé.*' He gestured to the flowers. 'For you.' He ducked his head and was gone.

For a moment Jane couldn't move. No American boy would have dared! They would have kept their head low, stayed at a distance, probably terrified some husband or father would run them out of town with a shotgun. She picked up the flowers – spikes of rosemary studded with starry blue flowers were mixed with deep red geraniums – and put them to her nose. The smell was sweet and bitter, real somehow.

Tucking the flowers inside her shirt, she made her way back to the empty bedroom. David and Simone had decided to take a trip down the coast. Slants of orange sunlight coming through the shutters striped the fusty, unmade bed. She placed the flowers in her underwear drawer, carefully covering them up with a couple of pairs of silky panties. At the back of the drawer was a huge crystal flask of Joy perfume that David had bought her on the way over, still unopened.

What had happened yesterday was almost obsessing her now, constantly stealing into her thoughts. She had woken that morning relaxed, with juice already flowing from between her legs. She'd turned to David and then remembered the reason for her obscure happiness: recalled the dark suntanned boy in the tree and the way his come had landed softly on her stomach. How, after he had run away, she had wiped at it with her hand and then experimentally touched her tongue on her finger.

Now, peeking through the shutters, she saw the painters' jumble of buckets and ladders below which told her they were about to begin work. She fished around in her drawer for her best white bikini, the bottoms like little shorts which outlined everything and made her rear look high up and firm like a boy's.

She was aware they were looking at her as she sat by the pool, sunglasses obscuring her eyes. Their movements were slower and more languid today as they painted. The four of them were soon naked to the waist, often pausing to drink out of large flasks of water while sneaking glances over their shoulders at her. Of course they wouldn't dare whistle or call out in French as they probably did to the local girls. Jane guessed the grandeur and wealth of the villa would be completely alien to them. But her lone presence by the pool made them slightly bolder in their glances – except for the boy from yesterday who kept his head resolutely down and worked more steadily than the others. From behind her sunglasses Jane tried to figure out how old he might be: eighteen maybe, perhaps a little older, close to her own age anyway. Jane stood up deliberately and poised to dive in front of the pool. She plunged with one easy movement into the water, her shadow making shapes on the bottom.

By lunch time she was growing pretty frustrated. She'd certainly grabbed the attention of all the others but *her* boy, as she had begun to think of him, was still working furiously with his eyes studiously averted. Her feeling of disappointment when they all lay down their brushes was intense. She closed her magazine and decided to cool herself down for a bit in the garden.

On her way down the steps she nearly fell over him. He was crouched behind the wall and pretended to do up his shoe lace when he saw her. But the guilty, miserable expression on his face coupled with the bulge clearly visible between his legs told a different story. So he'd been spying on her again! He feebly tried to cover the bulge with his hands but then gave up and stood awkwardly in front of her. Jane just about restrained the joyous smile that threatened to break out on her face. Then, staying cool, she swayed ahead, and with a tiny look over her shoulder she beckoned him to follow. Like a puppy being called, he obeyed.

Once inside the woods he tried to encircle her with his arms and kiss her. But as his slightly over-full mouth came towards her, she pushed him away. A look of hurt confusion came over his face and his arms dangled uselessly by his sides. He muttered something softly in French and approached her again, reaching out his fingers to touch her hair, her face, her mouth.

'No,' she almost shouted, and he stood back, surprised at the vehemence of her reaction.

She knelt before him and deftly undid the buttons of his trousers. Her knees grazed against the covering of pine needles on the ground, releasing their aroma.

The boy looked hopeful again and went to hold her head, to urge her mouth towards his cock. She noticed he wore nothing underneath and glimpsed the dark bush of hair. She held his hands firmly and drew them to his unbuttoned crotch. As she tugged at his trousers his cock sprang free. His balls looked hard and tight, the skin around them stretched taut and red. As she manoeuvred his hand his fingers touched the tip of his cock and he gasped, despite himself. Deliberately she placed his hand on his erection and stood up, unbuttoning her shirt and unclasping her bikini top as she slowly walked backwards away from him.

What had happened yesterday had almost happened to her dreaming self. She wanted to make it real, to savour every drop of the experience. Slowly she stripped off her bikini bottoms to reveal her dark bush, clipped to a neat stripe in the middle. The boy put his hand on the tree to steady himself. The sea boomed in the distance as she lay down, stretching her limbs and parting her legs slightly so he could glimpse the swelling opening between her legs. At last he seemed to understand and, grasping his cock he began to pump. The look of desire mingled with shame and confusion on his face, and he attempted to half hide himself behind the tree in a futile attempt to disguise his arousal.

Every inch of skin felt alive on Jane's body. She felt aware of it as never before, every crevice, every hole. The creases behind her knees and her scalp tingled. She could feel the air rushing up through her nose as she breathed and her stomach juddering with excitement as she let the breath go. She licked her lips and tasted the salty air.

In half of her mind she felt as if she must still be dreaming. Surely this couldn't be happening? It couldn't be her that set this scene up, forcing this poor young boy to humiliate himself again in front of her? But in another sense she had to admit to herself that she'd planned this meticulously through the night, just waiting for the chance to lure him into the woods again.

Under lowered lids she watched him. His shirt was damp with sweat now as his hand stroked firmly and rhythmically. Every second or so his thighs spasmed, thrusting his cock forward which jabbed the air like a gesture. His eyes were half closed, as if to concentrate on his pleasure and remove himself from the re-enactment of his shame. She wondered what he could see from his perspective; what his name was for what lay between her legs; how much of the swelling opening he could see from where he stood. Jane slowly rolled over, opening her legs wide to reveal her moist slit and his eyes flew wide open again.

The afternoon sun began to bake through the trees. He was close now, she could see. His lips were pulled back from his teeth and sweat ran down from his brow, running into his black hair. Her own body felt so hot and responsive even the tiny breeze tickled her cunt almost to frenzy.

In one way she craved the hard cock which curved in his hand. But she felt driven on to tease him, to perform, to play the scene out while fully awake so that she could memorise it for ever. She put a finger to her slit and stroked it experimentally, using the creamy moisture to slide her finger up and down. He breathed in sharply. The sight of her playing with herself was obviously too much for him. His thighs tensed even harder and he let out a choking sob as a jet of semen shot out in front of him and landed on the earth. He panted and rested his hand on his leg, bent in exhaustion.

Jane delved again with one finger into her slit and her finger emerged gleaming and slicked with juice. Suddenly she heard thin, distant voices from the other end of the pine wood. Quick as a flash the boy buttoned up his trousers and gallantly gathered up her clothes. She scrambled into her bikini while he hurriedly did up the strap for her from behind.

'Go,' she said urgently and summoned up her morsels of French: '*Allez*. Go.' The boy ran hard towards the sea.

Thank God they hadn't been bothered to look for her further. Jane had had a vision of Simone and David coming round the corner – Simone's spiky heels sinking into the soft ground of the woods – to find her, dishevelled and shaking, the jelly-like come sprayed on the ground close by. In the event, the heat had driven them back.

'We've found this fantastic little vineyard though,' David said, pouring the thick red liquid into a glass for her as they sat at the dining table. 'Here, try some.' The sun-spiced fruit smell overwhelmed her as she drank.

The next day she'd really rather have stayed inside, but in her state of paranoia she felt any pleas of sickness or headaches might be suspicious. David wanted to go through the script and he liked other people to read out the parts, to give him ideas about direction. Why he insisted on sitting around the pool Jane didn't know. Despite the shade of the large white umbrella, suspended like a balloon above him, sweat was already breaking on his forehead.

The picture didn't interest Jane. It was one of those overblown old Hollywood romances that Simone had once done so well in. Jane hadn't been given a role in it and she was glad: she was on the lookout for something that had the spirit of this bright, new age she found herself in, that turned black and white into colour. Simone interjected with occasional intelligent comments. She had been friends with David way back and he always brought her along, valuing her shrewd perceptions. She wasn't stupid, Simone, which was why Jane felt so uncomfortable when those big eyes kept turning to her – as if she could see the dirty little secret locked away in Jane's mind.

'I don't love you, not one little bit,' said Jane. The words were supposed to read like a feeble protestation, the doubletalk of a woman who would be finally won over. The script seemed especially outdated in this place, where film was branching out, experimenting with style, where Vadim had created Woman.

Only two of the workmen had arrived. They were pulling their shirts off to reveal sweaty, muscular backs. Jane's stomach churned – maybe he wouldn't turn up. Her ears strained as she heard the pop pop popping of his little Lambretta scooter as it revved up the little winding road to the villa. But he must have lent it to his work mate who parked the neat little machine in the drive. Her nerves felt strained to breaking point.

David looked up from his script. 'Look, there's only three today.' Jane was surprised he'd noticed. He called out to the distant men: 'Where's the other one, where's your friend?' They spoke a few words of French to each other.

'Michel,' one of them shouted back, 'he's late.' As if the Americans hadn't realised.

Michel, Michel, the name ran through her mind like a chant.

David flung down his script as if tired of it and the weight of the summer heat soon enveloped them. The air was so still that Jane noticed single sounds: a dog barking in the distance, the sound of the paint bristles scraping on the wall and of ladders dragged across the ground and of the young French voices as they teased and chatted. They stopped every once in a while and Jane could smell the musky scent of their cigarettes drift over like smoke from a bonfire.

Jane lowered herself into the blue cube of the pool to cool down and ducked her head under the water. It was silent, except for the rushing in her ears. When she emerged, water dripping from her brown skin, she saw, with a stab to her stomach, that he had arrived. He was working, stripped to the waist like the others, their canvas trousers spotted with mud and paint – the colours of the landscape.

Jane heard the little click click click of David's 16 mm camera. He trained it on Simone, who laughed and fluttered her hand in a wave, and then Jane, who stared sullenly into its lens. This moment will be crystallised for ever, she thought – in twenty years' time I will be able to look at the flickering pictures and see my face and remember the reason why I looked like that.

David stood up and trained the camera on the workmen. He sees it like a painting, thought Jane. She had to admit to the beauty of the scene: the four men's muscles moved smoothly as they worked, the occasional flash of dark hair revealed as they lifted their arms to paint. He fiddled with the zoom lens and seemed to focus on the single figure of Michel.

'Why are you doing that?' she said sharply, then bit her lip.

Although when they first arrived the Americans had complained loudly about the way the French disappeared after lunch and everywhere descended into deserted stillness, they had soon slipped into the way of it themselves. Now most afternoons they retired to white-painted bedrooms where fans whipped and cooled the air, to sleep off the effects of the sun, the alcohol and the unaccustomed heavy lunch.

Jane still hadn't got used to the idea of sleeping in the afternoons. Today she hung around the pool, occasionally ploughing up and down in the water to cool down. She'd just decided that her games with Michel must stop when she looked up and saw him standing at the edge of the pool, empty paint tins in his hand. The painters had nearly finished their work and he was clearing the debris which they had left behind.

The sight of his muscled arms in the torn white work shirt was too much for her. She smiled and beckoned him into the water. Michel pointed questioningly to the blinkered windows above them.

'They're asleep,' she said, folding her hands by the side of her head in gesture. She must be crazy, she thought to herself. Did she want to be caught?

He shrugged and dived in. She saw his brown shape descend to the bottom, his arms behind him as if in flight. David was probably snoring his head off by now and Simone slept at the back of the house anyway, she reassured herself. Anyway, all they were doing was swimming. The lie sounded feeble and tiny in her mind, like a quiet voice speaking in another room. He dived again and passed between her legs. She felt the rush of his body against her legs and her cunt. He emerged laughing next to her, his thick, black hair slicked back by the water.

All at once she felt as if a bomb had gone off in her head. The water seemed to brighten and sparks of light flew from it. Suddenly she didn't care. Some part of her wanted David to look out of the window, to see her being fucked by this beautiful young French boy, this life and flesh and blood, with his thick hard penis and his beautiful full mouth, to see that she was young and alive and laughing. The need to risk everything drove her on.

Diving under the water, she quickly undid his canvas trousers and pulled them free. They floated gently away, ballooning comically in the water. They swam together for a while, naked, diving through each other's legs and wrestling. As they stood face to face in the water he put his hard penis between her legs and his restless hands moved all over her body. Jane floated underneath the water while he passed over her, his cock sticking straight out into the water, looking somehow like an animal.

A dog barking in the distance seemed to bring him to his senses and he looked suddenly afraid. His eyes darkened and his cock wilted.

He glanced up at the windows. 'Come,' he said, 'dangerous.'

They swam to the side, retrieving clothing as they went. The wet fabric grazed their skin as they hurriedly pulled on their soaking clothes. Jane prayed they wouldn't encounter anyone on the way as they ran towards the woods.

Fear and lust and heat made them crazy. As they ran Michel touched and tackled her from behind. They reached the sand dunes, falling and laughing. They stopped to strip off his clothes and Jane could feel his cock bouncing on her back, on her behind as he urgently embraced her. She stumbled and fell to her knees and swiftly Michel slipped inside her, aided by her slick wetness. She gave a deep groan of pleasure which seemed to emanate unbidden right from her stomach. But he slipped out of her again. Pulling her to her feet he urged her to run again, to a yet more isolated place. White sand flew around their feet as they went.

He obviously knew the beach very well and finally they came to a secluded place which looked as if it had been untouched by human occupancy, as if its last inhabitants might have been strange amphibious dinosaurs which left huge footprints on the sand. Jane wondered with a pang of jealousy if he brought many girls here, local girls to be rudely fucked on the sand with their little summer dresses around their waists.

He was slicked by sweat all over. His hairless brown chest was gleaming and frosted with sand. She flung herself down and opened her legs in welcome. When she closed her eyes she suddenly felt, not the hardness she'd expected, but the slick of his tongue against her cunt. My God, she had never ... the action seemed more obscene, more animal somehow, even than fucking. He was drinking and licking at the salty juices which she assiduously washed away every day, taking in deep breaths of the odours that were supposed to be kept firmly at bay. She pushed him away. It seemed too much, too intimate somehow. She saw his face and his full lips were bright with her juice. Persistent, he went down again, this time gently, barely flicking her with his tongue. Sinking back onto the sand she let out a deep moan despite herself. She felt his tongue shamelessly stick right up her.

His rough tongue drove her wild. When she made

love, it had always been under covers, her underneath. Now she throbbed and pulsed and wanted to take him all ways, everywhere, all at once. That place between her legs hardly seen by any other person, he was now examining in the full light of day, playing with the tuft of hair that remained after her bikini line had been stripped away. It occurred to her that he may not have seen it like this before, the American way.

She had the sudden urge to expose herself completely. She turned over and stuck her behind right up in the air. She knew he could see her arsehole now, that secret, puckered place was right in front of him.

One of the first things she'd seen through the window of the car when she'd arrived in France were a pair of dogs fucking on the street. The dog's cock was long and thin and bounced over its mate's back, desperate to find its target. She'd felt ashamed at the time that the sight had caused a tingle between her thighs. Now she felt like some wanton female dog, straining upwards to be filled. She wondered if anyone else that she knew, Simone even, with her crisp clean clothes and perfect lipstick, had ever been fucked like a dog on the beach like this. She let her face fall in the sand, a few grains entering her mouth, and pushed her behind up even higher. Nobody, ever, had seen this much of her before – she felt completely exposed.

His penis bounced roughly on her mound and then slithered abruptly home. Jane felt a sudden rush, as if some rapid, gushing birth had happened in reverse. He fucked her quickly, his hips thrusting in the movement of a dog. Her pussy clenched and spasmed around his prick. Occasionally he leaned over her and paused to restrain himself, and cupped her hard little breasts in her hands, pinching the nipples between his thumb and finger.

He was muttering words of French as he thrust, the foreign words intercut by deep groans. His penis slid delightfully against her wet interior. The sun beat down mercilessly and she could feel the sweat from his body rain onto her back. Stars showered behind her eyelids and she felt a curious tingling over her body which mingled with the beat of the sea. The feeling was growing, spreading over her body and making her give involuntary animal cries. Finally it swept over her, as if a dam had suddenly been released. The strange feeling lapped over her so many times she was only partially aware of Michel crying out in his own climax. Finally, they lay exhausted on the sand. What had just happened she knew she had never experienced before.

She wandered into the kitchen of the villa and sat in a daze on one of the rough kitchen chairs, swinging her bare feet which slapped against the cool tiles on the floor. The housekeeper fluttered silently around her and a cat nursed its litter of kittens on the floor. A tiny grey kitten took one of its mother's nipples delicately into its mouth and sucked.

'Try this,' the housekeeper urged, placing a huge black olive into her mouth. Jane closed her mouth around the salty taste.

She had to get out. Almost in a frenzy she rummaged through the dirty clothes in the laundry room and found a crumpled little gingham cotton dress. She changed quickly, standing in the cool white room. Leaving a scribbled note to David – 'Gone for Drive' – she picked up the keys to the blue MG parked outside.

He would probably be horrified to see her, she reflected, as she drove far too fast around the narrow, bendy road. She knew where they all went. Simone and David had mentioned the little club where all the locals hung out. As she revved the car she felt like a prisoner on the run.

To her surprise Michel's face lit up when he saw her. The club was hot and sweaty and the band belted out Latin rhythms from the crowded stage. With relief she noticed it was dark enough in there to be hidden. They danced close together and she could feel his desire stirring again against her stomach. In a break from dancing they sat with his friends around a little table. Jane felt as though she could be back with her friends at home, hanging out in the milk bar after school.

'Are you a movie star?' one of his friends asked. She nodded. Her film had never been released in Europe and he clearly didn't believe her. 'I'm a movie star,' he said, swaying as he stood up to dance. 'We're all movie stars.' He put his arms around his friends. They all started laughing and Jane joined in. Laughing felt wonderful.

Later she fucked the friend, Jean, in the filthy little toilet of the club. If she'd seen herself doing this at the beginning of the summer, she reflected, she would never have set foot on the plane. The tiny room smelt of piss and several cigarette butts floated in a shallow scum of water in the washbasin. She perched on the tiny basin while Jean rubbed his cock up and down between her legs without entering her until her lips stood out wet and puffy. People kept hammering on the door and shouting in French, so he entered her swiftly and they fucked quietly and quickly, her raised leg banging against the wall.

It was late when she let herself into the silent hall of the villa. Simone stood there quietly as if she'd been waiting.

'You better go and talk to him,' she said gently. She

called up as Jane ascended the stairs. 'He's a special man you know.'

David was lit by the flickering images of the cine film he had taken by the pool. He shut it off when she came in and the machine whirred to a stop. He took her hand.

'Jane, my love, we were close once. When I married you I thought I could make everything all right. I realise now that was very wrong of me, very wrong.' He paused. Jane had been expecting an interrogation but he had tears in his eyes. She felt sorry for him suddenly.

'I've struggled for years,' he carried on, 'but I can't any more. This place it's ... it's taught me something.'

The summer suddenly fell into place and made sense. 'You're beautiful, Jane, and I can admire you like a picture. But really, you know I prefer boys.'

Immense relief coursed through her body and she squeezed his hands kindly. She looked deeply into the face that was thirty years older than hers and answered: 'Don't worry about me, David, not at all. You see, so do I.'

The Pearl Seeker

I'm taking off my knickers now, slowly. When I look down I can see my pussy splayed out on the chair. The lips look all red and shiny poking out under the hair. Black hair, thick and curly. My knickers are round my ankles now. Boy, they look really hot all tangled up with the thongs on my high heels that twist around my ankles, like restraints or something. I wish you could see it.

Hold on. I'm going to dip my finger in now. Fuck, that feels good, my finger's shiny and wet now. It smells all hot and salty. I'm tasting it, licking off the juice, every last drop. Can you taste it too?

Tanya grabbed her wine glass and took a slug to calm herself down before pressing the send button. The words went winging out across cyber space, like a quivering arrow seeking its target. There was a long pause before the reply came hurtling back. While she was waiting she tenderly stroked her aching cunt.

The words began to tumble on to her screen, so fast they looked like a row of soldiers falling over themselves.

That tasted good. But details! Give me the details. What colour are your panties, are you wearing a skirt and if so, how much is it pushed up, what style is it? I *need* to know.

Tanya smiled to herself – he was such a stickler, so assertive. She glanced down at herself before beginning to type, her fingers stickily catching with her own juice on the keyboard.

I'm baby-doll tonight. Sweetness and light. Little white blouse and a girlish string of seed pearls around my neck. Panties are white, of course, with pink flowers. Tiny blue skirt, like an ice-skater's, just pushed up enough to let my fanny peek underneath. Very horny fuck-me shoes: high-heeled white sandals, with straps tying up my ankles – you'd love them.

This time the reply raced back before she even had time to gather her thoughts.

Wow! That sounds amazing. My dick's so hard now I just can't help myself. What I've got in mind is coming round your throat, like those little pearls.

Tanya breathed in deep. Her hand flew between her legs and her finger began to work in earnest. She typed with the other hand, picking out the letters one by one.

Yes! Your spunk all round my throat, dribbling down my tits. I'm so creamy now my finger's just sliding over my clit. It's so big and tender I won't be able to hold it for much longer.

Tanya slumped over the keyboard, her long black hair brushing the letters. Her orgasm sped across the globe, like a sparkling comet set to crash to earth, a blazing trail of fire in its wake.

Afterwards they virtually cosied up to each other. Tanya typed that she couldn't believe she'd be meeting him for real – she was looking forward to it so much. There was a long pause before he replied. Two little words spelled out on the flickering screen.

Me too.

The plane cruised closer to Tokyo airport, slicing the cloud with its wings. Tanya felt a knot of excitement as she peered down through the tiny window. Somewhere, far down there, was James Shaw, aka the Collector – dubbed such by Tanya for his avaricious interest in pearls.

She loosened another button on her blouse. Christ, it was hot. But she'd kept her coat firmly wrapped around her for the whole flight, despite several offers from the air hostess to put it away in the overhead luggage. The coat made her feel secure, and anyway, if someone else handled it they might feel its unnatural heaviness from all the pearls that were stitched firmly inside the hem. When Tanya stepped out of the plane she could feel them weighing her down as if she was a goddamn walking treasure trove. She liked to keep them about her person; their secret presence gave her a feeling of security and, besides, customs was such a bore.

Tokyo shimmered in the spring sunshine as Tanya watched it speed past through the window of the jeep James had sent for her. The city was a crazy confusion of buildings: ramshackle old wooden structures crouched next to glittering steel skyscrapers. Tanya tried to figure out the signs from the few Japanese characters she knew to take her mind off the vague disappointment that James hadn't been there to meet her at the airport. Never mind, he was only a few short hours away: him and the pearls that he'd first emailed her about, the ones she'd been looking for for ages. She imagined him as a handsome eagle, guarding the pearls for her like a clutch of eggs.

For a few moments when she awoke she couldn't remember where she was. She unpeeled her face from the sticky plastic of the back seat of the jeep and sniffed. The invigorating salt smell of the sea quickly brought her to her senses and she tried to smooth out the creases in her skirt, tidying her hair by dragging her fingers through it. Hardly a vision of poise, she thought, rather hoping that she could have had a chance to freshen up before she met him.

Of course, as luck would have it, James appeared almost immediately. Her heart knocked double time. Better than she'd imagined in her wildest dreams. What a vision: tall and muscular with curly blond hair and wide-open blue eyes. Tanya practically scrambled out of the car.

'Nice to meet you at last,' he said, stretching out his hand in greeting. His voice had the modulated even tones lent by a public school education.

Considering the virtual intimacies they'd been sharing over the last few months the handshake seemed cold and formal. She searched for a spark in his eyes but he looked away, awkward and shy. Well, there was plenty of time for that. Tanya's eyes scanned the flat grey sea.

'Where are all the divers?' she asked.

'The ama will be back soon. It's only the second day of the season so it's too cold for them to stay out for long. Come inside.' He glanced at her. 'You look like you've had a really hard journey.'

Tanya's breath was taken away when she stepped into the old beach hut set back from the sea. It looked so unprepossessing from the outside, but inside he'd transformed it. It looked like an Arabic palace from another century: heavy velvet curtains shuttered the light at the windows and richly coloured rugs glowed on the floor.

He grinned at her shyly. 'I like to keep comfortable while I'm here,' he explained.

Fresh from the shower, she unpacked a slinky clinging black dress. This ought to get him going, she thought.

The personality he assumed on the net was so forceful, almost brutal. She'd expected some sharp-suited maverick who'd take her straight away, have his cock deep inside her within the first five minutes. Instead he seemed shy, withdrawn, stumbling over his words. But, God, he was beautiful though: those golden curls, the sensuous mouth, almost like a girl's. The expectant desire that she'd managed to repress throughout her journey bloomed between her legs, making her damp and sticky.

When she emerged back into the main room she saw that he'd set the table; tea lights winked and glittered among the bowls of rice and shining cutlery. Perhaps, she reflected, all was not lost. She sat down and inhaled the mist of fragrant steam that rose from the table.

'How long will you stay here?' she asked, to make conversation.

'Oh, I keep meaning to leave. But you know how it is. I always think there's one last perfect pearl out there that I'd be leaving behind.' She knew from his emails that his interest lay in size. The bigger the better – typical man. Those huge pearls always looked overgrown to her, as if they'd gestated for too long.

'Do you want to look before we eat?' he asked. A knot of expectation tightened in her stomach. She nodded silently.

He fished out a felt bag from a little drawer in the table. Almost reverently, he lay it before her. She folded back the material and breathed in sharply. Three perfect globes shone against the blue felt, the flickering tea lights reflected in their pinkish sheen. Tanya almost felt on the verge of tears – they were perfect, exactly what she had been looking for. For five years she had been obsessively seeking pearls with that particular pinkish sheen and of the right size and shape. There was just a tiny gap at the end of the necklace she had been stringing together – just room for three pearls.

'Are you pleased with them?' he asked, a little uncertainly.

She folded the felt back carefully, wrapping the pearls snugly back in their dark enclosure.

'Oh yes, they're beautiful,' she said softly. There was only one thing now to make her day complete. She decided to take the direct approach.

'Have you still got the panties I sent you?' she asked boldly.

James started and blushed, as if she'd bought up a dirty secret – which she supposed she had.

'I've course I've still got them; they're in the drawer.' It wasn't only pearls that he collected. Tanya had airmailed several pairs of panties to his beach hut. She remembered that he'd been very specific: only knickers that had been worn for a week would do.

'Perhaps we should eat first, and then...' His voice trailed away as she came to sit on the table in front of him, shoving the bowls to one side.

'The food looks delicious,' she said. 'I'm sure it will still be delicious in half an hour.'

He'd been telling her what he'd like to do with her for months. Now they were face to face all he seemed to be capable of was blushing and stammering. Tanya didn't like to feel cheated.

She pulled her skirt up, exposing her slim white thighs, and James's hands began to shake at the sight.

'All those things you said you wanted to do to me. Well, now's your chance.'

She tried to keep her voice soft and gentle, so as not to frighten him. Beads of sweat popped out on his forehead and he licked his lips as if they had suddenly gone dry.

'I'm, I'm not used to, I mean...' he stammered. 'On the net it's different. You can play someone else, but...' His voice trailed off as she raised her skirt another couple of inches. Her sheer black panties clearly showed her thick dark bush beneath.

'That's OK. We can take our time.' She was beginning to enjoy herself, playing the seducer.

Almost despite himself, he stretched out a tentative finger and lightly stroked her cool pale thigh. Her legs felt hard and strong to his touch, like marble.

'You don't have to do anything you don't want,' she crooned. 'Just touch, go on, touch.'

He reached his hand out again, like a boy about to be slapped for stealing sweets. His fingers skimmed the sheer black material of her knickers. Tanya's senses felt so stretched, so sensitive, that the soft touch sent shivers of desire through her body. She'd waited for this for a long, long time.

'Good, that's good,' she said sweetly. 'Now touch me lower down.'

Poor lamb, he was really trembling now. But he did as he was told and moved his hand between her legs. His fingers slid over the shiny, damp fabric. Tanya's lips hung down, swollen and heavy with desire. He let out a gasp as he felt the wetness.

'I'm going to take off my dress now,' warned Tanya. She guessed that any sudden movements might send him scurrying away like a frightened animal.

Sensuously, she unbuttoned her dress and let it slither to the floor. It lay in a heap around her pointy high-heeled shoes. James gasped again. She'd certainly dressed for the occasion: her sheer black basque matched her little panties and her white flesh and rosy nipples glowed enchantingly through the fabric.

She shook her long dark hair back from her shoulders and thrust out her smooth breasts. The string of pearls nestled in her cleavage, warmed by the heat of her body. She guessed the sight must be having some effect on him, judging by his cock which bulged obscenely in his trousers. Her body craved his touch now; ached for the feel of his full, curving lips at her breasts, on her cunt. Slowly, slowly, she warned herself.

She pulled aside her knickers so that the black bush of hair sprang up, released from its restraint. 'Touch again,' she whispered.

His fingers brushed against the fuzz of coarse hair. Almost by accident he touched her swollen clit and the action made her shudder with pleasure. 'I'm going to take these off now,' she said, unconsciously adopting the language she used on the net.

She hooked her fingers into either side of her panties and slowly pulled them down so that they stretched across her thighs, digging into her tender flesh. With one hand she parted her aching lips, letting the fingers of her other hand rest on her clit. Just a couple of strokes and she knew she would come. With great restraint she kept her hand still. The weight of it felt hot and heavy.

Surely, she told herself, no man could resist this sight spread out before him, as dirty and open as a centrefold. The sweat on his forehead had begun to trickle down into his eyes and he wiped it away with the back of his hand.

She reached her arms behind her and unclasped the string of pearls from around her neck. They'd performed this act many times over the net and it never failed to make him come quickly in virtual land. She shook off her knickers and put her feet on either side of him on the arms of the chair. Her cunt was practically thrust in his face now and his nostrils twitched a little as if he had caught a whiff of her salty fragrance. For a moment she dangled the pearls over her mound letting them bounce deliciously against her clit. Then she drew them across the whole length of her slit so the creamy spheres disappeared for a second, engulfed in her furled red lips, then re-emerged, glowing wetly with her moisture.

The sight seemed to galvanise him. He unzipped himself quickly and pulled out his cock. It stuck up obscenely between them. He grabbed hold of himself and began pumping in rapid, short strokes. Tanya kneeled between his legs and gently prised away his fingers. Closing his eyes he leaned back in the chair. The muscles in his face made involuntary twitches as she circled her own hand around his erection. His prick felt hot and dry to her touch.

She'd only given it a few firm strokes when he gave out a pained cry. His hips thrust upwards as he pumped out a rush of hot white semen. She quickly put her face up close, letting the come spatter over her face.

Slowly, she wiped the come down over her face and the swell at the top of her breasts, dabbling her fingers in it. She was just anticipating her own sweet relief when they both heard the sounds of high, light voices from the direction of the beach.

'Oh God, the ama are back,' he gabbled, quickly zipping himself up.

She was just about to say that she didn't care if a tribe of headless horsemen were about to gallop through the cabin when he leaped to his feet. Before she could say a word he'd disappeared out of the door.

She kicked the chair in frustration. Christ, most men would get down on their knees begging for what she had offered James on a plate. Reluctantly she dressed herself and wiped her face with a serviette before forcing a smile onto her lips to greet the divers. She was really interested in meeting these women – she'd read so much about them. Their timing could be better though, she reflected, as she followed James outside.

The divers had gathered in a little knot around James. One or two of them were dragging the little boats up onto the beach, leaving wide trails in the sand. As Tanya drew closer she could just make out the jumble of rubber flippers and face masks in the bottom of the boat.

Tanya could hear them calling, 'Mr Shaw, Mr Shaw, look what we found,' and 'You're gonna be very happy today, Mr Shaw.' Judging by the way James was backing off from the women circling around him like a pack of dogs, it wasn't difficult to see who had the upper hand.

As Tanya approached the women fell silent. Tanya found herself being scrutinised by a dozen pairs of curious eyes.

'Who's your friend, Mr Shaw?' asked one of the older women slyly.

James introduced Tanya to the women, who muttered and whispered to each other.

'Is she your girlfriend?' asked the same woman, laughing.

'No she's not,' blustered James. 'She's come over on business. Now, are you going to show me these pearls or not?'

The women spread themselves out on the sand and delved into their net bags to retrieve the day's catch. Shellfish, encrusted with sand, soon piled up on the beach: abalone and oysters lay jumbled up with lobsters which snapped their pincers open and shut in protest. With long sharp knives the women began prising the shells of the oysters open, looking for pearls. There was soon a comfortable hum of conversation in Japanese as the women worked, with only the occasional curious glance thrown in Tanya's direction.

'Look, look, pearl,' yelled one of the women.

James went over to examine it then shook his head. 'Too small,' he said.

'Perhaps you're interested in my other pearls then,' the woman teased, reaching up to pull at the neck of her thin wetsuit.

James backed off quickly and all the women burst into gusts of laughter at his discomfort. The laughter was so infectious that Tanya soon found herself joining in. Wave after wave of laughter made all the women double up and tears form in their eyes.

The ache between Tanya's legs throbbed as she turned over on the small hard bed. She'd spent a pleasant enough evening with James, eating and talking. But he hadn't approached her at all. In fact he seemed determined to put as much distance as possible between them after their encounter. Where was the character that she'd come to know so well on the net, Tanya puzzled. He must be in there somewhere, that demanding collector who ordered her to do such filthy things.

Tanya sighed and flipped open her make-up bag. There was nothing for it; she wouldn't be able to sleep in this state. She nearly hadn't brought her vibrator. She'd once heard a terrifying story of how some woman's vibrator had started buzzing away in the hold of the plane and of how security, thinking they had a bomb on board, went through every item in the luggage until they found the offending object, buzzing away merrily. Now she was glad she'd taken the risk.

The long shaft of blue plastic felt warm and familiar in her hand. She turned the base until the vibrator sprang into life. God, it sounded noisy in this tiny, silent cabin. Oh well, sod it, he could come and investigate if he wanted. Then he'd see what state he'd driven her into.

She threw back the covers and touched her clit gently with the vibrator. The relief was intense and her throbbing cunt responded immediately, tightening up with pleasure. The vibrations reached deep inside her as she guided the plastic shaft gently between her lips. The image of James lying in bed with only the thin wall between them stole into her mind. She imagined his beautiful lips parted slightly in sleep, his arm flung loosely across the bed and the sheet twisted around his body. A sigh escaped from her lips. Why did he have to be so bloody gorgeous? If he'd turned out to be some repulsive old man she could have quite easily taken her pearls and booked herself on the next flight home. It was as if he'd groomed her for months only for this – back to her trusty old friend again.

She sighed again and let the vibrator rest between her moist lips. It sent soothing waves pulsing through her pussy. She stroked it rhythmically until it was coated with juice and it slid in and out like the piston on a well-oiled machine. Tanya saw James's mouth again in her mind: the shape it made as he came; those girlish lips stretched out across his teeth. He'd exploded in a matter of seconds as if the orgasm had been waiting, pent up for months. She gritted her teeth as her stomach began to contract. Well, she knew how he felt. Her sex felt huge and swollen now and practically sucked at the blue plastic, as if she had a huge mouth between her legs.

The vibration spread across the tops of her legs and resonated deeply inside her. Suddenly, her hips thrust upwards, as if her salivating pussy wanted to swallow the vibrator whole, and her climax ripped through her, nearly lifting her off the bed.

When the tremors had died away she wiped the blue plastic with a flannel and returned it to its place, leaving it handily on top of her make-up within easy reach. The sound of the gentle waves permeated the little room as she fell into a deep exhausted sleep.

The sea was quite choppy as she wandered out onto the beach in the morning sunlight. The sun was sending sparks of light flashing across the swell of waves. Tanya warmed her hands around her mug of coffee as she watched the ama unload their kit from the transit van. They waved to her in friendly greeting.

'Tanya, hello Tanya. Come see the amagoya,' they called.

Tanya smiled and waved back. She carried her coffee into the amagoya, the little hut where they all prepared themselves for the day's work. The women were all busily sorting their gear, checking the seals on their diving masks and unfolding their thin wetsuits. The tiny hut soon warmed with the heat of bodies as the women began to strip for their diving clothes. Tanya politely averted her eyes from the hair tumbling over hard golden-brown nipples and from the riotous bushes of dark hair between their legs. But she soon gave up, realising how little they were bothered by their nakedness, even in the presence of a stranger.

'We think Mr Shaw likes you,' said the woman

who'd been introduced as Miyoko yesterday. The women all started giggling madly.

Tanya snorted. 'I think he prefers his pearls,' she said.

'But you're like a pearl, Tanya, with your white skin,' said another of the women. Tanya seemed to remember she was called Aki.

Tanya felt unexpectedly shy as the half-naked woman touched her face gently. The women giggled again at her discomfort and a smile soon cracked open Tanya's face. You couldn't help liking them and their lusty self-confidence.

Tanya watched as they smoothed the wetsuits over their muscular bodies. They all looked incredibly robust and fit, their muscles honed by the rigours of their perilous work.

'Come with us, Tanya. Forget about Mr Shaw, come out to sea with us,' said Aki.

The Pacific stretched out to the horizon as Tanya watched the black shapes of the ama under the water. In no time at all they disappeared to a depth where they were no longer visible from the surface of the water. Tanya practised taking a deep breath as one of the divers flopped over the side of the boat into the water. Every time she had to let her own breath rush out well before the woman reappeared, smiling and triumphantly holding up a crusty shellfish in her hand for everyone to admire.

Eventually Tanya plucked up enough courage to borrow a spare wetsuit and lower herself into the water. The sea felt icy cold through the thin latex. She paddled around just under the surface with the dark shape of the boat visible above like a large awkward sea monster bobbing around on the waves. Through her mask she could see the fluid shapes of the ama as they dived head first, like a shoal of black fish, until they were out of sight in the murky depths. The women were still out of sight as Tanya dragged herself to the surface, breathing deeply as she clung to the side of the boat.

'What's it like down there?' she asked Miyoko as the women all took a break, lying like seals in the sun to dry out.

'It's like a foreign land,' Miyoko replied thoughtfully, 'very dark and full of strange creatures. Many of them just lie there waiting to be picked like grass. But the abalone, now he's a different matter. They have to be fought with, pried off their rocks with tools.'

Miyoko leaned over and took out a huge shellfish, its thick mother-of-pearl shell the size of a plate. 'Abalone,' she explained with satisfaction, '40 dollars a pound it's worth. Sometimes they also carry pearls.' She winked at Tanya. 'A few more of these will pay for my divorce.'

Back on dry land the ama prised open the few oysters that had been caught during the day. Only one of the creatures yielded a tiny pearl. Tanya weighed it in her hand. It was the first time she'd held a pearl fresh from the ocean. It looked like a tiny soap bubble in her palm. Looking at the perfect shimmering sphere Tanya could understand the old belief that pearls formed from a drop of rain caught in the mouth of an oyster.

The amagoya felt damp and hot as they all dried themselves off, exhausted from the day's diving. Tanya noticed a picture, which looked as if it had been torn from a magazine, tacked onto the wooden wall. It was a highly stylised Japanese cartoon of a girl locked in unwilling embrace with an octopus. The girl's huge breasts pouted beneath the octopus's tentacles and her mouth formed an o of terror as the beast grasped her in its suckered limbs.

'What's that?' she asked.

'It's the devil fish.' Miyoko grinned at her. 'The big man of the sea. Count the tentacles and ask yourself where the eighth might be.'

Nearly every day Tanya went out to sea with the ama. They seemed to accept her easily and she looked forward to them arriving each day, catcalling and whistling to each other across the beach.

It certainly beat staying in with James anyway. His tall muscled body and blond curls still taunted Tanya. Several times he'd stumblingly suggested they repeat the experiment of that first night but Tanya declined the offers quickly. She could do without revisiting that frustration.

His eyes often followed her around the tiny cabin, barely repressed lust burning behind them. If that was the case, she asked herself, why was he so unwilling to touch her? All he had really wanted to do that first evening was look, to examine her nakedness while he drooled and wanked off, as if he was looking at a dirty picture.

Several times she'd heard him come into her bedroom at night while she pretended to be asleep. In a pantomime of disturbed slumber she'd fling off the covers, letting him see her nakedness. She could feel his presence staring at her for a long time before he crept away. She longed to be taken completely, forcefully even. But she was beginning to realise that sex for him was strictly a non-contact sport.

The best thing about the whole trip were the three pearls which were now stitched firmly inside her coat, snuggled in the soft lining. That and getting to know the ama. Tanya felt closer to them every day, particularly to Aki and Miyoko. Unlike most Japanese women, they pleased themselves, often bringing a bottle of saki in the evenings to share with Tanya. The women were fiercely proud of their work and the independence it gave them. Miyoko told Tanya about a beauty contest held in the nearby town with fake ama who paraded in see-through diving costumes and high heels.

'Can you imagine diving in high heels?' said Miyoko with a sneer. 'Those tiny girls wouldn't last five minutes out there.' And she slapped her own muscular thigh with satisfaction.

They were intensely curious about Tanya's relationship with James and one tipsy evening on the beach they began questioning her closely.

'Mr Shaw likes you, Tanya. His eyes follow you everywhere. Don't you like him?' asked Aki, looking up at Tanya with her warm humorous eyes.

Tanya doodled in the sand with her finger. 'Oh, I like him all right, but I don't know if he really likes me. It's . . . it's complicated.'

Miyoko and Aki had rolled over to face her and they both looked at her questioningly.

'It's just that he . . .' Tanya falteringly told the women everything that had happened so far. When she finished Miyoko sat up.

'Well, it's obvious what needs to be done, Tanya,' she said decisively. 'You have to seduce him in a way he can't resist!'

Perhaps this wasn't such a good idea, thought Tanya. Nervously, she applied some more lipstick in her compact mirror as she heard James's footsteps coming up the little path to the cabin. Oh well, it was too late to back out now. She smoothed her tight red dress over her hips. Dressed to kill, she thought, as she caught her reflection in the full-length mirror. She looked like a vamp from a silent movie with her black hair swinging out over her pale shoulders and her body like a flame in the clinging dress.

James's eyes nearly popped out of his head when he saw her.

'My God,' he exclaimed, his nerves disappearing for a second, 'you look fantastic.'

'Good evening, James,' she said in a seductive voice, a couple of decibels above the usual.

At the prearranged signal Aki and Miyoko leaped out of the bedroom, giggling wildly as if possessed. James looked at them aghast.

'What the hell's going on here?' he stammered.

Before he had time to say anything else the women grabbed him from either side.

'Let go of me,' he shouted.

Aki and Miyoko ignored his protestations and began manhandling him towards the bedroom. He struggled, but even though the women were tiny, he was no match for the powerful muscles formed by struggling every day with the force of the sea. The bedroom had been set like a stage with candles on nearly every surface, and the heady smell of burning incense clouded and perfumed the air.

Aki sat on his chest while Miyoko, quick as a trice, secured his wrists to the iron bed head with fine plastic rope. He began kicking his legs furiously.

'I think he'll need tying at the ankles as well, Aki,' said Tanya. Her cool exterior belied her rapidly beating heart.

Soon he was trussed up like a chicken and lay sweating and trembling on the bed.

'Let me loose, Tanya,' he said, tossing his head from side to side in a futile attempt to free himself.

'I don't think so. You see, I think you really want it. All that stuff you said over the net. It's there in you somewhere. It just needs ... liberating,' she explained sweetly.

He'd gone quiet as she spoke. He seemed to be considering her words. With one hand she lifted up her dress. Underneath, her lacy red crotch-less panties blatantly exposed the swell of her pussy.

'Come on, James,' she said in a soothing voice, 'how many times did you have me wearing these when we were thousands of miles apart?'

His eyes widened and fixed between her legs.

'Sweet Jesus,' he moaned.

Separating her lips with one hand she inserted a finger inside her pussy. She stuck the moistened finger into her mouth and sucked at the juice greedily.

'Do you remember how you said you could taste me, that night before I left?' she asked.

He nodded rapidly, sweat coursing down his forehead. She gathered more moisture from her swollen cunt and ran it over his dry lips. He stuck out his tongue to taste the juice. He seemed very aroused now, his cock forming a huge mound in his trousers. Tanya lifted one foot on to the bed and planted it firmly on his chest. Her sex opened out wide, gaping at him. She rubbed at herself, her thick dark bush with the swollen lips peeking beneath just inches from his face.

'Is he ready now?' asked Miyoko. Tanya nodded in response.

James's eyes widened in fear as the two women produced long thin knives from their belts. The blades, which they used to prise open the shells of abalone and oysters, winked in the candlelight. James began writhing and tossing again, trying to free himself from his restraints.

'It's safer if you keep still,' warned Tanya.

The women expertly sliced at his clothing as if they were gutting a huge fish.

'There, there,' soothed Tanya. 'They're not going to hurt you.'

Soon his clothes lay about him in tatters. His penis looked red and sore in its arousal and stretched up so it reached nearly to his belly button. Aki and Miyoko sat either side of him. Aki leaned over and grabbed his cock in her fist. It looked huge in her tiny hand. He gulped and shook all over as she shafted him up and down. 'No, get off me,' he muttered, his wrists chafing at the ropes. But despite his protestations his prick bulged even more, the veins standing proud down its length.

'I think he's ready for you, Tanya,' she giggled.

Tanya unzipped her dress at the sides and it fell to the ground. James gawked stupidly at her body clothed in the crotch-less knickers and tiny bra. She padded over to the bed and lifted herself over him, straddling his hips.

'We did this too, didn't we? In a virtual sense I mean,' she whispered.

James lifted his head to watch as she slid her soaking pussy over his erection. Soon his cock was bathed in the shining juices. Her sex lips pouted out from the opening in her knickers as she pushed herself down on his cock, sinking it inside herself.

'Tanya,' he gasped, 'I have wanted you, you know, so much...'

'Well, now you've got me,' she said, bouncing around on his prick.

Miyoko came up behind her and undid the strap of

her bra. Her tits plunged forward and he groaned as he watched them jiggling up and down in the rhythm of her movements. Miyoko's hands snaked around Tanya and held her breasts for a moment, squeezing the nipples into points. Tanya plunged up and down on his cock. Each stroke chafed delightfully inside her making her muscles contract tighter and tighter. She felt very close now and she bit her lip in an effort to restrain herself.

'Aki, take his balls,' commanded Tanya.

James looked up in alarm but closed his eyes and sank back down as Aki cupped her little hand around his huge hairy balls. Tanya could feel the other woman's hand grazing her buttocks as she sank down again on James's erection. She felt the first tinglings of climax at the roots of her hair.

'Squeeze him, Aki. Squeeze him harder,' she said.

James's lips stretched across his teeth as Aki complied. Tanya glanced down at him, trussed up and sweating on the bed while Miyoko brushed the hair gently back from his forehead. His whole body looked tensed to breaking point, the rope at his wrists biting red marks into the skin as he twisted and turned. Sometimes he muttered, 'No, no.' Then thrusting his hips upwards to meet her he would say, 'Fuck me, please, fuck me,' in a hoarse, dry whisper. Tanya felt she was taking part in some strange ritual with the three of them teasing and luring his reluctant sexuality into life.

The sight of his skin glistening with sweat and the rigid muscles straining in his neck and arms pushed her to the edge. She could feel ripples beginning inside her and she bounced on his prick with renewed vigour, an indecent sucking sound filled the room. When her climax came it nearly knocked Tanya sideways off the bed and she let out loud yelps of pleasure and triumph. Exhausted, she managed to keep moving until she felt James' cock thrust inside her and he gave out a long low moan as he came.

After a few seconds James's eyes opened. 'You bitches,' he said in a weak voice. 'You dirty bitches.'

Tanya put the phone to the airline down with a touch of regret before wandering out to the amagoya. She had already told Aki and Miyoko she was leaving and they had sighed regretfully.

'But we had such fun, Tanya!' said Aki, her eyes glinting naughtily.

It had been fun. But since the other night something seemed to have been liberated in James and he now followed her around like a puppy dog desperate to stick its nose up her skirt. Tanya wasn't sure she liked this new James any better than the old one. Despite the attractions of his lithe angular body and his angelic curls, he still wanted her to take the initiative every time. Tanya longed for a forceful lover who would take her with power and possession, not a cowering man begging to be dictated to.

Tanya found Aki and Miyoko in the amagoya, drying off after the morning's dive. She held out her hand. Two pearls nestled in her palm, one for each of them.

'This should pay for your divorce, Miyoko,' she said. Tears clouded Tanya's eyes – she was really going to miss them both.

Aki rubbed at her own eyes then straightened herself up. 'Let's not be sad,' she cried, 'we also have a leaving present for you.'

They led her over to the minibus.

'Where are we going?' asked Tanya.

'Ssh, don't ask questions. The present is a surprise,' said Miyoko.

The sea glittered to one side of them as Aki drove up the narrow winding road. Finally she parked the car by the side of a beautiful tidal pool which was still save for a few ruffles on the surface as the breeze blew over it.

The stones crunched under their feet as the women led Tanya to the edge of the water. 'Why have we come here?' asked Tanya, intrigued by the mystery.

Miyoko put her finger to her lips and then pointed to the blue water. 'It's the big man of the sea, the devil fish. This is where we come when we're feeling lonely.'

Miyoko took out a jar from her net sack and unscrewed the lid. 'Crab meat,' she explained, 'to tempt his taste buds.'

The two women gently undressed Tanya. The motions of their fingers lulled her into a voluptuous dream-like state and she let their hands move softly over her. How much she had come to trust them, she realised: as if, despite the distance of their lives, they were her long-lost sisters.

They heaped crab meat on their fingers and began smearing it over her breasts. The fishy smell mingled with the salt tang from the water. Tanya gasped as Aki gently parted her legs and applied some of the substance to her pussy, her small, deft fingers reached up into Tanya, pasting the sticky substance inside her slit.

They led her to the water.

'He'll be waiting for you, Tanya,' they said softly.

Tanya waded out into the warm water until it reached her waist.

'Further, further,' they cried from the shore.

She waded until the water came up to her armpits

and rested there. Despite the calming warmth of the water lapping against her body she trembled with anticipation. Half-willing, half-terrified, not knowing how or when.

It had seemed she'd stood for ever, the gentle motion of the water unable to soothe her trembling anticipation, when she felt a brush against her legs. The water rippled around her.

Tanya repressed a scream – of pleasure or fear, she wasn't sure which – as a well-muscled tentacle wrapped itself around her leg. Her new-found sisters waved and smiled encouragingly at her from the shore. She could hear their distant voices carry over the water.

Another tentacle curled around her waist and she screamed out loud, this time in terror. The limb held her firmly in place. The smooth snake-like arms slid over her body easily as another tentacle grabbed on to her other leg. Except for her arms she was immobile now. She shuddered and quaked in the unnatural embrace. Its presence felt so huge and powerful around her. She felt overwhelmed by the sheer size of it; by its huge writhing mass and by the strangeness of the unseen animal which had risen from the ocean and sought her out.

For a long while it held her there, its arms rippling over her body, caressing her up and down with its wriggling, tender motions. Exhausted from her fear and the insistent pulsing of its limbs she leaned back against the dome of its body. Its strength was such that her feet lifted from the floor of the pool, so she was held as if in a state of suspended animation. Despite her fear an almost involuntary pleasure burgeoned all over her body as time and time again the tentacles slithered over her.

All eight tentacles were wrapped round her now,

the tips of which all played with some part of her body. Suddenly, the octopus lifted her up a fraction more, at the same time opening and spreading her legs apart. Any resistant movement on her part was futile now. Her legs were stretched open almost to breaking point in the octopus's powerful grasp. She cried out again in terror and arousal as an arm explored between her legs. She remembered the drawing on the wall of the amagoya and Miyoko's words: 'ask yourself where the eighth tentacle might be.' Miyoko had explained that among the octopus's eight limbs was a sperm arm, a special elongated tentacle. Tanya could feel it now, tickling her labia, the tip moving curiously over her mound.

The tip wriggled in and out of her legs for what seemed like forever. She gasped every time she felt the enquiring touch snaking between her legs. Sometimes it flicked in and out and sometimes it writhed there softly for a while, transporting her to state of ecstasy every time it slid over her clitoris. She almost sobbed as again and again her climax threatened to explode at the octopus's jelly-like caresses. But every time the sensitive limb withdrew before it had a chance to send her spiralling over the edge.

She lay back against the creature, feeling its body expand and contract behind her, sending jets of water skimming against her thighs and bottom. She felt limp and exhausted from the lapping tide, the repeated, soft assaults on her body, and the climax which spun and spiralled inside her but never quite broke. Her long hair was plastered over her face and shoulders and her mouth tasted of salt. The creature's caresses were so protracted, so exquisitely drawn out, that Tanya found herself almost in a dream state. The lapping of the tide mingled with the throbbing in her body until she felt as one with the water and with the squeezing, prying creature who held her.

Suddenly the sperm arm delved into her pussy. After the long minutes of tender courtship Tanya nearly wept with relief and with the extreme sensation. The arm was as lithe as it was huge and made her cunt stretch and gape with its width. As the sperm arm moved and pulsated it sent shock waves across her body. Further and further up it went until she felt fuller than she ever had before, ever could with any man. She thrashed about in the restraint of limbs as she felt the tantalising arm wriggle inside her repeatedly until she was breathing in deep, long gasps. Finally the orgasm engulfed her body, its waves simulating the action of the water as she cried out over and over again.

Exhausted, she flopped back into her lover's strong arms. The sperm arm continued moving inside her spent body for what seemed like hours. Thoughts drifted through her head as she lay in the clutches of the monster. She had come here to these strange shores to find her pearls and to see a man. She had found her pearls but she had also discovered two women – women she would remember for ever. She had found her man but he had turned out so differently to her expectations. And now there was this – not a man, but an alien lover from the salty depths of the sea.

The sun was low in the sky and turning red when she finally felt a fluid jet issuing from the tentacle and a gush of sperm flood her stretched open sex. The steady stream went on and on, pumping in huge spurts inside her. Finally, when the creature's orgasm was exhausted, she lay back in its strong embrace, totally at peace, feeling the liquid pearls which swirled and swam between her legs.

Rain on the Tongue

'I'll take that one.' Crouched down on the floor she was just aware of the end of a walking stick pointing decisively to one of the badges spread out before her.

It was a good choice – a pair of soaring metal wings with a blood-red enamelled heart at its centre and a little clasp on the back to attach it to the motorbike. Wings and heart: that summed up biking for her.

As she looked up, the sun scorched Anna's eyes and all she could see was his bulky shape leaning on a stick. She stood up in one easy movement, the badges spread neatly on a chequered travel rug at her feet. His heavy leather biking jacket was open revealing a tattered and faded black T-shirt underneath. She took a cloth and pretended to buff up the sparkling metal, wanting to look a bit further.

'It's twenty pounds, this one. In fact I didn't really want to let it go, it's my favourite.' Mentally she'd priced it at fifteen this morning but she wanted to see how much he wanted it.

'That's expensive.' He smiled thoughtfully and shifted his weight onto his stick. 'But then, it's my favourite too.'

He ran his large square hand over his close-cropped hair as Anna wrapped the badge in a bit of old newspaper. Nose bent to one side and with a heavy jaw, he looked a bit of a bruiser, but this was offset by the blue of his clever-looking eyes, and then there was the injury . . . He was unashamedly staring at her.

'I'll give you my business card,' she said offhandedly. 'I've got all sorts of bits and pieces, some of them almost antique. There's a pile of stuff in the garage. If you ever want anything else just give me a ring.' The invitation hung in the air.

She held out the package while he fished around in his back pocket for the money and handed her two crumpled tenners. Leaning on his stick, he went off to join his mate who was lounging against a car, smoking. Anna hadn't noticed him before. The pair faded into the crowd and Anna followed his stocky frame with his slight limp until he disappeared altogether.

'One hour. I'll give you one hour to come back,' she thought. The idea of waiting more than that for a bloke seemed preposterous to her. But she was being generous; ten minutes was usually the max.

'Fuck you, then,' she said audibly an hour later as she began packing her stuff away into her capacious panniers. She hadn't sold much but she didn't care; she was hot and tired and horny. She counted out the meagre earnings for the day. These bike shows were more of a hobby really. She'd love just to travel round doing this all year but finances meant that at the moment it was strictly weekends.

Sparking her Fireblade into action she revved the machine unnecessarily loudly. Several men selling hot dogs nearby cheered as the engine burst into life and she spun past them, leathered up and hair flowing from underneath her helmet.

Back on the road she pushed the machine hard. Its pulsating body always felt like a horse to her and, like a horse, it sometimes had a mind of its own and needed to be controlled. The landscape raced past and the smell of wind and petrol fuelled her senses. Anna wanted to feel this exhilaration infect the rest of her life. She bit her lip as she thrust the bike round a particularly difficult corner. For one thing, the job had to go – one more week in that sodding place and . . .

The Volvo shot out in front of her, cutting her up badly. Why is it always fucking Volvos, she muttered to herself as she checked her speed and slowed down. She started laughing like a crazy woman – laughing and riding. The Volvo had done her a favour. Near misses made her love the world and think of all its sensual delights. Usually when riding she carried death on her shoulder as a warning. This time it nearly got her and she vowed not to be so careless again. For the rest of the ride the world seemed formed in brighter colours and the throb of the engine was like the sweetest thing she'd ever heard.

The next morning she washed the grease and grit out of her hair and was lying back in the bath looking at the ceiling. it was still coloured 1930s green, a remnant of when her Aunt Bethan lived there. Suddenly she noticed something strange about the surface of the bath water. It was just a tiny vibration at first but then the water started lapping in miniature waves as if responding to some invisible moon. Then she heard it clearly, the unmistakable sound of the Ducati engine, full-throated and gutsy. The sound seemed to thud through her body until she could hear it right underneath the window. Shedding water, she grappled with the handle on the bathroom window which seemed to have got stuck through disuse. She wrenched it open and leaned out, water from her hair splashing his unturned face as he pulled his helmet off.

She dressed quickly in classic biker-chick style: short skirt, grungy T-shirt, tights with more holes in them than fabric, huge, heavy boots right up to her knees with massive chrome clips studded up the sides and, of course, the well-worn leather jacket.

He was leaning comfortably against his standing bike, legs encased in leather which had gone slightly loose at the knees from the riding position. The jacket was heavy, padded leather designed for protection rather than fashion. Something she couldn't avoid noticing was the hardness in his trousers. Obviously her dripping, naked breasts hadn't gone unnoticed.

'Where's the wings?' she asked after admiring the Ducati. It was all black and chrome, like a huge expensive piece of jewellery.

'I don't put anything on the Duke but I think it might be kind of lucky so I'm keeping it in my pocket.' The silver flashed and the red glowed as he slipped it out of his pocket to show her.

'Do you want to see anything else?' She looked at him questioningly. She liked a man who didn't hide his feelings.

He didn't even feign an interest in the oddments of memorabilia stacked in cardboard boxes in her garage.

'I thought we could put some miles down.' He gestured towards the pillion seat of his bike.

'I don't ride on the back of anyone's bike,' she announced proudly, going to wheel the Fireblade out of the garage where, as usual, it crouched expectantly in the dark.

He stared at her hard as she swung herself on to the Fireblade, revealing quite a bit of leg. His tough charisma interested her. Biking for her was a way of satisfying her rebel heart and, if she was truthful, part of its appeal lay in being the furthest away from her starchy upbringing as possible. After all, weren't bikers supposed to be as bad as you could get?

'I'll lead and you follow and we'll see where we get,' she commanded as she turned the keys and the Fireblade roared in appreciation at being liberated from its enclosure.

Glancing sideways she noticed how he had to get on, swinging his damaged leg over the back. His stick was strapped neatly onto the side.

Once on the road Anna soon unwound. The riding was sweet today, the engine sucking in great gulps of air and gas and throwing out the power to the back wheel. The machine almost felt like an extension of her own body, relaxed and responsive. After about fifty miles they were well out into the countryside and the roads changed from relaxed dual carriageways to winding lanes which spattered stones into her visor.

The Ducati engine had such a distinctive thrum to it that Anna could hear it above the roar of her own machine when he rode up alongside her. He gestured to a roadside cafe in the distance and she nodded, using the shorthand that comes naturally to people who spend a long time in the saddle.

The cafe was as big as a barn, beautifully greasy and classically formica'd, just as Anna liked them. It was a hot day and the massive old fans slowly whipped the air about on the ceiling. A bored-looking waitress leaned on the counter reading *Hello* magazine and the only other customers were a beige-clad middle-aged couple who sat drinking tea and eating dried-out scones.

They sat at the other end and studied the menu. 'What will you have?' His stick leaned up against the bench next to him.

'Anything but fish,' she replied decisively. 'I hate fish. My company export tropical ones and I have to have a huge tank of them right next to me on reception. I swear to God sometimes I think they're all lining up to look at me.'

He raised his eyebrows. 'What do you do when that happens?' There was humour in his voice.

'I growl at them. Perhaps they think I'm a cat, maybe I'll even eat them one day, stick them in a pan and fry the fuckers up.' She bared her teeth in mime.

He looked at her hard. 'Come and sit over here.'

This took her by surprise and she felt a flush of indignation at being commanded. 'Maybe I don't want to,' she answered quickly.

He looked out of the window. 'No, perhaps you don't.'

Oh, that was clever, she thought, not pushing too hard too soon. She shrugged her shoulders and moved next to him.

'Now then, what do you like to drink?' he asked as he put his hand between her legs.

Surprised at his audacity she glanced down and could see his big roughened hand cradling her crotch. His fingers found one of the holes in her tights and, as if he was batting away an annoying bug, he ripped them firmly, exposing her little black lace thong. He hooked one of his fingers under Anna's knickers and stroked tenderly. She took an audible intake of breath and moisture tickled her cunt as the air blew over it and he delicately fingered her clit.

'Chocolate, do you like drinking chocolate?' He continued to finger her while looking at the menu.

She shook her head. 'Tea, I think.' Her voice had a little gasp in it as she struggled to control her speech. 'And something to eat.'

She could feel her sweet wetness begin to flow and

her nipples pucker up, aching for attention. Although the lack of preamble was exciting, there was also a feeling of ambush. But this was a vague notion in the back of her mind, not quite forming itself into a thought. She knew that if she wanted to she could get up and walk away, throw the bike into action and clear out. But she didn't. She succumbed to the delicious feeling of his hand between her legs while the waitress dozed on in her dreams of celebrity white and gold bathrooms.

He pushed one of his fingers slowly inside her, exploring her own particular space and wetness. She squeezed her pussy muscles tightly. She'd always spent five minutes a night practising her muscle tone and was amazed how quickly this special exercise regime showed its benefit. He breathed heavily in response. Withdrawing his finger slowly, he stuck it into his mouth, savouring her heavy juices.

Anna felt a high-octane excitement she hadn't experienced for a long time. While the world dreamed on they were carrying on their own little porn movie and the audacity of it made her blood race. When he unzipped his leathers and exposed his rigid cock under the table, her cunt bloomed in appreciation.

'Move onto my lap.' His voice rasped slightly now.

She checked quickly across the room then moved on top of him. He pulled her thong to one side and sunk his cock into her in one easy movement. Desperate to feel the delicious friction, the spark that lights the fire, he began to thrust his hips. She quietened him with a touch on the leg and picked up the menu, anxious to stall the waitress.

'Bacon,' she suggested, 'with loads of baked beans and toast.'

She squeezed her muscles hard around his swollen prick and he groaned into her shoulder. She carried on pumping.

'And pancakes, I think, with maple syrup.'

She was milking him in earnest now and, with each squeeze, her own pleasure escalated. He began to thrust his hips again but gently this time, hardly a movement at all. She drew his hand over to between her legs, wanting him to seek out her treasured nub. Eagerly responding, he used her wetness to slide his finger over her clit.

He was shaking under her now and she bent her head further over the menu. She felt so completely and deliciously full, as if nothing before had ever filled her up before. As she looked up the world seemed to splinter and break before her as she came, choking back her cries. Almost a second later she felt his thighs tense and she heard him moaning, 'Oh fuck,' into her shoulder as he spunked deeply inside her.

Dripping with each other's juices they moved apart, hurriedly rearranging their clothes. With a yawn the waitress slapped down her magazine and came over to them, pad in hand.

'What'll you have?' she asked sullenly.

It was only when their food arrived that she realised she didn't know his name. She thrilled at the sluttishness of it. She loved to be naughty, and enjoyed making men gasp and groan in pleasure at how bad she could be. She was usually disappointed at just how little it took.

'Graham,' he responded to her question and they shook hands sardonically.

They ate and chatted idly and then she smoked a thin cigarette which he rolled. She found out that he worked sometimes in a bike spares shop and sometimes from home doing repairs in his garage (it all sounded enticingly casual). Being interested in dreams she wanted to find out about his.

'Well,' he said slowly, 'I've been to Australia twice and I guess I want to explore the States next. I'd also like to fuck you again.'

When he said this he lifted his fingers to his nose and breathed in her scent as if it were some rare, mysterious perfume. Her well-brought-up senses quivered. His frank appreciation, almost bordering on crudeness, was fascinating.

Eventually they wandered back to their bikes through the hazy late-afternoon sunshine.

'D'you want to go back home or shall we go further?' His eyes played over her body lustfully.

Anna looked at the road in one direction and then the other.

'Sod it,' she said, 'everyone gets a bout of flu every now and again and I can feel a tickle in my throat.' She gave a broad healthy grin as she swung onto her bike and opened the throttle.

They stopped once at a village to buy a couple of sleeping bags and some food which she strapped on to the pillion of the Fireblade. She felt the wild urge to put miles behind her, as if she were fleeing from prison, and as if freedom was a destination around the next corner. She was almost disappointed when he gestured to the forest by the side of the road, wanting to stop.

They lay on the open sleeping bag eating slivers of ham straight from the packet and drinking wine. Anna was pleased to note that he had bought an expensive Claret, but he soon dispelled any notions of refinement by burping loudly and unashamedly. Anna giggled.

He rolled over and smiled, lines creasing the corners of his eyes. 'What do you look like under your armour?' he said, pulling at the zip of her jacket.

She loved her leather biker's jacket with a passion. Most of them were made for men but even the women's ones had very little room for breasts. She'd had this one made especially for her and it moulded over her full breasts perfectly, fitting like a second skin. There was the other side of biking which fired her almost as much as riding – the leather, metal, straps and buckles, the quasi-bondage porno look which made her feel like she was acting in some wild and seedy B-movie.

As he pulled the zip her tits in their skimpy T-shirt plunged forward appreciatively. He roughly yanked her T-shirt up to release them. She groaned and arched forward as he kissed and licked her, a delicious ache spreading through her sex.

'You're wild at heart, aren't you,' he said suddenly, watching her aching abandon, and then added almost as an afterthought, 'however posh you sound.'

He stood up suddenly and began to unbuckle his studded belt. 'I think you want to play some games,' he said softly, staring at her intently.

She had a sudden whiff from him of the open road combined with the musky scent of well-worn leather. The scent almost cast a spell on her and she noticed for the first time the tattoo on his upper arm depicting a writhing knot of snakes.

'I want to play for ever,' she returned forcefully.

Graham loosely unbuttoned his leather trousers. Falling to her knees, she opened his flies to reveal his stiff upstanding prick and a deep and angry scar which marked his hip and the top of his leg as far as she could she. It looked like a road leading to some unfathomable place. She began to gently kiss the scar, marking its path downwards.

'You know there's only two kinds of bikers,' he said softly, touching her hair. 'Those who've had their smash and those who are going to have it. I've had mine.'

He stripped her jacket and T-shirt off and deftly buckled her wrists together behind her back. Taking his stick, he whacked her gently on the bottom under her lifted skirt. It produced a delicious tingle which spread through her cheeks and made her clit stiff with appreciation.

He lifted her up on to his bike. Anna felt the sting of the machine's engine, not yet cold, against her legs. The bike lock clanked as he wrapped the chain around her bound wrists and secured her firmly to the handlebars. Pulling at her clothes he ripped off what was left of her tights and eased her knickers down.

Graham stood back. He fingered the end of his prick which jutted through his leathers as he savoured the sight.

'If you could only see how dirty this looks.' He smiled lasciviously.

All that she had left on was her huge biking boots and a pair of little lace panties which stretched indecently across her knees. Graham stroked his finger between her legs, relishing the feel of her lips which hung down, hot and heavy.

'Feel how wet you are,' he said in faux shock. 'You dirty girl.'

He smeared the gathered honey over one of her puckered nipples and then licked it off. The action sent waves of pleasure bolting through her body. The evening air was still warm and the slight breeze tickled her pubes, making her cunt ache even more for attention. She gazed longingly at his rigid prick.

'Fuck me now,' she pleaded. She felt as though she could devour his cock with every orifice.

He laughed and fell to his knees, letting his tongue play lightly on her clit so that she could feel his hot breath rasping over her cunt. The leather of the bike seat stuck to her as she leaned back, thrusting her greedy pussy out for him to tongue.

When her breath was coming so fast she was panting, he stopped abruptly and stood up. His heavy cock thudded against her stomach. Slowly and deliberately he entered her and then fucked her fast and furious. She thrashed in pleasure inside her restraints as he squeezed her bouncing tits. Her pleasure gathered and flowed and she smiled as she half remembered something from her Convent childhood; something about being broken against the wheel...

When she came she moaned deeply. The sound sent Graham's restraint over the edge and, after thrusting for another few moments, he climaxed, almost doubling up with the sensation.

She slept exhausted under the stars, the trees forming their complicated web above.

While he was still sleeping the next morning she called her firm from her mobile. Pinching her nose she imitated a women stricken down with flu hardly able to pick up the phone. The truth was, she giggled to herself inside, she felt like a sex princess who had just had the best fuck of her life. Punching the 'end call' button she found him awake, smiling at her complicitly.

Cleaning herself up with water from a freezing cold stream, Anna felt fresh and more awake than she had done for months.

They made their way into the nearest town to eat.

There were a few surprisingly chic shops and, after stuffing herself as if she'd never eaten before, Anna wandered off to explore. She'd soon fallen for a pair of bootlegged leather jeans cut low on the hips and, deciding to flex her plastic, she hurriedly chose a stringy black T-shirt to go with them. Chucking her old stuff in the gold-lettered carrier bag she emerged feeling biker-chick gorgeous from top to toe.

All that she needed now was some fresh underwear. The first shop she came across was one of those rather frilly sex shops meant for women. Figuring that she may as well be pure glamour underneath as well, she chose a few sexy little crotch-less numbers to be going on with.

Just as she was about to pay she noticed the sex toy section discreetly tucked at the back of the shop. Fascinated, she examined the dildos and vibrators set out like rows of fireworks, primed and ready to explode. Finally she settled on a long thin cute-looking dildo and a little something for him. She thrilled at the secret contents of her bag as she strolled down the street to meet up with Graham. She'd show him bad.

Graham walked easily without his stick today – he seemed to need it only when he was tired, or had been riding long distances; at the moment his limp was barely discernible. As the day rolled on it became smokingly hot so they decided to camp out again to save on cash. Anna rode in front, leading the way through little woodland paths to a dense, quiet place in the forest. Feeling hot, she searched out a tiny stream and paddled her feet in it, changed her knickers and combed her unkempt hair. Several twigs and leaves fell out like confetti and she realised they must have been there all day.

When she returned to their 'camp' Graham was already mellowed out with a half-empty bottle of wine next to him. It seemed a good time to bestow her gift.

'I haven't had one of these for years,' he exclaimed as he turned the chrome cock ring over in his square fingers.

Taking the lead, she deftly unbuttoned his trousers and clipped the cock ring with its little spring fastening firmly around his prick and balls.

'With this ring,' she intoned ironically.

She stroked his cock idly and it soon began to firm within its metal enclosure. The sight fired her up and she began to strip his boots and trousers off.

'You're one horny bitch,' he murmured contentedly as she stroked and licked him. She reached over and felt for the bike lock and belt which she had secreted under the sleeping bag.

'Your turn.' She smiled wickedly. 'Stand up.'

Before he could protest she slung the chain over a branch and had him firmly locked in the chain's embrace, his powerful arms stretched above him.

She slowly eased her leathers down to reveal her tufts of hair peeking through her crotch-less knickers. Graham groaned in frustrated pleasure, like a caged animal whose food is just beyond his reach. Anna reached for the dildo which had been stored with the rest of her cache. She tickled her clit with it and with one foot on a rock eased it inside herself.

Naked except for a tatty T-shirt, Graham looked huge and taut and menacing. Like a wild beast on heat he rattled his chains. The cock ring made his prick and balls stand proud, jutting out before him.

'Suck me,' he tried to command with the force of his personality.

Anna laughed. 'Maybe later,' she teased.

With this she pulled the dildo out and made sure he clocked the sheeny juices which smothered it. She slid it back in and began to slowly wank herself, opening her legs as far as possible to make sure he had a good view.

He howled in frustration. 'You're playing with my mind,' he stuttered, half-admiringly.

Anna abruptly stopped and pulled her leathers up. She had plans. She graciously let him lick her juices from the dildo and then went behind him and stroked his buttocks.

'You have a lovely arse,' she said, absent-mindedly kneading his golden skin.

'Do it,' he said simply.

Almost breathless she parted his buttocks to find the cute puckered button within. Gently at first she slid the dildo in. Being slim, it glided in and, as he groaned in pleasure, her confidence grew and she began sliding it in earnest.

She felt wild with excitement. Here she was fucking a big bad dirty biker up the arse as he howled in pleasure, 'Fuck me, girl, fuck me.' Pausing, she reached out her hand and grasped his prick, squeezing the end. His body went limp with pleasure in his chains and Anna quickly decided to let him loose before he went over the edge.

He laid her tenderly, stomach down, over her bike and eased her leathers over her thighs. Her cunt stood out rudely from the revealing knickers and he toyed with her clit before finally sinking his prick unceremoniously inside her. The enclosure kept him firm and hard and she could feel the now warm metal bump against her lips. Its stricture made him last and as he rhythmically pumped, huge and sweaty, her protracted pleasure seemed to lead to another place, a room she'd never entered before. He swore and sweated above her, muttering 'Jesus,' and 'Fuck, fuck.'

Shortly after, it began to rain. Anna moved to where the trees were sparse and stuck her tongue out to catch it.

The next few days were a blur of cheap B&Bs, roadsides cafés, hurried calls to Anna's employer, wanton sex and hard riding. She reflected that living was more real on the back of a bike. If it rained the ride became a death-defying journey across slippery wet roads. On the other hand, exquisite warm air carrying the tang of a far-off ocean could unexpectedly hit you like a cloud from heaven. Most people on the road in their metal cages were insulated from all the danger and joy. The freedom she sought was out there: on the perilous roads, in their dirty sex and in the passing through and moving on. She felt a small stab of disappointment when he finally suggested they should get back.

'I need to work some shifts and get some cash,' he explained regretfully.

'Yeah, I guess I have to get my life in order too,' she agreed.

Back to reality she had trouble settling her itchy feet. To her surprise she still had a job waiting for her. Her boss didn't even seem suspicious when she appeared looking fresh and brown from the open road. She even felt a bit guilty, until she was back behind reception and the presence of the creepy fish mindlessly roaming their tank began to bother her again. She turned her back on them. There was one particular little blue bastard which seemed to take pleasure in staring at her all day. Looking at her with his baleful eyes he seemed to be saying, 'I know where you've been. Not ill at all. You just don't *like* us.' Anna thought to herself, I'm going mad.

To cheer herself up she went out at lunch time and bought a copy of her favourite bike mag. As she flicked it over underneath the desk the ads caught her eye: Hire and Ride, Arizona, Nevada, The Californian Desert...

The estate agent said her house was worth a packet – property prices had rocketed in this part of town. The deal all went through surprisingly quickly but for some superstitious reason Anna kept it secret, feeling that as soon as she told anyone her dream would disappear like smoke in the wind. Whenever she had the urge to blab she pictured it in her mind, the smoke rushing away from her over valleys and rooftops.

About a week before the contract was due to be signed she felt a pang of guilt as she sat drinking tea by the open French windows. Her Aunt Bethan had always loved the garden and Anna almost saw her, misty like a watercolour, out in the drizzly fresh greenness. Anna had always been the favourite and Aunt Bethan had left the whole house to her along with a few rings and premium bonds. But then she remembered her Aunt talking wistfully about 'the freedom young girls have today' and she knew she was doing the right thing. Her Aunt seemed to nod and smile approvingly from the garden before firmly deadheading a geranium and fading away.

It was all rain on the tongue and you had to catch it when it fell.

She knew what she wanted. It was the hot white droplet that seeped from his cock when he was hard and horny, the buttery firmness of leather rubbing her nipples and the jet of hot semen as he came over her stomach. It was Marlon Brando, Easy Rider and speed and the landscape forming a blur and hot chrome and Bruce Willis looking up from his bike all handsome and laid back, saying, 'Zed's dead, baby, Zed's dead,' to his sexy French girlfriend.

She blasted up on her Fireblade. It was due to be sold in a couple of days and she was riding it as much as possible, to ease the pain of parting. She rode up to the store where Graham worked. He was leaning on his stick, discussing one of the bikes with a customer. He looked up but didn't seem surprised. It was one thing she'd noticed about him, he never seemed surprised.

'Come to me, baby,' she yelled, hoping to embarrass him. He grinned and laconically walked over.

'I'm clearing out of here in a week or two,' she confessed. The contract on the house was signed and she was just waiting for completion so she figured she could break her pact of silence.

'I expect you'd like me to come with you,' he said with cheerful arrogance. She tried to look careless but a big grin spread over her face.

'Where are we going?' he asked as he swung his damaged leg over to ride pillion.

'Somewhere,' she said firmly, 'where there is absolutely no water, and not a fucking fish in sight.'

A Classy Piece of Rainwear

Dear Mrs Woo. I sound your name in my head as if beginning a letter. Dear Mrs Woo, I still don't know how you really spell your name – I think of it like the word for ritual flirting. I want to thank you for those times. You opened a door for me then, you really did. I might never have known about those dark places if you hadn't shown me. If I actually wrote to you now, sitting here on my narrow bed in the halls of residence, what would I say? Dear Mrs Woo, your name tolls like a bell to me across the distance between us.

Keraaang! The comic book noise played in my head as my skateboard whizzed down the pavement, the shops and colours of the Chinese quarter melting into each other like paint as I shot past. The extra wide pavements here were like open boulevards built for skateboarding pleasure. Wheee! Past the tattoo parlour, the Chinese restaurants (nasty rumours of dog chow mein), and of course, Mrs Woo's shop – *All Provisions* – white plastic lettering on red with crisscrossy Chinese writing underneath.

My wheels sounded like grinding bones beneath me as I performed a graceful arc and flipped the board up with my foot, deftly catching it in one hand. Like everywhere else, we were moved on almost daily here, mostly by Mrs Woo. At least three times a week she'd come screaming out, broom in hand, and literally sweep us off the streets. A tiny Chinese siren – in appearance as well as sound – she looked like a miniature ageing Hollywood goddess, her black hair puffed up in an elaborate swirl, her tiny feet in high, clicking heels. Whenever she left the shop, even on her street sweeping missions, she would wear an old shiny mac, patterned with black and white asymmetrical squares. It was like a relic in a museum dedicated to the 60s, or to Mary Quant, and it looked strange in the way that glamour from a different age always does.

Sometimes we would softly call insults to her. Mostly we just moved on. One day my friend Stevie called out to her: 'That's a classy piece of rainwear, Mrs Woo.' Pausing in her frantic click back to the shop she turned and smiled at him, one hand reaching up to pat her hair.

This particular (and later I would come to regard as fateful) day, rain started washing softly down as I attempted a difficult diagonal turn. Perhaps it was the wet pavements that did it, I don't know. Mrs Woo came screaming out as usual, like some vicious, tiny motorbike, all black and silver and PVC. Cruuunch! The impact felt feather-light to me, but Mrs Woo crumpled and fell to the ground, her arm bent behind at a weird angle. She looked like a swastika drawn onto the pavement with chalk.

Drawn by the promise of disaster, a crowd began to gather, muttering like a hive of bees. I gathered up my board and ran, glancing back long enough to see the crowd clustered around Mrs Woo, and something else – it was Mrs Woo's broom still waving madly above their heads.

I awoke the next morning in the thrall of a dream about exquisite Chinese women dancing and swirling around me as I lay immobile, strapped to a bed. As they skipped and fluttered past they took off their shimmering clothes, dropping each one on my hard cock which stuck out, unnaturally large, straight above me. The dream dissolved just as Mrs Woo appeared from a mystery door, beckoning me (with her good arm) in what I felt was a most disturbing fashion.

I cursed as I woke, trying to cling on to the dream. My cock felt tender and swollen, even the light touch of the duvet cover seemed unbearable. I could hear my parents moving around downstairs as I circled the ache with my finger and thumb and began to stroke. Sweet explosions thudded down my legs and up my stomach at my own tender touch. Biting my lip to suppress the sound, I jerked off quickly and quietly, the impression of the dream still behind my eyelids. But even as I pumped up and down, it was with the knowledge that the relief would be short-lived. How long would it be until my wayward prick would stir painfully again? I gave it an hour – tops.

The come shot out across the sheet just as my mum shouted up the stairs to wake me. I sighed and scooped up the gloopy mess before getting dressed. As I left, dad was outside washing the car.

'Won't be long before you have a real job, Josh,' he called out cheerfully after me.

It was true. At the moment I was caught in a strange adolescent neverland, skateboarding and still doing a paper-round, but checking out college prospectuses and attending droning career meetings as well. Like I had a foot in two different worlds.

Today the paper-round seemed a particularly oner-ous task for I knew, secreted among all the heavy slabs of newspapers in the bag Mr Roberts had ready for me, would be the paper for Mrs Woo. Very light and rolled up in the middle, it was covered in dense Chinese characters and felt like some pre-biblical text, imparting knowledge somehow more precious and important than the rest. I'd tried to cry off after breakfast.

'I'm too old to be doing a paper-round,' I'd grumbled to my mother. 'I'm calling Mr Roberts to quit.'

'Nonsense,' she replied firmly, pushing me out of the door. So that was that.

About an hour later I found myself in front of her door, stupidly looking at the thick black gaffer tape that had mysteriously appeared overnight and now sealed up the letterbox. Suddenly, Mrs Woo appeared inside, putting her face close to the window. For a moment it looked like a face underwater, the hanging packets and bunches of vegetables behind her a dancing oceanic backdrop. She lifted her finger and with a sharp movement beckoned me in.

I'd never been inside her shop before. It didn't smell of food, but of dust and spices. Her arm was in plaster and it appeared far too big for her, like some extraterrestrial life form had wrapped itself round her body and which she would now have to drag around.

'These kids.' She gestured with contempt towards the door. 'They push things through my letterbox.' I'd never heard of any trouble like this before and I had the horrible idea that she was lying.

On the counter were two tiny cups and a teapot. It looked like a dolls' tea set. I bowed my head waiting for the telling off, the mention of parents, even police. Instead she poured a yellowish liquid into the cups and pushed one towards me.

'I'm going to tell you a story and I'll do it in as western a way as possible so you understand,' she said.

I looked hesitantly towards the door. But she rapped her knuckles sharply on the counter calling me to attention and pointed to the stool next to her behind the counter. She spent a few moments staring out of the window at the sky, as if gathering energy from some invisible source.

'It starts with a beautiful girl. Beautiful, but quite desperate, living on nothing but her wits. One day she was travelling across a barren place in China and she came across a small blue pool of water. The blue was very bright, like your eyes.'

Mrs Woo leaned forward to examine my eyes and I blushed miserably.

She continued briskly: 'The girl took a string from her pocket, put her last half of rice ball on the end and dangled it in the water. It was her last morsel of food.' Mrs Woo's voice turned tragic when she said this, as if reading from the script of a silent movie. 'But against the odds she had a bite and quickly landed a bulging silver fish on the shore.'

I imagined the girl and the fish and the tiny shore, like a postcard made from fabrics, the kind where the colours change when you tilt it to one side. For a moment her hand fluttered against my leg in a contact I assumed must be accidental.

'She slit the fish open with her penknife and found five gold coins inside. She washed the fish-guts from the coins and gobbled up the fish – everything except its bones and insides. While she ate, she noticed the level of the water going down, as if the sky was drinking it up. Pretty soon, the little lake disappeared, leaving just a stain on the ground.

'She used the money wisely. Oh yes, she was a practical girl. She travelled to the nearest big city and used her charms to join a dancing group, the kind that entertained important men.'

'Like a geisha?' I asked.

She frowned at me for the interruption. 'Geisha girls are Japanese,' she corrected me. 'The group entertained important men, powerful men that belonged to the party. The girls always began the entertainment with a little dance. They were so charming and light on their feet they looked like little blossoms being blown along by the wind. As the music played, they took off their little garments piece by piece, letting them drop on the laughing men.'

The hairs on the back of my neck stood up. Could this woman see into my dreams? I shifted uncomfortably on my seat as my cock stirred at the memory. Her hand brushed my leg again. Surely the touch wasn't intentional, I thought. But when her hand continued its passage upwards, I began to doubt it.

She carried on: 'As each piece came off, a little more got exposed – a pert breast peeking out maybe. The men's eyes would fasten on to it like glue, watching as it shamelessly bounced in time to the dancing.'

Mrs Woo laughed a little. An uncomfortable sound. Keeping her eyes fixed out of the window she reached up further. The shock made my heart knock when she cradled her hand over my groin. She began to stroke, almost abstractedly, at the growing bulge.

'At the end of the dance,' she continued as if nothing was happening, 'the girls gathered in a huddle to draw lots. In a pot were scraps of paper that each man had dropped in with his name on it.'

I held my breath as she stroked, her little fingers dancing over my cock, which throbbed and grew in response. Nobody had ever touched me there before.

A smile played across her lips. 'There was always an air of great excitement in the room at this point in the evening. You could see the sweat forming on the men's foreheads and they all loosened their ties, as if they had trouble breathing. As one of the girls' hands dipped into the pot to choose a name, all the men would lean forward, straining their ears to hear who it might be. When the name was read out, the other men would slap the selected one on the back, congratulating him and calling him "a lucky dog".'

Her hand paused, leaving an ache of desire between my legs. The whole situation was utterly beyond my comprehension. I had the inkling that if I moved or protested, she would remonstrate with me sharply, as if telling off a wayward child. And she scared me, she really scared me. Fear and lust kept me rooted to the spot.

Mrs Woo's eyes remained focused through the window as her hand returned. This time she fumbled at the zip. I almost stopped breathing as she pulled my zipper undone and smuggled her hand inside my pants. Her fingers worked over my cock which was almost bursting now. Just the thin covering of my boxer shorts lay between me and her.

No inflection in her voice betrayed what she was doing to me as she continued.

'A space would form around the chosen man and all the girls would descend upon him, like a flock of pretty birds. Soon he would be in ecstasy as the girls fluttered around him, touching, caressing, kissing. Bit by bit his clothes were removed until he lay naked on the ground. One girl cradled his head in her lap while the others attended to the rest of his body, the little tongues licking at him until he cried out in pleasure.'

The hand disappearing inside my jeans worked expertly. I bit my lip hard. I was so keyed up that I feared I would come, right there and then. Her words formed a rhythm in my head as she pawed at me.

'These girls were graceful, yes, but they were expert

too. They did things wives would never dream of doing. As one nestled over his penis, another would sit astride his face, letting him lap at the little opening between her legs.'

A flush began to mark Mrs Woo's face and neck and her hand worked harder, digging her fingers into my cock. The sensation nearly doubled me over, but I was terrified any noise or movement from me would break the spell, snapping her back to the present. I had the awful feeling, if broken from her trance, she might suddenly yell at me for being a dirty, filthy boy. As if it had been me who unzipped myself and placed my erection in her hand.

'The girls took it in turns to crouch over him, all the other men craning to look, their jealous sighs washing around the room like water. Each girl slipped his penis between her legs until it disappeared inside her, shafting on it for a few moments before another pretty sparrow would take over. This would go on until he had the juice of maybe eight girls mingling on him.'

My cock was throbbing almost to the point of pain now. Suddenly, Mrs Woo yanked down my boxers and liberated my prick from its enclosure. It stuck up like an obscene pointing finger between us. The elastic of my pants snapped back over my tense balls, squeezing them painfully. She circled her hand around me and began to shaft delicately up and down with exquisite precision.

'Of course, what the man didn't know was that there was a prize for the girl who retained his precious fluid. Some bauble, a watch maybe, or a dainty comb for her hair. Each girl had exactly one minute to dance on his penis, timed by the clock on the wall. During her minute the girl would use all her skills to cause his climax, working her tight, little muscles like a ballerina up and down him. Our heroine, it has to be said, won many prizes in her time ...'

I could contain myself no longer. Mrs Woo's fingers felt so practised, so expert, that out of nowhere my balls tightened. For a second my prick seemed to grow even bigger than before and I shot a streak of hot sperm over her tiny hand.

Almost in surprise, Mrs Woo studied her brimming handful. Just then the phone began to ring in the back of the building. She stood up, briskly wiping her hand with a piece of kitchen paper torn from a roll on the counter, and went to answer it.

Shame and confusion fell over me like a cloud. I quickly zipped myself up. Mrs Woo's voice chimed in the background as she spoke in Chinese to whoever was on the phone. I took a swift look around. Her broom was propped up behind the counter and for some reason it made me shiver. I'd come to regard it almost as a second Mrs Woo, or at least a lieutenant in her army. Hanging on a peg was her plastic mac, her cracked and shiny shell. On impulse I reached up and unhooked it before I left, shutting the door quietly behind me.

That night I lay in the bath for a long time, mostly to avoid my parents. My thoughts raced and tumbled. Exactly how old was Mrs Woo? I found it hard to imagine: fifty maybe, sixty, perhaps even more? The delicate girls from the dream-story danced and fluttered, performing their ritualistic fucking in my head. In the state of arousal that I experienced daily I was sure I could have fucked all eight girls in turn, climaxing into each one. Then I remembered the long jet of spunk spraying out over Mrs Woo's hand and I groaned out loud with a mixture of shame and horniness.

Drying myself on the bed, I glanced almost shyly down at my own body. My muscles had hardened and delineated over the past year. Despite the paper-round and all the childish activities that pointed elsewhere, it was now definitely a man's body. Dark hair sprouted around my balls and lay in a fine fuzz across my chest. Just looking at myself made my cock stiffen. I put my head in my hands despairingly. What kind of pervert got off at looking at himself?

Mrs Woo's coat poked out from the gym bag where I'd stuffed it. In the shadows it seemed to take on the aspect of a living thing with its shiny head rearing accusingly at me from within the bag. I pulled the mac out and spread it across my legs. The cold of the plastic warmed as I ran my hands over its length, like a cold body being brought back to life. I felt almost as if *she* were there, sprawled across my naked legs.

The cool plastic warmed again from my heat as I slipped it on. Loose and hanging on her, it stretched tight across my chest and shoulders. Breathing in, I fastened the buttons, and the fabric yawned and creaked as it strained across my body. The coat held me as tight as if I was tied in rubber bonds. My fingers slipped and slid as I ran my hands over the coat and the heat from my body made the material exude a faint chemical smell of plastic.

Strapped down, my prick hardened painfully inside its enclosure, straining as it unfurled against the fabric. The coat slipped against the sheet as I lay, face down, on the bed. I felt swamped in heat and sweat began to form and trickle down my back. There was a gentle knock on my bedroom door and I started within my plastic skin. I quickly drew the duvet up to my neck.

'Josh, there's tea in the pot downstairs,' my mum called through the door.

I cleared my throat. 'I'll be down later,' I said, trying to make my voice sound normal.

I heard her footsteps down the stairs. The heat had intensified under the cover and sweat slicked my whole body now. I pinched my lips together to repress a groan as I thrust my hips up and down, my cock shafting inside the coat. The impression of Mrs Woo's hand seemed to grip around my hard on. I thrust harder. What would she do if she saw me like this? Perhaps she would lift the coat and expose my naked buttocks, scolding as she whipped me soundly with the belt. My mind spun with the image. Her presence filled the room. She was like a tiny queen, I her subject. I had instinctively known that morning as she wanked me off that one word, one foot out of line, and I'd be in trouble. I wondered how it was that someone so tiny could exude such power.

Lifting myself up, I fastened the belt so that it buckled across my groin and strapped my cock down tighter. Face down again I thrust my hips faster, the buckle of the belt pressing deliciously into my hard cock. I felt almost insane with lust as I pumped. I thought of the delicate dancing Chinese girls as I thrust, the buckle scoring my cock. Each one swayed over me in my imagination, daintily lifting their skirts and lowering their juicy little openings onto my cock, swallowing me up in their sweetness. I felt those girls could double in number, treble even, and they still wouldn't be enough to contain my lust.

Suddenly, in my mind's eye, Mrs Woo appeared in the background, sitting straight and stern on a chair, directing the girls how to sit astride me, instructing them how to form a ladder with their muscles inside to increase my pleasure. I was lying back on silky cushions as they all writhed and contorted just for me.

My buttocks tightened at the thought and, with a muffled cry, I spilled jet after jet of come inside the coat. The tight garment squeezed the wetness up to my chest.

Over the next few nights I took to sleeping in the plastic coat in a strange homage to Mrs Woo. She was the furthest I could imagine from the drowsy suburban land which I inhabited. Her world seemed dark and dangerous: delicate in its culture, but ruled over by tiny dictators in exotic costumes. On waking I'd be bathed in sweat with my cock already springing to attention. However many times I jerked off (and it was many, many times) the relief was always short-lived. It wasn't long before my wayward cock would stir again, begging for attention.

When I delivered her paper at the weekend, Mrs Woo's submerged face appeared again at the window. Inside, the tea was already on the counter. I'd spent the last week in a lather of arousal and confusion and I'd hoped and feared she would be waiting for me. She mentioned nothing of the theft of her coat, but settled me down in my place behind the counter.

'I know you've been waiting for the next part of the story,' she said.

How could I deny it? My experience with Mrs Woo had taken my permanent adolescent arousal to fever pitch. I sipped the tea which tasted of flowers. Nothing appeared to have changed in the dark shop: the little packets and tins, the broom, even the dust seemed to be in the same place. Mrs Woo folded her hands in her lap.

'And then . . .' She carried on as if she'd never left off. 'And then, one day one of the powerful men decided to take the girl home. He realised she was something special and wanted her all to himself. He employed her as a maid, but it has to be said –' Mrs Woo giggled: the effect was both fascinating and disturbing '– it has to be said, her duties were often of the bedroom kind.

'The powerful man liked to surprise the girl while she was at some menial task. While she swept the wooden floors or wrung out the washing, he would steal up behind her, pressing his penis against her back and rubbing himself against her like a dog in his desperation.

'She didn't always make herself available. Oh no, she knew the value of a scarce commodity. Whenever he came up to her like this the man would be in a terrible stew – his wife was always around the house somewhere. If the girl decided to push him off that day then all he could do was retreat with his penis all hard and heavy, like a dog that's been kicked for jumping up at you.'

I sympathised with the man. My own cock was already bulging inside my jeans. Mrs Woo sat neatly on her stool with her plastered arm resting on the counter. She wore a tight red dress today that came nearly to her ankles. An aura of mystery and danger hung around her. She reminded me of a sharp silver knife kept in a red velvet-lined box.

'Of course she didn't always reject him,' she continued. 'Sometimes she would hop onto the kitchen table and spread her legs wide, pulling up her clothes so he could see her little red opening, all prettily fringed with black hair. When that happened, oh, the man would be in ecstasy: trying to still his sighs so his wife couldn't hear, his eyes rolling around like a madman. But she always made sure her own pleasure came first. She'd push him to his knees so that her slit was right by his mouth, and make him lick it all over. He'd use his tongue until it felt just right and then she'd hold his head in that place, so he wouldn't move from it.

'The poor silly man might be terrified of his wife chancing upon them, but it made the girl tingle with excitement. The sound of the other woman's footsteps on the wooden floor above made her heart race and her juice flow even faster. When she had finally received her own pleasure she would graciously allow the man entrance into her delicious, moist cave. He would thrust in and out of her quickly, his penis shining like a fish as it darted. It made her giggle the way he kept glancing over his shoulder expecting to see his wife appear. And she almost laughed out loud at the thought that the family would be sitting around that very table for their dinner in a few short hours.'

Mrs Woo's eyes were shining and a flush had crept up from the neck of her red dress. Again, without a glance at me, she thrust out her hand and began to knead my stiff cock under my jeans. I tried to keep as still as possible – just a small sigh escaped. Although her hand sent sharp needles of pleasure across my cock, I felt desperate for more this time. I wondered briefly if I could make her take me in her small painted mouth. Then I realised with great certainty that there was no way I could make *her* do anything.

'As time went on,' Mrs Woo continued, 'the girl became bored and took to playing games to achieve her excitement. She smuggled into the man's bed at night, with his stupid wife lying right there next to him. Of course, the man was terrified, but he could never resist. And anyway, resisting her would make more noise than the act of love. So, trying not to make a sound, he'd lie between the two women and sneak his hungry penis inside the girl while his wife snored away beside them.'

I longed to reach out and touch Mrs Woo as she spoke. Looking at her red painted mouth made me want to put my fingers under her dress and feel the lips between her legs. My prick felt monstrous, huge. Teased by her fingers, it seemed to grow bigger and bigger until I nearly doubled up with the pain of it being jammed tight inside my jeans. I looked at her tiny narrow hips. Surely I would be too big for her, I thought – she might break in two if I tried to put my prick inside her. The thoughts ran through my head but I stayed absolutely still, hardly breathing. Her face began to darken as she spoke.

'The girl started to believe the wife suspected her. Oh, she became a real thorn in the girl's side. The wife began to treat her as a skivvy and encouraged her nasty little brats to do the same. The girl, with her exquisite hands, was forced to wipe their horrible little bottoms and beat the dust out of the futons until her poor arms ached.

'One day, when the wife was being particularly cruel, the girl decided she'd had enough. She'd heard about a powerful dragon that lived in a cave above the city and she resolved to visit it to see if there was any solution it could offer.

'She climbed the mountain all night until she found its cave. She knew it to be the dragon's cave because the glow inside from his fire could be seen from a mile away. She trembled as she entered his cave and even more as she explained the situation.

'When the dragon asked her to strip down naked (he hadn't seen a naked woman for more than fifty years) she did as he asked, even though her hands shook as she unknotted her clothing. The dragon bathed her in his warm breath, caressing her with his heat-scorched tongue. She let him fuck her right there and then, as he had promised a solution to her terrible predicament. Lying on the damp floor of the cave, she was terrified when she saw his huge, scaly prick. Terrified it would break her in two . . .'

Here, I blushed at my earlier thoughts.

'But he was careful with her. When he entered her she thought she would die of ecstasy. She'd never felt so full before and the scales of his magnificent penis fretted and rubbed inside her delightfully, his huge balls swaying to and fro. He seemed to carry on for hours, taking her to new heights of dizzy pleasure, until she screamed out in climax. He was such a thoughtful lover. He only took his pleasure when he was sure she'd had hers: moving up and down until he came with a great snort of fire from his nostrils, drenching her in dragon seed.'

Mrs Woo withdrew her hand from my prick, leaving an aching void. Her hand snaked up the red dress and moved briefly between her legs. For one moment I thought she was going to rub herself shamelessly before me, seeing to her own pleasure before pushing me out of the door in a state of obvious agitation. But she led me by the hand to the back of the shop and, like a willing little lamb, I followed.

The room at the back managed to appear cluttered and bare all at once. Cartons and boxes with Chinese lettering stamped on the sides were stacked haphazardly against one wall, and a battered-looking sofa was pushed against another. A calendar advertising honey, with Chinese characters crisscrossing the jar in the photograph, decorated the wall. I noticed the calendar was two years out of date.

'What are you going to do with me?' I asked weakly.

She laughed, and instructed me to stand in the middle of the room. I towered over the tiny woman but somehow I felt completely at her mercy – as if she'd sucked the spirit right out of my body and had it stored in a little box somewhere.

Her hands flew to my zip. Although one arm remained encased in plaster, her fingers were as lithe as butterflies as she unzipped me, pulling my pants and trousers down around my thighs.

Sighing, she licked her lips. Her greedy eyes fixed on my knob which jutted out before me.

'What a fine boy you are!' She giggled, almost girl-ishly. She ran her hands over my buttocks, the plaster grazing against my skin. My muscles tensed at her touch.

'Have you ever ... been inside a woman?' she asked, looking up at me slyly.

Pride nearly made me lie, but I shook my head feebly. Her lips tremored in excitement at the news.

'Sweet boy,' she murmured, with a hint of triumph in her voice. She cupped my balls in her hand. My prick pulsed at the sensation and seemed to grow another inch!

She blew gently on my knob and the sensation made me groan out loud. My arms dangled uselessly by my sides. I felt dizzy with lust and humiliation, standing there with my hard-on exposed and my jeans around my thighs like some naughty little boy about to be spanked.

Slowly she unwound the red scarf from around her neck. It fluttered down from her hands and rested on my outstretched cock, like a flag hanging from a pole. I clenched my fists at the soft sensation. The touch of the silk was maddening in its delicacy. A gleeful smile played across her lips as she stood back to examine me.

'Does that feel nice?' she asked, her eyes flashing with a wicked gleam.

It was as if my power of speech had been taken away. I nodded dumbly. She kneeled before me again, wrapping the silk around my swollen cock. Gritting my teeth, I desperately tried to hold on. The touch of the scarf was like a soothing hand on a tender wound, almost agonising in its sensation. My buttocks clenched and unclenched. Just one touch, I thought, one touch and I'll lose it. I tried to parse French verbs in my mind: *Je suis, tu es, il est, elle est, nous sommes* . . .

Her hand gripped my cock, the silk like a soft glove around me. She slid her hand along my length and my balls hardened. Her practised hand rolled along my cock again. This time it was unbearable and, with an agonised cry, my hot spunk escaped, shooting in a jet over the scarf and her hand. It seemed to go on for ever. I cried out again in humiliation as the sticky fluid carried on coming, seemingly limitless in its supply. Finally I slumped forward, exhausted.

I was too terrified to look at her. I bowed my head expecting a tirade of abuse about my uncontrolled response. Instead she said simply, 'You clean yourself up, and wait there.' I found it impossible to gauge anything from her voice.

Mrs Woo disappeared out into the shop and I bleakly surveyed the damage. Sperm seemed to be everywhere: spilled over the discarded scarf, spattered over the floor, dribbling down the front of my jeans. For some stupid reason I didn't use the scarf, even in its sullied state, to clean myself up with. She was so unpredictable that I was terrified if she caught me cleaning myself with it she might be angry at me for further soiling her possessions.

I trembled as I imagined her capable of anything: telling my parents that I exposed myself to her, or telling Mr Roberts at the newsagents that she'd found one of his boys wanking in the back of her shop. I guessed she would be very adept at playing the vulnerable old lady.

In desperation I wiped at the mess with my hands, smearing it down my jeans. Once I'd made myself decent I sat heavily on the sofa with my head in my hands. I'd hoped today ... What had I hoped? That I would finally be allowed entrance to that mystical place. That she would allow me to swim inside her and I could emerge from her shop changed, having finally tasted the universal secret. Instead I'd folded at the first touch – shaming myself with my uncontrolled mess.

She reappeared with one of the tiny cups in her hand. Steam rose from the cup and seemed to hang in front of her face for a second like a translucent curtain.

'Drink this up, it'll make you feel much better,' She purred.

The sweet yellow tea revived me to the point where I dared to steal a glance at her. She was leaning back on the sofa with her legs neatly crossed, looking at me almost indulgently.

'You boys,' she chortled. 'So impatient.' It was only much later that I realised the implications of that plural.

I drained the cup. The tea seemed to have an almost magical effect, sweeping away my exhaustion in one stroke. In an almost motherly fashion she began to unbutton my shirt. She ran her hands over my chest and over the broadness of my shoulders.

'You're a fine, fine boy,' she said. For the first time she appeared excited and her iron control slipped slightly. Her cheeks flushed and she bit her lip.

Already my dick stirred again. I wondered, almost in awe, how many times I could come in a day – five, ten, fifteen? My sperm was a constant, sweet burden.

I gasped as she pulled her dress up above the tops of her thighs. Her mound was smothered in dark hair which disappeared in a crease between her legs. I put my hand out, burning with desire and curiosity. As I touched the tiny lips that protruded between her legs she moaned, and her eyes rolled back in her head. They felt softer than I expected – the glossy images from magazines always looked so hard and cold. I felt a surge of pride: at last I'd touched a woman there.

She moaned again as I explored her wetness. I felt ten foot tall – it was my touch that was making her writhe and moan like that! She lay down on the sofa and rested her head carefully on the arm, as if she didn't want to disturb her elaborate hair style. Her plastered arm rested snugly by her side.

When I hesitated for a few moments, she explained, 'You can mount me now.'

As I stripped off my jeans I felt a stab of anxiety again as I looked down on her tiny body. My cock stuck out huge in front of me. *Surely* I was too big for her. I'd split her in two with my throbbing prick. But she lifted her arms up impatiently, opening her legs wider so I could see the gape of her sex as it stretched open.

She felt like a tiny light bird as I entered her, almost as if her bones were hollow. With a rush of desire and relief I felt her juicy slit expand to fit me, opening up and swallowing my cock. Cupping my buttocks from behind, she dictated a rhythm to my thrusts. It was just as well – the feeling was so new and sweet I would probably just have pumped wildly away.

I glanced at her face as I moved in and out. The flush was creeping up her neck but she looked serene with her eyes closed and her lips parted. I raised myself further up on my arms, terrified that I might crush her. As I looked down I could see my cock gleaming wetly as it disappeared in and out between her legs. My breath was sounding in loud pants now and each thrust magnified my desire tenfold.

Without opening her eyes she pushed a hand down between her legs and stroked herself with one finger, using rapid, tiny movements. The flush on her neck spread and darkened and a series of small cries fell from her lips before she sank back on to the sofa.

I felt I was drowning in her wetness. Her cunt contracted around me sending quivers of electricity up and down my cock. The feeling washed over me and with a triumphant yell I came, pumping more and more come inside her until I was completely drained.

When I left the shop a few minutes later I nearly danced down the grey, wet pavement.

Back in my bedroom, it didn't take long for my desire to rekindle itself. The sight of her coat brought the experience in the back room of her shop sharply into my mind. I slipped it on again. The smell of it was almost becoming like a drug. Its slippery folds acted as an instant aphrodisiac. I tied the belt firmly around my penis and then tugged at it with rapid, hard motions as I jerked off quickly and quietly.

The night before I was due to deliver Mrs Woo's paper again I went to a party with Stevie. Bottles of vodka and snogging couples littered the floor and furniture. To my surprise I soon started chatting to Rebecca who I'd fancied from afar for ages. She swept her long brown hair from her shoulders and stuck out her little tits as I talked to her. I even made her laugh!

After a couple more vodka and cokes she led me up to one of the bedrooms. We instantly fell on each other. She shoved her tongue right into my mouth and clutched at my groin. When she undressed I gasped: she was beautiful, truly beautiful. Her pearly skin glowed and her swollen rosy nipples showed through the hair which fell about her.

We fucked on top of the piles of coats stacked on the bed with a chest of drawers pulled across the door to foil intruders. Her pussy felt moist and sweet and I ached to put my sperm inside her. Just a tiny part of me missed Mrs Woo's cleverness in the act, and the expert working of her muscles. I knew I had a lot to thank her for. Before now, even the girls who were rumoured to do it with *anyone* hadn't wanted to do it with me.

As I settled down on the stool in Mrs Woo's shop the next day, the surroundings felt almost familiar to me. As was our ritual she picked up where she'd left off.

'The dragon gave her some powder. It was very special, magic powder, imbued with ancient spirits and demons. As instructed, the girl put a pinch of it every night into the wife's noodles. Pretty soon, the old wife's face began to crack, like the glaze on an old plate. The magic dust was drying her out like a fish left out in the sun. Oh,' Mrs Woo raised up her eyes and nearly clapped her hands together, as if remembering some exciting game. 'All the man had to come home to at night was her sad old cracked face mooning over the table at him.

'The powder was very special, very potent, and in the end it just melted her away. She took herself off into the corner of a room one day and, poof, just melted away.'

I shifted about on my seat. The story was starting to make me feel uncomfortable. With Mrs Woo's attachment to the girl in the story, I'd taken that character to be herself. She'd carefully placed the whole story in a world of magically appearing money and deadly spirit powders. But if the girl was Mrs Woo's younger self, what did that mean? That she was a thief and a murderer?

Mrs Woo seemed to notice my fidgeting. I felt impatient for the end today, so we could visit the back room again. I felt more confident than ever before with her and I no longer sat quietly, hardly daring to breathe. Two women in one week had made me feel invincible.

'So what happened in the end?' I asked.

Mrs Woo looked at me nastily. She didn't like interruptions.

'The girl married the man and lived happily of course.' She seemed to have lost interest, not only in the story but in me. Despite my earlier impatience I felt cheated of the ending. She hadn't even tried to make it sound convincing. Perhaps I'd expected to learn some moral, some important lesson in life, like in Aesop's Fables.

'But how . . .' I began.

'How, why?' She turned her face to me, mimicking my voice.

'But what's the point of the story, what's the real end?' I persisted.

'The point of the story is ...' She gripped me tight around the wrist, her hand surprisingly strong. 'The point of the story is, you stupid child, that it's women who rule the world and always have.'

Visit the Black Lace website at
www.blacklace-books.co.uk

LOOK OUT FOR THE ALL-NEW BLACK LACE BOOKS – AVAILABLE NOW!

All books priced £6.99 in the UK. Please note publication dates apply to the UK only. For other territories, please contact your retailer.

NOBLE VICES
Monica Belle
ISBN 0 352 33738 9

Annabelle doesn't want to work. She wants to spend her time riding, attending exotic dinner parties and indulging herself in even more exotic sex, at her father's expense. Unfortunately, Daddy has other ideas, and when she writes off his new Jaguar, it is the final straw. Sent to work in the City, Annabelle quickly finds that it is not easy to fit in, especially when what she thinks of as harmless, playful sex turns out to leave most of her new acquaintances in shock. **Naughty, fresh and kinky, this is a very funny tale of a spoilt rich English girl's fall from grace.**

HANDMAIDEN OF PALMYRA
Fleur Reynolds
ISBN 0 352 32919 X

Palmyra, 3rd century AD: a lush oasis in the heart of the Syrian desert. The inquisitive, beautiful and fiercely independent Samoya takes her place as apprentice priestess in the temple of Antioch. Decadent bachelor Prince Alif has other ideas. He wants a wife, and sends his equally lascivious sister to bring Samoya to the Bacchanalian wedding feast he is preparing. Samoya embarks on a journey that will alter the course of her life. Before reaching her destination, she is to encounter Marcus, the battle-hardened centurion who will unearth the core of her desires. **Lust in the dust and forbidden fruit in Ms Reynolds' most unusual title for the Black Lace series.**

Coming in December

THE HEAT OF THE MOMENT
Tesni Morgan
ISBN O 352 33742 7

Amber, Sue and Diane – three women from an English market town –
are successful in their businesses, but all want more from their private
lives. When they become involved in The Silver Banner – an English Civil
War re-enactment society – there's plenty of opportunity for them to
fraternise with handsome muscular men in historical uniforms. Thing is,
the fun-loving Cavaliers are much sexier than the Puritan Roundheads,
and tensions and rivalries are played out on the village green and the
bedroom. **Great characterisation and oodles of sexy fun in this story of
three English friends who love dressing up.**

WICKED WORDS 7
Various
ISBN O352 33743 5

Hugely popular and immensely entertaining, the *Wicked Words*
collections are the freshest and most cutting-edge volumes of women's
erotic stories to be found anywhere in the world. The diversity of themes
and styles reflects the multi-faceted nature of the female sexual
imagination. Combining humour, warmth and attitude with fun, filthy,
imaginative writing, these stories sizzle with horny action. Only the most
arousing fiction makes it into a *Wicked Words* volume. This is the best in
fun, sassy erotica from the UK and USA. **Another sizzling collection of
wild fantasies from wicked women!**

OPAL DARKNESS
Cleo Cordell
ISBN 0 352 33033 3

It's the latter part of the nineteenth century and beautiful twins Sidonie and Francis are yearning for adventure. Their newly awakened sexuality needs an outlet. Sent by their father on the Grand Tour of Europe, they swiftly turn cultural exploration into something illicit. When they meet Count Constantin and his decadent friends and are invited to stay at his snow-bound Romanian castle, there is no turning back on the path of depravity. **Another wonderfully decadent piece of historical fiction from a pioneer of female erotica.**

Coming in January 2003

STICKY FINGERS
Alison Tyler
ISBN 0 352 33756 7

Jodie Silver doesn't have to steal. As the main buyer for a reputable import and export business in the heart of San Francisco, she has plenty of money and prestige. But she gets a rush from pocketing things that don't belong to her. It's a potent feeling, almost as gratifying as the excitement she receives from engaging in kinky, exhibitionist sex – but not quite. Skilled at concealing her double life, Jodie thinks she's unstoppable, but with detective Nick Hudson on her tail, it's only a matter of time before the pussycat burglar meets her comeuppance. **A thrilling piece of West Coast noir erotica from Ms Tyler.**

STORMY HAVEN
Savannah Smythe
ISBN O 352 33757 5

Daisy Lovell has had enough of her over-protective Texan millionaire father, Felix, and is determined to get away from his interfering ways. The last straw is when Felix forbids her to date a Puerto Rican boy. Determined to see some of the world, Daisy goes storm chasing across the American Midwest for some sexual adventure. She certainly finds it among truckers and bikers and a state trooper. What Daisy doesn't know is that Felix has sent personal bodyguard Max Decker to join the storm tour and watch over her. However, no one can foresee that hard man Decker will fall for Daisy in a big way. **Fantastic characterisation and lots of really hot sex scenes across the American desert.**

SILKEN CHAINS
Jodi Nicol
ISBN O 352 33143 7

Fleeing from her scheming guardians at the prospect of an arranged marriage, the beautiful young Abbie is thrown from her horse. On regaining consciousness she finds herself in a lavish house modelled on the palaces of Indian princes – and the virtual prisoner of the extremely wealthy and attractive Leon Villiers, the Master. Eastern philosophy and eroticism form the basis of the Master's opulent lifestyle and he introduces Abbie to sensual pleasures beyond the bounds of her imagination. **By popular demand, another of the list's bestselling historical novels is reprinted.**

Black Lace Booklist

Information is correct at time of printing. To avoid disappointment check availability before ordering. Go to www.blacklace-books.co.uk. All books are priced £6.99 unless another price is given.

BLACK LACE BOOKS WITH A CONTEMPORARY SETTING

☐ THE TOP OF HER GAME Emma Holly	ISBN 0 352 33337 5	£5.99
☐ IN THE FLESH Emma Holly	ISBN 0 352 33498 3	£5.99
☐ A PRIVATE VIEW Crystalle Valentino	ISBN 0 352 33308 1	£5.99
☐ SHAMELESS Stella Black	ISBN 0 352 33485 1	£5.99
☐ INTENSE BLUE Lyn Wood	ISBN 0 352 33496 7	£5.99
☐ THE NAKED TRUTH Natasha Rostova	ISBN 0 352 33497 5	£5.99
☐ ANIMAL PASSIONS Martine Marquand	ISBN 0 352 33499 1	£5.99
☐ A SPORTING CHANCE Susie Raymond	ISBN 0 352 33501 7	£5.99
☐ TAKING LIBERTIES Susie Raymond	ISBN 0 352 33357 X	£5.99
☐ A SCANDALOUS AFFAIR Holly Graham	ISBN 0 352 33523 8	£5.99
☐ THE NAKED FLAME Crystalle Valentino	ISBN 0 352 33528 9	£5.99
☐ ON THE EDGE Laura Hamilton	ISBN 0 352 33534 3	£5.99
☐ LURED BY LUST Tania Picarda	ISBN 0 352 33533 5	£5.99
☐ THE HOTTEST PLACE Tabitha Flyte	ISBN 0 352 33536 X	£5.99
☐ THE NINETY DAYS OF GENEVIEVE Lucinda Carrington	ISBN 0 352 33070 8	£5.99
☐ EARTHY DELIGHTS Tesni Morgan	ISBN 0 352 33548 3	£5.99
☐ MAN HUNT Cathleen Ross	ISBN 0 352 33583 1	
☐ MÉNAGE Emma Holly	ISBN 0 352 33231 X	
☐ DREAMING SPIRES Juliet Hastings	ISBN 0 352 33584 X	
☐ THE TRANSFORMATION Natasha Rostova	ISBN 0 352 33311 1	
☐ STELLA DOES HOLLYWOOD Stella Black	ISBN 0 352 33588 2	
☐ SIN.NET Helena Ravenscroft	ISBN 0 352 33598 X	
☐ HOTBED Portia Da Costa	ISBN 0 352 33614 5	
☐ TWO WEEKS IN TANGIER Annabel Lee	ISBN 0 352 33599 8	
☐ HIGHLAND FLING Jane Justine	ISBN 0 352 33616 1	
☐ PLAYING HARD Tina Troy	ISBN 0 352 33617 X	
☐ SYMPHONY X Jasmine Stone	ISBN 0 352 33629 3	

To find out the latest information about Black Lace titles, check out the website: www.blacklace-books.co.uk or send for a booklist with complete synopses by writing to:

Black Lace Booklist, Virgin Books Ltd
Thames Wharf Studios
Rainville Road
London W6 9HA

Please include an SAE of decent size. Please note only British stamps are valid.

Our privacy policy
We will not disclose information you supply us to any other parties.
We will not disclose any information which identifies you personally to any person without your express consent.

From time to time we may send out information about Black Lace books and special offers. Please tick here if you do <u>not</u> wish to receive Black Lace information. ❏

Please send me the books I have ticked above.

Name ....

Address ....

....

....

....

Post Code ....

Send to: Cash Sales, Black Lace Books, Thames Wharf Studios, Rainville Road, London W6 9HA.

US customers: for prices and details of how to order books for delivery by mail, call 1-800-343-4499.

Please enclose a cheque or postal order, made payable to Virgin Books Ltd, to the value of the books you have ordered plus postage and packing costs as follows:

UK and BFPO – £1.00 for the first book, 50p for each subsequent book.

Overseas (including Republic of Ireland) – £2.00 for the first book, £1.00 for each subsequent book.

If you would prefer to pay by VISA, ACCESS/MASTERCARD, DINERS CLUB, AMEX or SWITCH, please write your card number and expiry date here:

....

Signature ....

Please allow up to 28 days for delivery.